Sailor Eyes

(The Lost Manuscript of Alexander Hackett)

Written by

Alexander Hackett

Sailor Eyes (The Lost Manuscript of Alexander Hackett)

Written by Alexander Hackett

FIRST EDITION

Editor-in-Chief: Steve William Laible, MBA

Prepared for publication by Vicky Rummel

Published by The Kodel Group, LLC
PO Box 38 - Grants Pass, Oregon 97528
KodelEmpire.com (info@kodelgroup.com)

Imprint: Empire Holdings

Summary: Sailor Eyes, the lost manuscript of Alexander Hackett, written circa 1953 is a fictional account of life on the Cape outside Boston, Massachusetts in the 1850s. It follows the lives of an aristocrat ship builder, his debutante daughter, rugged and brave ship captains, widows and a young man who has sailor eyes. Courting story lines are weaved into this charming tale of land, sea and heart. The manuscript was passed down for generations and eventually forgotten until it arrived without ceremony at the passing of the late author's wife. The grandson, William Turrell, wishes to honor his step-grandfather, who passed in 1970s, by publishing the manuscript as was intended. A polished, finished novel may follow.

Library of Congress cataloging in publication data: Hackett, Alexander. Fiction.
Library of Congress Control Number 2014902525

ISBN 978-1-62485-005-9

Printed in the United States of America, Europe, Asia and beyond...

Foreword

I, William E. Turrell, do hereby give my best recollection of Alexander Hackett's life and how he was involved with the Turrell family, as my step-grandfather.

Alex, as he was known to us, told the story about his being a cabin boy at a young age and coming from France by way of England to the Americas on a "square rigger ship". He said he went back to England on a sailing ship and returned to the Americas because he loved the country. He said most cabin boys were runaways or had been kidnapped. The young boys were desired because they were small, didn't eat too much, and didn't take up too much space in the Captain's cabin. Cabin boys duties were to keep the Captain's cabin clean, laundry done, bed made, bring them food, and make sure that no one took anything from the cabin.

Alex settled in the Boston, Massachusetts area and lived with some people that took him in. He said he had heard of ships going to California by way of the "Horn of South America." It was a long trip and he saw a lot of the shore line of the Americas. On this return trip he was drawn to write stories about going to California on a sailing ship, so that part of history would not be forgotten.

Alex said he settled in the Massachusetts area and worked at building sailing ships. He related he would sail down the East Coast and visit other ports of call. This adventure gave him the desire to move further south. He liked history and became fascinated with various stamp collections of people he knew. He said that is how he met Raymond Webster Turrell and Amy W. (who was a novel stamp collector). The three kept in contact with each other over the years.

Amy W. Turrell contacted Alex after her husband past away and in the 60's they became close friends. They married and lived in St. Petersburg, Florida, where he had a home. He liked St. Pete (he called it that), because he could go to the beach and watch the waves. He had one book published and this was his second book called, "Sailor Eyes." Alex died in the late 1970's where upon I received his weathered and tattered manuscript from my grandmother, in its original type-written (typewriter) form.

In January 2014, I contacted Steve Laible, Publisher of the Kodel Group, about possibility of getting my grandfather's manuscript published. Before this time I had no idea how to get the manuscript published. But, how I wished to honor Alexander Hackett's work by bringing sailing ship history to the public as was his wish.

William E. Turrell

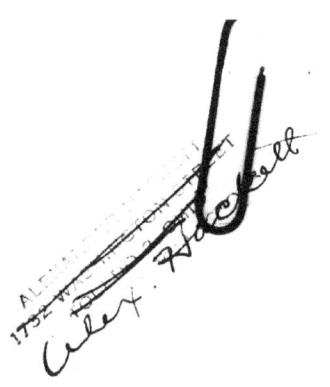

"Sailor Eyes"
by
Alex. Hackett

From the top of a tall mast on Mars Hill, a blue square of bunting
fluttered in the morning air, while on the streets of Eastham Village
people were hurridly making their way in the direction of Central Wharf.
A light breeze blew in from the ocean bringing with
it the smell of seaweed, but as it fanned its way along the village streets
and out over the broad medows, gracefully bowing the willow branches as
it passed and humming a song of summer, the odor quickly changed to that of
fragrant flowers, for it was the month of June, in The year 1853.

the gold rush was at its peak, and along
the waterfront ranged vessels of every rig imaginable hastily being
equipped to carry freight and passengers around "The Horn" to California,
for by this time the sturdy inhabitants of Cape Cod had become firmly
convinced that the latter trade was more lucrative than chasing whales; and they
had eyes for nothing but ships and sailors.
That year marked the beginning of the clipper era in Massachusetts,
and the shipyards teemed with busy workmen fashioning with skilled hands
the lofty ships which were afterwards destined to carry the house-flags of
their respective owners into every remote part of the seven seas. But
even with all the excitement relative to the discovery of gold in California,
the people of Eastham never lost interest in the arrival or departure
of a Boston packet, for the event was usually associated with either romance
or tragedy, thereby keeping the fire of village gossip constantly aflame.

On the day our story opens, the flag on Mars Hill was the signal that a packet had been sighted; and half the population of Eastham ~~to say the~~ ~~least were~~ was waterfront bound to see it dock.

"By Jupiter! There's two of 'em and its a race, " exclaimed a grizzled old whaler pointing a stubby forefinger at two glistening spots of white which were now plainly visable above the horizon. "Look at 'em come! "

Swiftly the packets drew nearer throwing a shower of white spray over their sharp bows as they luffed into the wind, and many were the comments as to their identity for as yet they were not close enough to be recognized.

"One of them's the Firefly," suddenly shouted a boy, who perched on a piling some three feet above the heads of the crowd, had appointed himself a committee of one to report their progress. "She's racing with Cap'n Bowden's Hornet and I hope he beats her. "

A wave of intense interest caused the people to stirr uneasily, and many of them voiced the desire to see their favorite win by loud shouts of "Come on Firefly! , Show him your heels Cap'n Bowden! " There were also several young ladies present whose gay-colored parasols fluttered in unison with their hearts at the mention of the Firefly for she was captained by a dandified young man named Alfredo Sanchez.

"That there Portuguese can sure sail a schooner! " exclaimed one old sailor . "Look! She's taken the wind plumb out of the Hornets sails." The captain of the Firefly, as the two schooners neared the wharf had suddenly put his wheel hard-down and manuevered his vessel close to the stern of his opponent completely becalming him, then quickly slacking off his sheets he had raced down by the Hornet to windward and again coming into the wind slid gracefully in alongside the wharf hardly touching the framework so skilfully was the movement executed.

"You got the best of me that time you young jackanapes," shouted a stout red-faced man from the deck of the Hornet as she drifted down by the Firefly, too far distant for a line to be thrown on board. "But you done it by a trick."

"It was not a trick, Captain Bowden," replied the captain of the Firefly showing a set of gleaming white teeth. "It was what you say in English good seamanship. I was too smart for you. "

That the Firefly's captain lacked in years he made up for in good looks and a capacity for being very popular with the ladies, and it would have been said by his rivals, of whom he had many, that his face bespoke arrogance and cock-sureness. He was garbed in white bell-bottomed trousers topped by a shirt of the same color open at the neck and tastefully garnished by a black silk handkerchief tied in a square knot. On his head he wore a wide-brimmed hat of straw from which dangled two narrow streamers of ribbon, shading a swarthy face. On the whole he presented a most striking and dandified appearance.

"I wish to thank you, Captain Sanchez, for a most delightful trip and the thrill of my life, " observed a passenger stepping forward with her hand extended. "It would be a pleasure indeed if you would dine with us one evening this fall after Priscilla and I have returned to our home in Boston. My husband is Donald McKane, the shipbuilder and I am sure that you two would have a great deal in common. "

Sanchez acknowledged the invitation with a courtly bow, his black eyes at the same time wandering in the direction of a fair-haired girl standing beside Mrs. McKane. The girl smiled as their eyes met and turning to her mother said. "Please introduce me mother. I have heard a great deal about Captain Sanchez, and can hardly wait until next fall for an opportunity to meet him. "

"My daughter Priscilla, " Mrs. McKane somewhat reluctantly volunteered after a moments hesitation which did not escape the keen eyes of the Friefly's master.

"My mother was not the only one who was thrilled by your skilful handling of the Firefly, Captain Sanchez," observed the girl after making a courtesy which would have done credit to a queen. "I am sure that I have inherited my father's liking for ships and " - Here she hesitated blushing deeply. "And the sea" she finished, quickly regaining her composure.

"I was very much in hopes that you were going to include sailors, " returned the captain simulating an air of disappointment.

"They are very much a part of of the ships and in all fairness they should not be left out . " returned the girl lowering her eyes to escape the steady gaze of the captain. "I hasten an apology. "

"Come , Priscilla,the gangway is out and we must be going," interrupted Mrs. McKane a trifle impatiently.

A shadow of annoyance crossed the captain's dark face but quickly disappeared. "It would be better perhaps if you and your mother waited until all the other passengers have disembarked, " he suggested in a low voice. "I should not be pleased to see a fair lady like yourself jostled by the crowd. "

"We would be most happy to do as you suggest, Captain Sanchez,were it not for the fact that the Widow Dennison is on the wharf, " replied Priscilla. "It would be very unkind of us to keep her waiting. "

"You cannot however deny me the pleasure of seeing you and your mother safely down the gangway, " rejoined Sanchez offering each of the ladies an arm.

"Make way for the captain " shouted a small cabin-boy springing out of nowhere and mounting the steps leading to the gangway like a monkey. "Make way for the captain. "

As the party were slowly descending the gangway a playful gust of wind suddenly whisked Priscilla's parasol from her hand and sent it sailing like a balloon out over the end of the wharf.. With an exclamation of surprise she halted and watched her orange-colored possession turn gracefully over in midair and land on the surface of the water handle-up. Her attention then was turned to a group of people shouting words of encouragement to a swimmer heading in the direction of her property. Breathlessly she watched his progress paying little heed to what was being said around her in regard to obstructing the passage of other people down the gangway.

Eventually the swimmer reached the parasol and after closing it began the return journey back to the wharf, and by the time Priscilla had reached the foot of the gangway he stood there confronting her like a retriever,with the parasol in his hand. "You will find it a bit watersoaked Miss. " he grinned."But I thought it a sin to let such a pretty thing go to waste so I went after it. "

"You were very gallant, " observed Priscilla holding out her hand graciously, and I am at loss for words with which to adequately express my appreciation. "

"You needn't bother about thanking me at all, " rejoined the young man. "I didn't go after that parasol afxyours for anything like that. I went after it just because I couldn't help myself, I guess,just because it was yours. "

"You are very complimentary" returned Priscilla blushing."I am in hopes that I shall see more of you while I am in Eastham. "

"You will. " replied the young man quite positively. "I've heard all about you from the Widow Dennison. She only lives about a stones throw from our house. "

Captain Sanchez standing close by could no longer restrain himself. "Here hand me that parasol,my good fellow" he said insolently. "Haven't you any manners? "

"That remains for your betters to decide ," rejoined the young man calmly. "I was under the impression that this parasol was the property of the young lady, that is unless you happen to be carrying one yourself these days. I would not put it past you," he concluded grinning broadly in the direction of Priscilla.

The captain of the Firefly clenched his fists and for a moment it looked as if he would throw himself upon the young man who so calmly stood there facing him, then the tension was relieved when Mrs. McKane stepped forward and taking the parasol added her thanks to those of her daughter. Captain Sanchez, smothering his anger with an effort, then escorted the ladies over to where the Widow Dennison was standing after which he retraced his steps back to the gangway of his schooner.

Meanwhile the young man had taken his stand at the foot of it and was awaiting his return. "Well, what are you hanging around here for? " queried the captain when he had arrived within speaking distance. "The passengers are all off and there are no more prarasol's to rescue. "

The young man's face flushed a deep scarlet, but with an effort he controlled his voice and replied evenly. "I won't deny that I made a fool of myself jumping in after that girl's parasol, Sanchez, but when you get the idea into your head that you are God almighty just because you happen to be a good sailor and captain one of the fastest packets in the Bay, you are all wrong and something should be done about it. "

"And what would you suggest my would-be cock of the walk," sneered the captain assuming a belligerent attitude with his feet spread far apart.

"I would teach you manners for one thing, " rejoined the young man clenching his fists and taking a step forward. "You have a lesson coming to you sooner or later , and I might as well be the one to give it. "

"Hold on a minute Danny, " exclaimed Captain Bowden of the Hornet, stepping forward. "This is my fight as much as it is yours. You go along home and leave this game -cock to me. "

"I think that you are wrong about this being your quarrel, Cap'n Bowden, " responded Danny firmly. "This is a personal matter that has to be settled one way or the other by myself. This turkey-gobbler has to be taken down a bit. "

"Strictly speaking it ain't my quarrel,that's a fact, Danny, but I heard what you said about his manners; and having had a few samples of them before now I feel that I should be the one to take him down a peg."

"Why you damned old prattler, " snarled the Firefly's captain! I can lick you with my hands tied behind my back".

"No you can't,son, and you'd best not try it if you know which side your bread is buttered on, " replied Cap'n Bowden, his steel-blue eyes fixed fearlessly on Sanchez. "I didn't make the quarter deck through no cabin winder and I used to polish off a couple of sweet-singing birds like you every morning before breakfast when I was mate in the Black Ball Line. "

"Speaking of birds you can warble some yourself,you old bag of wind, " sneered Sanchez. "If it wasn't for showing you up before all these people I would turn you wrong-side-out and hang your skin in the rigging of my schooner. "

At this sally Captain Bowden uttering a bellow which would have done credit to a mad bull charged on the master of the Firefly, who,a trifle uncertain as to the outcome and not wishing to be manhandled in the presence of so large an audience,nimbly evaded the onslaught beating a hasty retreat up the gangway.

"Now you've gone and scared him away, " grinned Danny. "I was all cocked and primed to take him down a bit when you stepped in. "

"Never mind son you'll get a chance at him sometime when I'm not around," replied Captain Bowden consolingly. With that he turned and shaking his fist in the direction of the Firefly's quarter deck where stood the cause of all their trouble, turned and walked away.

. . . .

Daniel Payne Griswold otherwise known as "Danny" to his intimates, was the son of Annie Elizabeth Griswold a widow of some nine years standing. His father, the late John Gardner Griswold, had been a God-fearing product of Cape Cod, who for many years had sailed the seven seas in quest of whales as master and part owner of the bark "Grampus".

In the days preceding Annie Griswold's widowhood her feelings while her husband was absent on a voyage were not unlike those of her neighbors whose men had gone down to the sea in ships. The long month's and sometimes years, of his absence were carefully checked off in the "Old Farmers Almanac", a book which stood next to none with the exception of the family Bible, and it was a gala-day indeed when some ship arrived at her home port bringing a letter from John.

When a year had passed, which often happened without bringing a word from the absent one, Annie Griswold would wonder as she lay awake nights in her bedroom facing the sea, with the rote of the surf on the beach constantly in her ears, whether she possessed a husband or not, and was always very much afraid some morning she would awaken to find that it was only a product of her imagination.

Then the crowing event of her life happened, the birth of her son Danny, who from the very first moment of his arrival wrapped his tiny fingers around her heart never to let go, necessitating an addition to her nightly prayer, that he might never, under any circumstances, follow in the footsteps of his father.

It was no easy task Annie Griswold had set herself for the boy's whole environment smacked of the sea. It began as you followed the shell-lined walk from the highway to the front door of Danny's home, and you were not obliged to hold one of the shells which bordered it to your ear to catch the imaginary sound of surf beating on a tropical shore, for it would come to you on the wings of a light summer breeze stealing through the clumps of syringa on either side.

And, as if that were not enough, you would see as you continued up the walk the figure-head of a ship mounted on a pedestal in the center of a broad lawn, the figure of a woman dressed in a long flowing robe with one hand shading her eyse. With little effort perhaps you could have imagined seeing this figure mounted just above the cutwater of some clipper ship, peering- always peering, out into the storm-tossed waters as if on the lookout for harbor lights or the dangers which beset the pathway of a ship at sea. Yes and perhaps you could go still farther with your imagining and visualize this fair lady of wood and the ship she graced lying at anchor in some far-away Eastern port and smell the fragrance of sandalwood and spice.

As you entered the rambling white-painted house with its green blinds by the front way and turned to your left in the small vestibule, you would still find yourself surrounded by reminders of the sea, for as soon as you stepped into the parlor your eyes would light on the model of a full rigged ship under a canopy of glass resting on a small mahogany table at one corner of the room, and as soon as your eyes had become accustomed to the shadows cast by a late afternoon sun you would observe on the walls more ships both painted and photographed... Stern, dark - bearded men stared down at you from out gilded oval frames, and upon closer inspection you would be able to decipher, although the ink has faded considerably with age, what had been written across the mat at the bottom.

"Captain Ezra Griswold, age 25. Master of the ship "Southern Cross." Ephram Griswold, age 30, Who died serving his country during the war of 1812, while a seaman on the privateer "Harpie"." There were many others of course besides those of the sea and sailors, but they all seemed to shrink back into the shadows as if fully aware they were only playing second fiddle . Was it to be wondered then that Annie Griswold found it so hard to smother her boy's desire for a thing which was so obviously a family inheritance?

On a summer evening shortly after Danny had reached his ninth birthday, Captain Griswold, returning from a trip to Boston, slowly negotiated the path leading to his back door, and there was a broad smile on his face when he greeted his wife who was standing on the step. "I have good news for you, Annie," were his first words.

"It cannot be that you have given up the water, John, " replied his wife her voice trembling with emotion. "You know that would be my most sincere wish of all, and the one if it came true that would make me the happiest."

"No, I have not given up the water, Annie, " returned Captain Griswold, placing his arm affectionately around his wife's shoulders. "But it is pretty close to it, " he added hurridly. "I have made up my mind to spend the rest of my days on soundings, and have traded my share in the Grampus for a fishing schooner called the "Watchman"."

"That will mean that you won't be away from home more than three or four weeks at a time, "rejoined Annie Griswold happily. "In comparison to the length of time you used to be away, this will seem like nothing at all. "

"It will be long enough for you to get sick of having me under foot, " observed Captain Griswold, "but I guess you wouldn't be so calloused about my goings and comings as Mrs. Bates over in Wellfleet was about her husband. She met him at the door after he had been gone four years, with a bucket in her hand. 'Now you're home you might as well go and fetch me a pail of water!'", she says before had even time to say hello. "

"Here comes Danny!" suddenly exclaimed Annie Griswold, turning with a smile on her face to greet her son.. "Captain Bowden has been making him a new boat" she said in an undertone to her husband, the smile leaving her face. "I wish he would not talk to Danny so much about sailors and boats for it puts strange notions in his head, John, notions that I had just as soon wouldn't be there. "

"You can't ever stop Danny from being interested in the sea, " replied Captain Griswold, taking the boat from the boys hand and gazing at it critically.. "You might just as well try to stop the tide from coming in. "

"Just the same I shall never give up trying, John, " answered his wife with a determined look in her eyes. "Having one sailor in the family is quite enough for me. "

"Don't you think that is a pretty nice boat father? " queried the boy proudly. "Cap'n Bowden says its a model of a new packet he is going to build. "

"Yes, its a mighty fine boat, Danny, but don't Captain Bowden need it to build his other one by? "

"No, he's got another much bigger than that" replied the boy quickly. "It's about that long," spreading his arms as far apart as he could get them.

"You and Cap'n Bowden seem to be pretty good friends, Danny. Is it because you see more of him than you do of me? "

"I guess so, " replied the boy thoughtfully. "He teaches me things about a ship and you don't, " he added after a moments silence.

"I'm sorry, son. " said Captain Griswold in an apologetic tone of voice. "I should much rather have the credit of teaching you those things myself than to have someone else do it, but your mother does not favor your being a sailor. She needs you at home, Danny. There has to be someone around the house to protect her while I am gone you know. "

" Cap'n Bowden says that I am a pretty good sailor right now," observed
the boy proudly. "I can tie all sorts of knots, box the compass and - " .

"It's growing late and past your bedtime Danny", interrupted Annie Griswold
hurridly. Please put your boat away and go to your room. Mother will be right
up to hear you say your prayers. "

"The sea is in his blood Annie, and you will never be able to change him
even if you should live to be as old as Mathuselah, " remarked Captain Griswold
after the boy had turned obdiently and gone upstairs to his room.

That night after Danny had finished his prayer and was kneeling beside
the bed he added with all the sincerity of a boyish heart. "And please, dear God,
make me a good sailor like my father and Captain Bowden. " It was then that
Annie Griswold realized for the first time how great the odds were against her,
and after tucking him in she too knelt beside the bed and prayed for strength
to combat this insidious thing which had become so firmly planted in her boy's mind.

. . . .

Captain Griswold brought the Watchman on to Eastham and fitted her out for
the fishing banks, and while this was going on Annie Griswold was more content
than she had been for years.... Then there followed several trips to the banks
which proved quite prosperous but uneventful... Finally, while Captain Griswold
was home from one of his trips, one evening he laid down the paper he had been
reading and said to his wife, "I think, Annie, I will turn the Watchman into a
Boston Packet this winter. Don't you think that she would make a good one? "

"She most certainly would, " was his wife's prompt reply. "And that would
mean having you home more than ever," she added happily. "It would be a good idea. "

"Yes, you could figure on me being home at least three nights a week and
all day Sunday , " replied her husband thoughtfully. "I'll make one more trip
and then tie her up for the winter. "

It was in mid -September when this conversation took place, and a strong autumn wind blowing in from Bay whistled a discordant note through the branches of the elms just back of the house... "It begins to sound winterish", remarked the captain after they had listened to it for a while in silence.

"If you only knew how lonesome it sounds when you are away John, and we sit here, Danny and I, waiting for you to come home,you would never leave us, " returned his wife gravely. "When you tell me that you are going to give up the sea for good it will be the happiest moment of my life. "

"After I make one more voyage your troubles will be over, Annie, " rejoined the captain cheerfully. "Nights after that when it blows like this the "atchman will be tied-up alongside some good wharf as snug as a bug in a rug. "

"It won't be long now before we we'll be having the "line gale" observed his wife as an extra heavy gust of wind shook the house, rattling the windows noisily. "I wish you would haul the Watchman up now and not go out to the banks again. "

"If everyone stayed at home just because they were afraid of bad weather there wouldn't be any fish caught," returned the captain. "Why Annie if I let a little thing like bad weather stop me I'd be the laughing stock of the village. "

"Just the same I wish that you weren't going going John. I guess that we could stand what the neighbors might say about your being afraid. You have followed the sea years enough to prove that ten times over. "

"I was thinking Annie " - here the captain paused to clear his throat... "I was thinking that it would be a good idea to take Danny along with me this trip. If its going to be my last it would give him a chance to see what fishing is like. He could make up the few weeks he would lose in school easy enough. "

Every trace of color vanished from Annie Griswold's face and she stared at her husband as if he had suddenly gone bereft of his senses.. "Take Danny with you," she observed tonelessly . "Take him out on the fishing banks at this time of the year! "

"Why yes Annie, " replied the captain. "You know that he's been teasing to go for month's, and I don't see any harm in it. If he don't go with his father he will be going with someone else before long, just as sure as you're a foot high. "

"You don't see any harm in his going, " repeated his wife. " "Well I do John Griswold,she almost screamed,rising from her chair her cheeks flushing a deep red. "The only way he will go will be over my dead body! "

"There there Annie, " soothed the captain. "You don't have to get so het-up about it. Of course I won't take Danny if you're not willing to have him go. "

Annie Griswold resumed her seat her eyes filling with tears. "You know that I would fight like a wildcat to keep that boy of ours from being a sailor, " she observed in a more settled tone of voice.

"I don't need to be reminded of it, Annie, " rejoined the captain with a shrug of his shoulders. "I've heard it times enough. But some people here in Eastham think that you've bit off more'n you can chew. "

"And one of them is Captain Bowden, " returned his wife quickly. "He's the salt of the earth where kindness is concerned, but like all the other men here on the Cape his horizon is bounded only by ships and the sea. "

"He means well enough by it though, " responded the captain. "He can't help having sailor eyes any more than the rest of us can. "

"Sailor eyes," his wife repeated in an undertone. "Yes, that's the name for it John. Its the disease I've been fighting all these years and didn't know it. "

"Most of the men here on the Cape couldn't have any other kind of eyes even if they wanted to, " rejoined her husband wisely. "They all look to the sea for their living Annie. "

"You are right John, " acknowledged his wife quickly. "But we mustn't let Danny get that way. "

"Well, it's a matter that will take a heap of figuring to straighten out, " rejoined the captain rising from his chair and reaching for the oil lamp on the mantle. "I'm going to bed Annie. We could argue from now to doomsday and it wouldn't get us any place. "

. . . .

Three days later Captain Griswold sailed for the fishing banks, while from a high point of land jutting out into the Bay his wife wife and son witnessed his departure. " I wish that I was on the Watchman with father, " remarked the boy longlingly, as he watched the schooner's hull gradually disappear below the horizon. Why didn't you let me go with him mother? "

"I need you here at home dear, " was the reply. "Mother would not know what to do with herself without a man around the house, " was the reply. "You wouldn't want to go, not if mother couldn't get along without you. Would you Danny?" she went on giving his curley head a gentle pat.

"I am not so sure about that, " was the reply. "I guess if there were more of us in the family I wouldn't be missed so much, " he ended t oughtfully.

"Who put such a notion as that into your head . Why do you think that if you had another brother or two that I would think less of you.? "

"Cap'n Bowden, " answered the boy quickly. " He said there were a lot
of boys in his family, and when he ran away to sea he wasn't missed at all. "

"Captain Bowden is a fine man Danny, but you cannot always take what he
says for granted dear, " replied his mother. "He has what your father calls
sailor eyes. "

"What are sailor eyes, mother?"

They are eyes that see nothing but ships and sailors Danny. We all
have them here on the Cape. "

"Yours seem to be all right mother, " rejoined the boy looking
up into her face curiously. "I don't see anything the matter with yours. "

"It's only an expression dear, " smiled his mother smoothing his hair
back from his temples. "You will find out what it is all about soon
enough. "

"Sailor Eyes," the boy kept repeating slowly to himself as with
one small hand in his mother's he trudged beside her down the hill
in the direction of the white house with the green blinds.

. . . .

Two weeks later a storm swept the New England coast with a devasting
force. From Provincetown to Chatham the seas beat upon the shores of the
Cape as they had never done before within the memory of the oldest inhabitant,
and on the nights when the storm was at its worst Annie Griswold prayed with
all her heart and soul for the safety of her husband and his vessel, which was
being tossed about at the mercy of the wind and sea, somewhere in the vicinity
of Georges Banks.

"Danny, Oh Danny! Promise me that you will never go away to sea,"
she begged, hugging the boy tearfully to her bosom, while in her ears sounded
the fearful din of the breakers pounding away at the beach outside. "Do you
hear Danny. Promise mother that you will never go. "

For sometime the boy remained silent, as if considering the import
of the answer which he was about to make, and action hardly expected from
one so young... Then he slipped down from her lap and confronted her sturdily.
"If I made a promise like that I should have to keep it, wouldn't I mother? "
he queried looking straight up into her eyes.

"Yes, Danny," she replied ,not a little off balance by the intensity of
his gaze. For some reason unknown to herself at the time she felt that she
was being judged , and for the first time in her life she harbored a feeling of
uncertainty as to the fairness of her plea...

"Then I won't promies mother ", was his defiant reply.

That night Annie Griswold learned that one of her boy's most distinguishing
traits was the courage of his conviction. "He is young", she reasoned hopefully..
Perhaps when he grows older he will see things in a different light.

....

The storm eventually blew itself out,and the sound of the breakers
beating on the shore grew less disturbing. From Highland Light to Woods Hole
the coast was littered with wreckage,a greater part of which had long-laid buried
in the sand. Deep-down into the graves of long-forgotton ships the grinding
force of the sea had penetrated bringing them once more to the surface, a mute
spectacle of the toll exacted by the gods of the deep from those who dared to face
them... And then as the morning sun rose higher in the heavens, it shown down on groups
of people huddled together on the shore,talking in low tones and pointing out
to sea. Far out on the horizon a tiny speck of white was visable, which for hours,
at least so it seemed to the watchers,it had made little progress in any one
direction.It was the first sail sighted since the storm , and there was little
wonder at the excitement of the people, for a large fleet of fishermen were
absent on the banks.

Annie Griswold with the first faint streaks of dawn rose from her bed and prepared a hasty breakfast for herself and Danny. She wasn't a bit hungry but managed to force down a cup of coffee and a small piece of toast, while Danny was eating his, "Where are we going mother? " he asked sleepily.

"Out on the Point to watch for your father, " she answered, gazing abstractedly out of the window at a bank of crimson and gold clouds that tinged the East.

"Do you think he will be coming home today? " asked the boy as he pulled on his small reefing-jacket and turned the collar up arounf his ears, for the air outside was tinged with frost.

"Yes Danny I am sure he will, " she answered without hesitation. But to have explained to him or to anyone else her reasons for being so sure would have been extremely difficult. She only knew that a voice - Johns voice, had called to her in the wee small hours of the morning and said "I am coming home today Annie. " That was all she had to go by, but to her way of thinking it was enough, and she wanted to be one of the first to welcome him.

Out on the Point clutching Danny's hand feverishly within her own, Annie Griswold hungrily scanned the horizon for signs of the Watchman, while all around her stood the wives of other men who like her John were out there beyond that vast expanse of dismal water, and as she gazed into their haggard and distracted faces her heart went out to them with sympathy and understanding, for they too like herself were watching and waiting for a ship which perhaps might never return.

The speck on the on the horizon grew larger as the breeze freshened gradually assuming the outlines of a fishing schooner minus her topmasts and bowsprit. Between the stumps of her once tapering spars a piece of canvas had been triced up ,evidently in an attempt to replace the sail which had been carried away, and as she steered a lumbering course across the harbor one could observe plainly that her decks had been swept clean of boats. ...

"It looks like the Osprey", somebody remarked.

"No it ain't, " argued another. "The Osprey's got a white stripe 'round her gunnel. "

"It looks to me like the Hawk out of Truro," voiced a grizzled old fisherman. "Only she'd be making her home port with the wind this way. "

"She's too big for the Hawk," observed another. "She's just about the right build for the Martha White. "

"It ain't any of them vessels," commented Captain Bowden . "You fellers couldn't see a bear on your eyebrow. That there schooner is the Watchman and she's been having a tarnation bad time of it. "

Annie Griswold,overhearing the remark, moved over to where the speaker was standing. "Do you really think it is the Watchman,Captain Bowden, " she queried eagerly.

"I sure do ma'am, " was the reply. "There ain't no other fisherman sailing out of the Cape with a hull as clean and shining as hers. "

"Thank you,Captain Bowden, " replied Annie Griswold very much relieved. "Danny and I will hurry right down to the wharf so as to greet my husband as soon as he arrives. "

Captain Bowden walked beside them down the hill and it could easily be seen that he had something on his mind, something that caused him a great deal of inward agitation,and when they reached the fork in the road that led to Annie Griswolds house he stopped short in his trac ks and said. "There's going to be a big crowd down there on the wharf when the Watchman gets in,and,like the old shay Alonzo Prebble drives 'round town in,it ain't going to be any too safe. "

"Perhaps we had better go home then and wait for him there, " replied Annie Griswold thoughtfully. "I am sure my husband would not want us to be standing around on the wharf if it isn't safe. "

"No, he wouldn't," quickly agreed Captain Bowden. "He'll be ashore in in two shakes of a lambs tail after he gets her alongside. "

For a moment Annie Griswold hesitated and then she chose the road leading to her home. "Tell John I'll be waiting for him", she called back over her shoulder.

. . . .

"Somethin' tells me she's had more trouble than losing a stick or two and a few sails, " muttered Captain Bowden to himself as he hurried down the road. "I wouldn't let that woman go down there and find that somethin' had happened to her husband for all the money in Eastham. "

Reaching the wharf Captain Bowden climbed quickly on board the Watchman and spoke to the first man who happened to be in his way. "Where's Captain Griswold? " he asked. "Why ain't he up here on deck while his vessel's docking? "

"He's down below, " answered the man in a strangely subdued tone of voice. "He won't be able to come on deck any more,leastwise not without being carried. He's dead. "

Captain Bowden quickly removed his peaked-cap and bowed his head for a moment reverently. "It will be a sorry day for his widow, " he remarked as he straightened up.

"Yes, and there'll be a lots of others besides her weeping their hearts out when the toll of this gale's counted, " rejoined the man tonelessly.

"How did it happen? " inquired Captain Bowden.

"A piece of the foretopmast hit him when the gale first come down on us off George's, " replied the man. "He wouldn't stay below after that like we wanted him to, but was bound and determined to look after his ship... And her looked after her too, " the man added after a long silence, during which he seemed to be living the struggle all over again. "If it hadn't been for him we'd all be out there now washing around among the codfish drowned to the last man. "

"Then he didn't die right away after the topmast hit him, " observed Captain Bowden.

"No, he hung on for quite sometime after that, rejoined the man. "But every little while he would spit up a mouthful of blood. We all did our very best to make him go below but he wouldn't budge an inch. We had caught a full load of fish before the gale struck us, so after we got the storm-trys'l on her the captain took the wheel. 'Boys' he says with a grim smile, 'We've got what we come out here after and some besides, so you just lash me to it and I'll pilot you home. ' " It was a sin to do it , Mister, after the beating he'd taken from the gale, but he was captain and what he said was law; so we obeyed orders. " Here the man paused and stared aft as if he still visualized the captain ~~still~~ standing at the wheel guiding his schooner home......

"He was a brave man and had what it takes to be master of a ship, " remarked Captain Bowden solemnly.

"He had God with him too, " observed the man piously. "He was with him at the wheel of this schooner and helped pilot us in. "

"What makes you so sure of that? " asked Captain Bowden.

"I'll tell you what happened and then you can judge for yourself, " replied the man. Then he was silent for quite a while evidently figuring on how to begin......

"All that night the schooner was driving like a race-horse towards home, and every now and then one of us would go up and peak out the companionway door at the captain standing there at the wheel like a statue. We did that thinking that if he wanted one of us to relieve him he would call out... Then when it began to grow daylight we all went up on deck to have a look for land and try to persuade the captain to go below, and you won't believe it, Mister, but there was Billingsgate Point right under our port bow and we was heading straight into Eastham Harbor... " Here the man paused and wet his lips with his tongue.

"How soon after that did Captain Griswold die? "

"That's where God come in, " answered the man, trying hard to stifle a note of awe in his voice. " He must have died soon after we lashed him to the wheel, Mister, for he was as stiff as a frozen codfish when we cleared him from it. "

....

Captain Bowden his brows contracted in deep thought slowly negotiated the road leading to Annie Griswold's home, the bearer of sad news. "By Tophet", he muttered under his breath. "I'd rather be boiled in oil than be doin' this. What in Sam Hill am I goin' to say when I get there?". At first he had decided upon going to the front door, but when he reached the path leading to the back door he automatically turned into it. "Nothin' but strangers ever use the front door, and she'll mistrust somethin' is up the minute she sees me. I want to break it to her gently. " His steps made a loud crunching noise in the gravel . "I wish I wasn't such an elephant. She'll hear me coming, " he grumbled under his breath.

Annie Griswold did hear him coming and met him as he rounded the corner of the house. Her sleeves were rolled up and her hands were covered with dough. "I thought it was John, " she remarked with a disappointed look on her face. "I was just making him a pan of sour-milk biscuits, and planned to have them ready for him, hot right out of the oven. "

"He sure would have liked them ma'am, " returned the captain, trying with but little success to conceal the note of sadness in his voice.

"Something has happened to him or you woudn't be looking at me like that , " rejoined Annie Griswold. "He is dead and you have come to tell me about it, " she continued, her voice trailing off into a sob.

"Yes, he's gone on his last voyage. ma'am. Gone to meet his Maker, " replied Captain Bowden solemnly.

And so in this manner the passing of Captain John Griswold was written into the annals of the sea, leaving his widow more determined than ever to prevent her son from following in his footsteps.

To say that Captain Silas Bowden was a thorn in the widow's flesh while the subject of Danny's future was being considered was no exaggeration. The captain, a bachelor, lived all alone in a cottage just up the road from her, and his influence over the boy, as we have mentioned before, was a never-ending source of worry. But in passing let us say that Captain Bowden was the soul of honor, and no one on the Cape knew it better than Annie Griswold.

And now that we have familiarized ourselves with some of the events associated with Danny Griswold's childhood let us again go forward to that day in June on which our story opens and again meet him in the character of youth.

. . . .

" I almost had a fist fight with Captain Panchez of the Firefly today, mother, " remarked Danny Griswold in a slightly embarrassed tone of voice, as he laid aside his knife and fork preparatory to rising from the supper table. "If Captain Bowden hadn't interfered we would have been at it hammer and tongs. "

"How did it happen. Danny? " queried his mother, sensing that he had something on his mind that he wished to tell her. "Did you start it? "

"Yes, I did, " was the quick response. "Sanchez got on his high-horse when one of the Firefly's passengers lost her parasol overboard and I fished it out for her. "

"I don't see anything in that to fight over, " returned his mother. "You were only doing the lady a favor, Danny. "

"It was what Sanchez said when I brought the parasol back to the girl that started it. 'Here hand me that parasol, my good fellow! Haven't you any manners?' " At this point Danny imitated him. "The girl must have thought that I was one of his lackey's, and I wasn't going to let him get away with it so I told him a thing or two. "

"But you shouldn't have lost your temper over it with ladies present, " mildly reproved his mother. "Who was the young lady, Danny? "

"A Mrs. McKane and her daughter Priscilla from Boston. They are going to stay with the Widow Dennison. I didn't say too much while they were all standing on the gangway of the Firefly, but after Sanchez had escorted the ladies over to where the Widow Dennison was standing on the wharf and returned to his ship, I gave him a piece of my mind. "

"And almost came to blows over it, " commented his mother. "Do you think that was right?" she finished chidingly.

"I would have had it out with him right or no right, if it hadn't been for Captain Bowden getting in between us. That fellow thinks he's the cock of the walk around Eastham and needs taking down a bit. "

"But you shouldn't go around with a chip on your shoulder, or the people will began to think that you are a bully, " admonished his mother. "Mrs. Dennison was telling me about her expected company. She said the husband of the woman built ships but you wouldn't be interested in that, Danny. "

"I am not so sure about that, " returned her son rising from his chair.But as far as being a bully is concerned I shall only be one when it is absolutely necessary,you can be sure of that. "

"Well, I am glad that you did not come to blows with that man, and I shall thank Captain Bowden for stopping it the very next time I see him, "

"He likes praise from you mother,and thinks you are the only real woman on the Cape," rejoined Danny with a grin.

The Widow Griswold blushed and began to hurridly clear away the dishes.. She was well-aware of the rumor being circulated around Eastham that Captain Bowden was"setting his cap"for her. "Are you going to the store. Danny? " she inquired abruptly changing the subject.

"Yes, I am going down for a while, " was the reply. "Everybody and his grandmother will be there, and if's more interesting than a town-meeting to hear them talk. "

"You won't let it interest you enough to make you want to go out in one of those ships,will you, Danny? " she returned eyeing him with a look of apprehension. "You won't suddenly take it into your head to go away and leave your mother all alone. "

"You know that I want to go, " was the reply."You have known it ever since I was knee high to a grasshopper. You have no idea how hard it is for me to stay at home while all the other young men of my age have been going to sea for years and soon will become masters of ships. If I should go eventually you will have only yourself to blame for holding me back as long as you have. The sea is my rightful heritage and some day I shall have to go down to it. "

Danny's way to the store led past the Widow Dennison's house, and just as he drew abreast the Rhododendron hedge which separated it from the road he heard the sound of footsteps coming hurridly down the walk..

"It's that girl from Boston, " he muttered under his breath, "and she probably has a letter for me to mail or something. " He quickened his steps and began to whistle.. Then the notes grew fainter and suddenly stopped as the girl suddenly rounded a tall syringa bush and stood confronting him. Danny came to an abrupt halt.

"Aren't you the boy that rescued my parasol this afternoon?, " she greeted him smilingly.

"I'm not a boy, and I don't like being called one, " answered Danny, a red flush of temper showing for a moment on his face.

"Oh, I'm sorry! " exclaimed the girl apologetically. " I was under the the impression at first that you were .. But one can be easily mistaken, " she added after a short pause.

"What made you think that I was a boy? " queried Danny, eyeing her defiantly. "I'm six feet tall and as big as any average man in Eastham. "

" I - I guess it was because you haven't a mustache, " the girl answered hesitantly . She was not a little taken back by the aggressive way Danny addressed her, for as a usual thing most young men secumbed immeadiately to her charms and were as putty in her hands.

"I'm eighteen and strong enough to do any man's work, " rejoined Danny squaring his shoulders . "I'll bet that you would not like to be called a girl, and you don't look to be a day older than seventeen. "

"Now that you have put me in my place I don't suppose there is any use of my asking you a favor, " smiled the girl. "I was going to ask you if you would please mail a letter for mother,but now I am very much afraid you will think it an imposition. "

Danny blushed. "I didn't mean to be so abrupt when you called me
a boy, " he said, holding out his hand. "I'll mail the letter for you
gladly. "

The girl after thanking him turned away, and Danny watched her
until she disappeared from view. "She's one of the nicest girl's I have
ever met, " he thought as he continued on his way to the store. "How I should
like to be captain of a ship and have her for a wife. "
....

The general store and postoffice combined of Eastham was run by a
retired shipmaster named Ezra Coffin, and it was there at one time or
another gathered almost every member of the village to gossip, trade, and
seek recreation. It was a theatre one might have said where the people
witnessed the beginning and the end of both tragedy and comedy. The walls
of the store were draped with oilskins, souwesters , caps, mittens and
cardigan-jackets;while on two long counters at the sides rested everything
pertaining to the wardrobe of a sailor and the needs of a housewife when
Jack was absent on a voyage. Boxes of dates, figs, prunes, dried apples on
strings,starch,soap, chewing tobacco, clay pipes,jack-knives, knives in a
leather sheath such as sailors carry around their waist,wooden pails of candy,
preserves, and tamarinds in syrup, brooms mops and washboards all jumbled
together, but easily located by Cap'n Ezra with the unerring instinct born of
long-practice. In front of the counters a line of bags,boxes,and barrels
served a twofold purpose,that of stowage and seats for the idlers. On an island
of sand in the middle of the floor,held in place by a barrier of two-by-fours
stood a big airtight stove,rusty and grim in summer,but spreading warmth and
cheer when the blustering winds of winter swept the Cape.In a large barn-like
room at the back a hogshead of molasses mounted on skids dripped sticky sweetness

from a spigot into the gallon measure beneath, while surrounding it, barrels
of pork, corned beef, tripe, and salt mackerel, all jostling each other for
space in order to get as far away as possible from the contaminating influence
of turpentine and kerosene oil, completed a picture of the interior.

The building a long, rambling one-story affair painted white , stood near
near the waterfront where Cap'n Ezra could see everything that was going on in
the harbor from his front porch, and a better place could not have been found for
one so steeped in the lore of the sea to spend the winter of his life. He was
spry as a cricket at eighty , and his face embellished by a snow-white goatee and
mustache, reminded one very much of weathered leather. "You don't need any banking
around your store winters, Cap'n Ezra, " a neighbor remarked one day. "You've got
enough junk piled around it to keep the cold out. " And so he had, for on both
sides and at the back there were piled a miscellaneous assortment of anchors,
capstans, chains, windlass parts, dead-eyes, single and double blocks, channels
and ring-bolts, almost to the window sills.

. . . .

Danny Griswold arrived at the store and paused for a moment beside the
old hitching-post , scarred by the teeth of many a cribbing horse. Here he
turned the letter given him to mail face up and noted the address on it in his
mind. "Donald McKane Esq., Shipbuilder, Stackpole House, Boston, Massachusetts, "
"I wish I could build ships, real ships like this man is doing, " he thought. A
faint odor of lavender greeted his nostrils and he held the letter close to his
face and smelled it. Then he visualized the face of the girl that had handed it
to him. "She's not like the girl's here on the Cape, " he reasoned. "I don't think
it would make any difference to her whether I was a sailor or not , " and this
point having been settled in his mind he turned to another. "I guess she's had a
lot of schooling and knows a lot of nice people in Boston. She probably wouldn't
look at me the second time if I was up there. " This new thought somewhat discouraged

him , so with an effort he put it out of his mind and entered the
store. Zeke Bacon, Cap'n Ezra's hired man was busy postmarking the
outgoing mail, and the thud of his stamp resounded from behind the
thin partition which separated him from the public. "Here's another
for you to belabor Zeke, " said Danny with a smile as he pushed the
letter through the slot under the window.

"Seems to me I've heard of that man before, " remarked Zeke as
he picked up the letter and scanned the address curiously.. "By thunder!
Now I've got it. He's the one that is building that new clipper up in
Boston called the"Red Jacket".

"His wife and daughter's rustacating at the Widow Dennisons,"
volunteered Danny. "They come down this afternoon on the Firefly. "

"I reckon we ain't had summer folks like them down here for
quite a spell, " returned Zeke as he postmarked the letter with great
care and placed it in the bag. "They're pretty big potatoes up Boston way. "

"They are not a bit stuck-up though, and I hope they will stay all
summer, " rejoined Danny as he moved away from the window to make room for
another customer.

The store as usual at this time of the evening was crowded with
people enveloped in a blue-grey haze of tobacco smoke,men in the various
seasons of their lives, lounged about on boxes and barrels discussing the
all-important subject ,ships; while near them stood the small boys who
were fortunate enough to be allowed the privilege of listening to their
conversation,staring with opened-eyed admiration at these men;who ,matching the
bravery of their brothers of the covered wagon, had chosen an equally hazard-
ous route to California around Cape Horn.

"Hello, Danny, " greeted Captain Ezra, peering out from behind a pile of rubber boots on the counter. "How's your Ma? "

"She's fine, Cap'n Ezra. "

"It's a tarnation pity that she won't let a likely lad of your age go to sea, " observed the captain eyeing Danny's broad shoulders appraisingly. "I wasn't any bigger than a tadpole when I first went. "

"Hello, Cap'n Ezra, " saluted a tall, broad-shouldered man striding up to the counter. "They want a mate for the bark "Sunrise". But he has to be able to jump over the fore yard every morning before breakfast, " he added after a brief pause. "I thought you would be able to fill the bill".

"By cracky I'm your man if they'll lay it down on deck for me, " was the quick rejoinder. A chorus of laugh's followed, for Cap'n Ezra had the reputation of being the wittest man in the village.

"Come on, Cap'n Ezra, spin us a yarn," someone suggested. "There ain't any buisness goin' except ship-talk. "

Captain Ezra shook his head. "I don't know any. I'm plumb storied-out. "

"Oh, come on Cap'n and give your imagination a fair wind, " voiced another.

"Speaking of imagination makes me think of a feller who used to come down here preaching about it from Boston, " observed Cap'n Ezra thoughtfully. "I had just come home from a long voyage in the bark Martha Brigs, and having no place to go in particular one night I went over to the Town Hall to hear him. He said that everybody that believed in it was seven kinds of a fool and ought to have his head examined. He said nothin' was so unless you had it right before your eyes in black and white. After the meeting was over Obediah Prebble invited him over to his house for the night . It was pretty hot when the feller went to bed, for it was in the

month of August,but bein' pretty well tired out with his rantin' he
falls off to sleep in a jiffy... Then about three in the morning he
wakes up,so he said, sweating like a bull, and feeling there wasn't any
window open in the room,he crawls out of bed an' starts hunting around
for one. It was darker than a stack of black cats and it took him quite a
while to find one, and when he did he couldn't open it, so he finally locates
one of his boots, and by that time he was so desperate for the want of air,
that he takes the boot and smashes the glass out. He said after that he could
feel the fresh air blowing in on his face, and he went off to sleep like a
baby in a crib. " Here Cap'n Ezra came to a full stop, and clearing his
throat gazed mildly at his audience.

"I don't see anything funny about that, " someone remarked.

"Neither did that feller who was preaching about imagination, "
grinned Cap'n Ezra."When he woke up the next morning the winder was staring
him right in the face without a scratch. He had gone and smashed the looking
glass hitched to Mrs. Prebble's bureau. "

"I'll bet he didn't preach any more about imagination in Eastham
after that " somebody remarked.

Cap'n Ezra chuckled. "You're just darned tootin' he didn't.
After he had paid Mrs. Prebble the price of a new looking glass , he went
off down the road, winged out, and that was the last they ever saw of him. "

After Ezra had finished his yarn a rich barytone voice started
humming "On The Banks of the Sacramento" a sea -chantey very popular at
the time , and soon the store vibrated to the words and chorus sung as
only men can sing it who have felt the braces of a lofty ship in their hands,
beating to the Westward around Cape Horn.

"Blow,boy's blow,for Cali-for-nee O.

There's plenty of gold so I've been told.

On the banks of the Sacramento ".

This naturally brought the conversation around to the all-absorbing topic of California. "They say that Abner Harrison's turned his brig into a eating-house out in "Frisco ", remarked a sailor perched high and dry on a cracker barrel. "He's got her moored to the end of a wharf an' doin' a land office business. "

"He sure knows which side his bread is buttered on, " observed another sailor.

"Abner Harrison was one of the slickest dancers on the Cape," added Cap'n Ezra as he carefully selected a broom spill to clean his pipe. "It wasn't so long ago that he and I used to dance each other down over at the town-hall. " (It might be said in passing that Cap'n Ezra still led the grand march at all the dances) .

"I'm loading my ship with picks an' shovels, " voiced a tall darkly-bearded man, who was seated on a nail keg whittling a piece of soft pine. "I reckon they need 'em out there. " The captain who had spoken had established a record on his last voyage to the Westward, 90 days from Salem, Massachusetts, to San Francisco via Cape Horn.

"My owners figure on getting 'em goin' and comin', " obserbed another captain dryly. "I've got more dudars in my ship's hold than you can shake a stick at. Cradles, teething-rings, coffins and grindstones, clocks and dict-ionaries, melodeons and cabinet organs, tombstones an' printing presses, an' — " Here he ran out of wind and stopped abruptly.

"By Tophet" exclaimed Cap'n Ezra coming out from behind the counter. Everybody in this town's gone plumb crazy over California. Silas Bacon was in here yesterday mornin' an' he says to me ' Ezra, I guess I'll have to be gettin' up my anchor an' headin ' out Cali-for-nee way. I know it's stuck pretty deep in the mud but I guess I can break it out somehow. "

"For heaven's sake, I says. What started an old coot like you thinking about California? "

"The Old Lady, " he replies with a sheepish look on his face. 'She come out of the buttery last night carryin' on like no pitch hot. 'Silas ' she says . 'The provender's getting low an' one or t'other of us has got to go 'round Cape Horn, an' I ain't a goin'. "

"How old is Silas? " inquired one of the men thoughtfully.

"He'll be 96 his next birthday, " chuckled Cap'n Ezra. "Do you want to take him out with you as mate? "

On his way home that night from the store Danny's thoughts were evenly divided. One minute they were on the Widow Dennison's summer boarders and the next of shipping on some vessel bound to California.

. . . .

A warm summer morning with a gentle breeze sweeping in, clean and fresh from the sea. A country road yellow in the sunlight ,lined with elm and poplar,shading neatly -painted frame houses ,nestled snugly away behind clumps of lilac and syringa. Roses everywhere in great profusion,red,yellow, pink and white, glistening with dew and filling the air with subtle fragrance. In the distance one can see a small white church partly hidden in a grove of pines, and from its belfry they can hear the clear vibrating notes of a bell.

Along the road, dust-laid by an early morning shower ,walk the God-fearing people of Eastham in the direction of this house of worship, for the day is Sunday and they seek solace from the earthly problems that trouble both mind and body.

Broad- shouldered darkly bearded sea captains, attired in blue suits,
their coats decorated with brass buttons, parade majestically in the middle
of the road, while by their side walk gentle, sweet-faced women clinging
proudly to their lord and master's arm. Silks from the Orient flutter in
ever-changing color modestly hiding the womanly contour of their bodies
from view... On their heads rest small bonnet's held firmly in place by bands
of ribbon tied in a bow under the chin.. Shawls of a gossamer texture cover
their slender bodies while the hands which hold the parasol aloft is silken-mitted.

In the rear walk the younger members of the family, the older girls
counterparts of their mother's in dress, many of whom cling timidly to the arm
of a sun-tanned sailor-beaux, who, as they walk along discourses mainly of his
adventures in foreign climes.. And then in turn come the small boys and girls,
the former in roundabout and Eaton collar, their face's shining from the effect
of a vigorous scrubbing with soap and water, the latter in short tight-sleeved
dresses, their heads surmounted by wide-brimmed Leghorn hats trimmed with flowers,
walking sedately in emulation of their elders, and all trying as best they can
to check the out-pouring of their childish spirit in order to conform with the
solemnity of the day.

......

Danny Griswold as usual escorted his mother to church that day and sat
beside her in the pew. They were early and the minister had not as yet taken his
place in the pulpit, but lingered near the vestibule door, greeting his flock with
a broad smile of welcome as they came in. Inside the church the congregation shifted
uneasily in their seats, and occasionally addressed one of their number in a
breathless undertone... The creaking of a seat as someone reached for a hym-book,
and the rustling of the leaves as it was slowly being turned ,were magnified a
thousand fold in the tomb-like stillness. Through the open windows came sounds of
the wind gently stirring the pine bows, interrupted at intervals by the notes of
a robin 'calling for rain',

As Danny sat there in the pew his thoughts were centered on Priscilla McKane, and at the sound of steps coming down the aisle he would turn in his seat expectantly... He was positive that she would be there, for the Widow Dennison was a devout church-goer and would surely bring them with her to the service... They came at last, the Widow in the lead attired in her Sunday best, mustering her charges much the same as a hen would her chickens, and filled with the importance of having the cream of Eastham's boarders in tow, bowing majestically to the right and left as she proceeded down the aisle. Mrs. McKane kept her head modestly bowed as she walked, but not so her daughter, who, the embodiment of Boston's prevailing fashion, held her head high , glancing boldly out from under the wide brim of her hat in a way that made many a young sailor man's heart rock as in a heavy sea when their eyes met.

Danny watched her progress down the aisle with bated breath, but when he saw the captain of the Firefly overtake her and pass some smiling remark in a low tone , for the first time in his life he suffered a pang of jealousy. The pew directly in front of them was the Widow Dennison's and as they paused before it he heard the widow mincingly invite the captain to sit with them. "The darned old gossip", he muttered under his breath. "Why don't she mind her own business. " Before that he had fully intended to smile pleasantly when he caught Priscilla's eye, but now he looked the other way, a hot flush of anger mantling his cheeks.

"Isn't that Mrs. McKane and her daughter, Danny? " inquired Mrs. Griswold in an undertone.

"Yes, " replied Danny shortly.

"Mrs. McKane is a very attractive woman, and a very sensible one, I should imagine, " Mrs. Griswold continued not having noticed her son's embarrassment.

"She has more sense than that chatterbox of a Widow Dennison ",
rejoined Danny. "When she asked Sanchez to sit with them she acted
like the Queen of Sheba. "

"Hush, Danny. The minister is taking his place in the pulpit, "
admonished Mrs. Griswold in a whisper.

All through the sermon which was aggravatingly long, Danny
watched the captain of the Firefly casting amorous glances in
Priscilla's direction until his blood fairly boiled with anger. He
was in such a disturbed state of mind that when Captain Bowden came along
with the contribution-box he didn't even acknowledge his friendly salute.

The service over at last Danny left his mother with a neighbor and
hurried outside to take his stand near the church steps. It had been his
intention to ask Priscilla if she would take a walk with him that afternoon
out on the Point,but when she came out of the church in earnest conversation
with Sanchez whose charms seemed to have completely captivated her, his
courage left him and he edged farther back into the crowd watcing the people
leave the church.

"She's rolling down to St. Helena with eighteen cloths in her
lower studdin's'l and no change out of a dollar, " remarked a tall,broad -
shouldered man,glancing at Danny quizzically. "Didn't you rescue that
clippers top hamper from the Bay yesterday, Griswold. "

"I sure did, Cap'n Bacon, but I would never make a fool out
myself that way again," replied Danny. "I don't want anything more to do
with girls as long as I live. "

"So that's the way the wind blows, " smiled Captain Bacon. "She's a trim sailing packet, Danny, and I wouldn't mind convoying her myself if it wasn't for Naomi here," he went on glancing at a pretty, dark-haired girl at his side. "How about it Naomi. Do you think I could cut that packet-sailor out who has the Boston girl in tow.' "

"I am pretty sure you could if you set your mind to it, Arnold, but you had better not try it out while I'm around, " smiling replied the girl.

"Laying all jokes aside, Danny. How would you like to go out with me in the Red Jacket? I 'm looking for a likely lad about your size," said Captain Bacon turning serious and giving Danny's shoulder a friendly pat.

Danny gazed at him for a moment in silence, hardly believing his ears. "It's the one thing I have been wanting to do all my life, Cap'n Bacon. I would go in a minute if it wasn't for mother. But she wouldn't let me go sir, I know that very well without asking. "

"After what happened to your father I can hardly blame her. I probably shouldn't have suggested it, " replied Captain Bacon. "But if she happens to change her mind, Danny, the Red Jacket is loading in Boston and there will always be a berth open for you in her while I am in command.

Danny thanked him and moved dejectedly away, while far down the road he glimpsed Priscilla and her escort walking arm in arm, followed at a discreet distance by Mrs. McKane and the Widow Dennison. "I wish that I had that fellow some place where I could give him a good licking, " muttered Danny as he started off across the fields on a short cut to Captain Bowden's home where he was always sure of finding relief from his troubles.

. . . .

Captain Bowdens small cottage stood well back from the road,sheltered quite comfortably from the north winds which swept the Cape in winter by two towering oak trees. It was painted white like Danny's but there the resemlance ended,for the blinds were a bright red. "If my neighbors don't like to look at 'em they can shut their eyes when they go by, " he was wont to remark when some unthinking person happened to criticise their color.

Next to the sea Captain Bowden loved his flowers. "I didn't get my fill of 'em when I was a boy , " he would tell you as his gaze wandered proudly over the well-kept beds in his front yard. " I used to lay awake nights when my ship was pitchin' an' tossin' out there on the ocean and think of them pretty things blooming back here on the Cape .Sometimes I could almost smell 'em. "

On either side of the front windows lilac bushes reared their branches, in season a mass of purple,sweet-smelling flowers, a veritable land of plenty for the bees.. And yes, there was another thing dear to the old man's heart, a marsh not far distant from the house where in the early spring,just after the frost was out of the ground,frogs peeped a joyous chorus of relief from a long cold winter. " I never could forget them peepers, " the captain would remark with a thoughtful look on his face."I've heard 'em in many foreign countries but they never sounded quite so good any place as they do at home here."

It would not have been a real seafaring man's home if the grounds had not displayed something pertaining to the sea however which could have met the eye. In Captain Bowden's case it was a weathervane, the model of aclipper ship,perched high over the gable of his house, her bows heading into the wind.

Danny reached the house far ahead of Captain Bowden and seated himself
on the back steps to await his arrival. The bees hummed steadily as they
darted here and there among the flowers, and the captain's big yellow cat
Barnacle,disturbed from its noonday nap under the lilac bush by the back
porch, rose lazily to its feet arched its back, and then stretching to its
full length,yawned sleepily showing the carmine roof of its mouth, after which
it settled back on its haunches a picture of contentment.

"I wish that I didn't have anything more to trouble me than that cat,"
sighed Danny... The animal seeming to sense Danny's state of mind rose
majestically to its feet , and after stretching again strolled over to where
he was seated and began rubbing against his leg purring loudly. " I guess
Barnacle you would help straighten this matter out if you could, " said Danny
stroking the cat's back gently. The cat stuck its tail in the air uttering what
could have been taken for a sympathetci mew.. Danny continued stroking its back
turning over in his mind Captain Bacon's offer.....He could visualize the Red
Jacket's tall tapering spars,her brightly holystoned decks, and the network of
ropes which composed her running-rigging.. In his minds eye he could see the
clouds of billowing white canvas hanging from her yards.. He could also hear
the wind humming in her stays and smell the salt breeze mixed with tar so dear
to a sailors heart... The voices of his ancestors were calling him - calling and
pleading for him to accept his rightful heritage.

Feeling thirsty he went over to the well and lowered the bucket down
into the cool refreshing water beneath.. The creaking of the windlass as he drew the
bucket to the surface deadened the sounds of Captain Bowden's approach, and when
Danny turned with the filled dipper in his hand the former stood confronting him
with a broad smile of welcome on his face."Was you waiting for me,Danny,or only
getting a drink of my aqua pura on your way home? " he queried as he stooped to
give Barnacle a friendly pat.

" I was waiting for you Cap'n Silas, " Danny replied in voice which trembled with emotion. "I guess I need your advice today more than I ever did before in my life. "

"Well Danny,maybe you've come to the right place,and maybe you ain't," replied Captain Bowden stroking his white chin-whisker reflectively. "What's on your mind son? "

"Captain Bacon has just asked me if I would want to go out in the Red Jacket with him, " rejoined Danny coming directly to the point. "It's the chance of a lifetime,Cap'n Silas,and I want to go. "

"I know how you feel, " replied Captain Bowden, after a long silence during which he was going over the matter carefully in his mind. "I know just how you feel," he repeated. "But how are we goin' to get your mother to feel the same as we do about it? "

"I don't know," returned Danny quickly."But I thought you might think up some way of getting her consent. "

"She wouldn't listen to me,Danny,no more than she would you. The only way would be for you to run away and that would break her heart. If she ever had an idea that I ever suggested such a thing to you though she would never speak to me again. "

"Running away wouldn't be anything new," rejoined Danny. " I can name a dozen men here on the Cape who ran away to sea when they were boys. Why you did it yourself Cap'n Silas. "

"So I did Danny, but my ma had four boys and we sort of spelled each other staying home. You are the only one your ma's got and that makes it a hoss of another color. "

"Of course I didn't figure on leaving mother without someone to look after her, " replied Danny thoughtfully. "I was sort of figuring that you might do it,Cap'n Silas.. That is if I made up my mind to go. "

"Come on into the house Danny, " said Captain Bowden ,his face
clouded by perplexing thoughts. "We can talk things over more comfortable
in there. "

One could have likened the sitting-room of Captain Bowden's home to
that of a curiosity shop, for every inch of space was utilized to accommodate
some relic of the sea. Over a square,oak table in the center a brass lamp
hung suspended from the ceiling,while from it dangled a flying fish its
wings out-spread ,swinging slowly to-and- fro in the breeze from the open
window,its varnished body glistening in the sunlight.. The table itself was
littered with a varid assortment of books and papers,many of them musty with
age. A well-thumbed book on practical navigation by Bowditch, a pile of "Old
Farmer's Almanac's,rolls of charts filled with numberless tiny holes made from
the sharp points of a divider as they had traced out the position of some ship,
and last but not the least a copy of the "Lady's Book" a magazine very much
in vogue during that period on the Cape,in which by way of introduction Mr.
Godoy the editor averred "that his magazine should be a shrine for the offerings
for those who wish to promote the mental; moral and religious improvement of
women. For female genius it is the appropriate sphere. It will contain a new and
elegant engraving in every number – also music and for ladies' muslin work and
other embellishments, " etc.

At first one would have wondered why this magazine graced the table of
Silas Bowden bachelor, but as it was carefully hidden away beneath a pile of
Topliff's News Bulletins,one could have assumed and not been too far out of the
way ,that he was secretly posting himself as to the idiosyncrasies of the opposite
sex.

The walls of the room were literally covered with pictures in frames
and out,of brigs,barks, schooners, Arab dhows and pinkey's ,each elbowing the
other for space. The painting of a bluff-bowed North Sea fishing boat on the

"Dogger Banks",rubbed shoulders with the famous Liverpool packet Dreadnought ,
while a lofty Black Ball liner with all sail set and a bone in her teeth,
towered majestically over a picture of Captain Bowden's latest possession,the
Hornet.

A long brass telescope hung over the mantel and beneath it rested a
quadrant encrusted with pea-green verdigris by the moisture of the seven seas,
flanked by curios of ivory, jade,and ebony,bits of coral,shells, lacqured
boxes and silken fans. There were other shelves in the room, all dust-covered
and neglected,upon which rested models of junks with their sails of matting
spread to catch the wind, Japanese swords and daggers, Chinese slippers
embroidered in blue and gold,small statues of tigers, elephants, dragons and
Buddha's, Shinto priests and what not, all peering out of some dusky corner
as if seeking liberation from a prison.

It was to this room Captain Bowden invited Danny and motioned for him
to be seated in a large rocker near the table.. This ceremony over he began
to search his coat pockets for smoking tobacco, and eventually finding it he
started to whittle the plug,his brows puckered in deep thought....

" I guess you didn't hear me,Cap'n Silas when I spoke to you about
looking after mother,if I should go out in the Red Jacket? " observed Danny
breaking the silence.

" I heard you all right,Danny, " answered Captain Bowden after he had
struck a match and applied it to his pipe. "But that's a job I ain't so
sure she will agree to having me perform. "

"Not wanting to run away,Cap'n Silas, I thought you might go over home
this evening and talk her into letting me go. You could do it if anyone could,
for She thinks that you are the salt of the earth. "

Captain Bowden seated himself near Danny and there was a scared look
on his face. "I would rather poke a stick into a hornet's nest than to
try and coax your ma into lettin' you go to sea, " the captain returned
hurridly. "Why she's so set against your goin' that she wouldn't ××××× speak
to me again for the rest of my natural life if I even mentioned it. "

"Then there is only one thing left for me to do, and that is run
away", rejoined Danny. "I am old enough to know my own mind,and it is no disgrace
for me to follow the sea as you and my father did. I have been saturated with
the atmosphere ever since I was a small boy. It's my rightful heritage,Cap'n
Silas. "

To plead Danny's cause with the Widow Griswold was the last thing in
the world that Captain Bowden felt like doing; but on the other hand he wished
to be loyal to her son,for it was he who had helped plant the seed of desire
in the young man's heart for the sea. He had listened to the call of the sea
himself when a small boy and had answered it just as Danny wanted to do now.
Captain Bowden was dangerously close to the breakers so he went off on another
tack. "I was a long way off my reckoning,Danny,when I come home and found you
waiting for me, " he remarked with a friendly twinkle in his eye. "I thought
you had come over to talk to me about that Boston girl. "

Danny's face turned a deep red,and his eyes flashed with anger."I don't
want anything more to do with her, " he replied. "She's gone plumb crazy over that
fellow Sanchez. They are as close as two peas in a pod. "

"I wouldn't be so sure of that," replied Captain Bowden. "It would
be no more than natural for her to be friendly with him seems she come down
on his schooner, and setting in a pew with him through a sermon ain't goin' to
give him the inside track either,not if I'm any judge of females. "

"She walked home from church with him, and they went as thick as
the fog coming in off the Banks, " rejoined Danny. "She only has eyes
for sailors like everyone else here in Eastham except mother. That is
why I want to go out in the Red Jacket Cap'n Silas. "

"Why don't you stay home and try to get on the right side of her
this summer, " suggested Captain Bowden. " Her father is a big shipbuilder
in Boston and this fall he might help you get a ship,if you still wanted
to go to sea. "

"Yes,it is all over Eastham now that her father is quite a famous
shipbuilder", repiled Danny. "Zeke Bacon found it out when I mailed a letter
for Mrs. McKane last night, and it didn't take him long to spread the news."

"And he was helped considerably by the Widow Dennison, "
chuckled Captain Bowden.

"She's another one I don't like, " growled Danny. "Butter
wouldn't melt in her mouth when she has summer boarders in tow. "

"She reminds me of old Sarah Tupper over in Hyannis. " observed
Captain Bowden with an amused twinkle in his eye. "She used to keep summer
boarders , and right away after they had arrived from the city she would
take them out visiting the neighbors. That woan used to tramp from one end
of Hyannis to the other,startin' in just as soon as she got her breakfast
dishes washed. With her flock at her heels she would start by calling on
her next door neighbor. ' How nice your garden looks Mrs. Rotch ' she would
say with a simper.'I have never seen such pretty roses in all my life'. And
then her flock would shanty a chorus of 'Oh,how pretty' . After that Mrs
Tupper would work her way into the house and compliment Mrs. Rotch on her
cake or pie, and the poor woman would be so flattered that she couldn't help
offering them some. Then after they had gorged themselves they would pass

on to another house where it would be beans or somethin' like that. Mrs.
Tupper saved more money that way on vittels than you could shake stick at. "

"Mrs. McKane didn't seem very pleased when the Widow Dennison
invited Sanchez to sit with them, " remarked Danny after a long silence.
"But her daughter was all smiles. She looks to me very much like a flirt."

"She's a high-stepper all right, but I don't think that she's a
flirt, Danny. " returned the captain thoughtfully. "All the girls up
Boston-way act like that ,but most of 'em don't mean any harm by it. Her
father's about as square as they come, and it stands to reason that his
wife and daughter would be the same. "

"I guess neither one of them could have said very much against
Sanchez sitting there even if they had wanted to," said Danny. "It was
the Widow Dennison's pew. "

"So it was, " agreed Captain Bowden . " I guess maybe you're
making a mountain out of a mole-hill Danny. "

"I'm pretty sure of one thing though, Cap'n Silas, and
that is, Priscilla McKane don't have eyes for anyone but a sailor,"
rejoined Danny . "And that is why I am more determined than ever to be
one myself. "

"I know just how you feel Danny, an' if I had any influence
at all with your mother I'd use it,but if you do make up your mind to
go you can be sure that I'll keep my eye out for her all the time you're
gone, " replied Captain Bowden.

"I know that you will Cap'n Silas, and it will be a great
relief to know that Mother is being looked after while I am away. I have
quite sometime to think it over, and perhaps I may change my mind before
the Red Jacket sails. "

Danny Griswold stayed away from the vicinity of the Widow Dennison's
home for several days after his talk with Captain Bowden, and busied himself
with his lobster pots at the Cove, during which time Priscilla was constantly
on his mind but he stubbornly refrained from going any place where there
would have been a chance of his meeting her. In spite of this seeming lack
of interest however, when at home he watched the road eagerly for a glimpse
of her ,and if by chance he saw her about to pass the house, he would scurry
like a frightened rabbit to the parlor window and from behind the curtain
watch her go by. He might have continued this game of hide and seek indefinitely, but as it so-happened destiny intervened one night and rather
unexpectedly brought them together again. While coming home from the store
rather late he was suddenly aroused from his reveries by the sound of excited voices
issuing from within the sacred precint of the Widow Dennison's. home He stopped
short in his tracks and listened... Something quite out of the ordinary was
taking place there could have been no doubt, for as he listened a woman's voice
pierced the night air calling for help... The night was pitch dark and the sound
sent a shiver running up and down his spine, but without a moment's hesitation
he hurried through the already open gate and hurried up the front walk,
negotiating the steps of the porch when he reached them two at a time. The front
door being wide-open he stepped inside and as he did so discerned the figure of
a man groping blindly about in the hallway. "Wash all this rumpus goin' on, "
the man was muttering in a thick voice. "Can't a feller come home and go upstairs
to bed without everybody makin' such a fuss? "

Danny recognized the voice at once as belonging to Sam Wortle , a shiftless
fellow who lived over at the Cove. In a highly inebriated state of mind he had
mistaken the widows house for his own domicile , and inocenlly enough was trying

to find his bedroom. "Get out of this, " growled Danny ,grabbing the
bewildered Wortle by the collar and forcing him towards the door."Go
on down to your boathouse and sleep it off. "

In the meantime the Widow Dennison was standing at the head of the
stairs , a lamp held high above her head, and screaming at the top of
her voice,while behind her stood Mrs. McKane and Priscilla...

Danny pushed the drunken man outside and closed the door after him,
then he turned his attention to the frightened group above. "It was only
Sam Wortle" he called up reassuringly. "He was'drunk as a fiddler' and
looking for a place to sleep it off. "

"Sakes alive! " exclaimed the widow. "I never heard of such goin's on
in all my life! He come up the stairs after we were all asleep, and when he
got to the top he tumbled all the way down to the bottom, and it sounded as if
the house was bein' shook from its foundation. " Here she paused to catch her
breath... "He must have knocked over all the chairs in the parlor and we thought
the end of the world had come, " she concluded.

"He won't give you any more trouble, Mrs. Dennison, " Danny replied with
a smile. "I'll go right out and see that he gets a good start for his boathouse
where he usually goes to sober off. "

"You always turn up at the right moment Mr. Griswold, " remarked
Priscilla ,peering out from behind the widows shoulder. "I do not know what we
should have done if it hadn't been for you. "

"Sam Wortle wouldn't hurt a flea, " was Danny's laughing reply as he
turned to go. "He's one of the most harmless men in Eastham. But in the
future it might be a good idea for you to keep your front door locked, " he
called back to the Widow Dennison over his shoulder.

. . . .

"It only seems as if it were yesterday that I stood out there on that headland and watched what was left of my father's schooner come drifting into the harbor, " Danny remarked to Priscilla as he pointed in the direction of a high bluff which projected far out into the water. On the morning after Sam Wortle had mistaken the Widow Dennison's house for his own she had followed Danny down to the Cove and was seated on an upturned bucket intently watching him repair lobster pots.

"Then your father followed the sea, " observed Priscilla as she watched him shape and deftly place a willow rib in position. "If I had been born a boy I would have followed it too, " she finished thoughtfully.

"All my ancestors were sailors, " Danny rejoined quickly. "History says that one of them discovered and named this Cape in 1602, " he went on proudly. "Only the name was spelled Gosnold instead of Griswold them. "

"I guess almost every man and boy here on the Cape has something to do with the sea, " returned Priscilla reflectively. "Father thinks that it is the most wonderful calling in the world. He says that the men that sail his ships are like the wood he puts into them . It makes men out of the boys that go down to the sea in them, Real men, " she added as an afterthought.

"There are exceptions, " replied Danny as he nailed a lath in place. "I know quite a few people who wouldn't rate the title of a man if they went to sea all their lives. It takes a lot besides good clothes and a lot of conceit to be a sailor. "

"When will you be going away on another voyage? " asked Priscilla. She was quite well-aware that he had yet to make his first one, for she had thoroughly probed the Widow Dennison regarding the matter.

"Miss. McKane, I have never been outside of this harbor in anything but
a sailboat in all my life, " confessed Danny an embarrassed flush mantling
his cheek.

"It's a shame that you did not have a chance to travel and see the
world as Captain Sanchez did . I think that he is one of the most interesting
men I have ever met. " remarked Priscilla. "Are you going to stay here and
fish for lobsters all your life? "

"No,I'm not, " answered Danny irritably. Just then the hammer missed
the nail he was driving and struck his finger a glancing blow. He shook his
hand several times and then placed the injured finger in his mouth.

"Oh you've hurt yourself! " exclaimed Priscilla.

"I's nothing", returned Danny. "I'm not sissy enough to let a little
thing like that bother me. "

Priscilla realizing that she was on thin ice tactfully changed the
subject. "I blush for shame when I think of how we looked standing there at
the head of the stairs last night , " she said. "It was very fortunate that
you happened to be passing the house as you did or Mrs, Dennison would have
died from fright. "

Danny grinned in spite of himself. "She did look funny with her
curlpapers flying every which way, " he replied. "With the sense of a bedbug
she might have known that it was Sam Wortle on one of his sprees. "

"She was scared nearly out of her wits, and all she could do was
stand there and scream for help, " laughingly replied Priscilla. "Mother and
I thought the end of the world had come. "

Danny busily engaged in fitting a lath to the framework was silent
for a time, while Priscilla idly traced strange characters in the sand with a
stick and patiently waited for him to finish.... The task over Danny straightened up and said, " They call that the "Widows Walk " up there Miss. McKane,"

he said, pointing again to the bluff. "When there's been a bad storm here on the Cape,the wives of the men who are absent go up there and watch the harbor for their return. Some don't come back at all, and some dead like my father. "

"Oh Danny how sad! " exclaimed Priscilla,her eyes filling with tears. And the suddenly realizing that she had called him by his first name she blushed a deep-red. "It came out before I thought," she hastily apologized.

"And it sounded awfully good coming from you, " was Danny's ~~hasty~~ rejoinder. "No one in Eastham ever called me Mr. Griswold before, and every time you said it I could not help but think that you were making fun of me. "

"But I wasn't,"denied Priscilla. "I shouldn't ever think of calling Captain Sanchez,Alfredo, and he has been much nicer to me than you have. "

"I'm sorry, " returned Danny. " I guess living here in Eastham all my life has made me unusually self- conscious and small. But I don't want to be that way if I can help it. Mother has always been against my going to sea, and I guess that is the cause of my being so disagreeable at times. "

"I know that it is not right to even suggest such a thing, Danny, but why didn't you run away like many a boy has done when their parents objected to their going. "

"I wanted to badly enough, but I was too cowardly to make the attempt." was the reply. "The sea is my rightful heritage,Priscilla, and nights after my father died, when it was blowing a gale of wind outside, I used to sit on the cellar stairs in the dark and listen to it howl around the house. I fancied myself on the deck of a ship, and I could hear the hiss of the angry seas as they boarded her and washed aft.. The call of the sea was in my blood,Priscilla, and when I could not stand it any longer I used to get up off the stairs and come down here to the Cove and stand for a long time listening to the surf beat against the rocks.. Mother thought I did it for devilment, and she used to whip

me for getting all wet and bedraggled. I never told her though how hard it was
for me to keep from running away, for she would have never understood. I shall
never forget the look on her face when they brought my father home nine years
ago and when I think of what happened I cannot blame her for not having sailor
eyes like all the rest of us. I want to go, Priscilla. God knows I do. But not bad
enough to break my mothers heart. "

Priscilla on the verge of tears drew a daintily emboidered handkerchief
from a small reticule she carried and gently applied it to her eyes. "I can hardly
blame your mother for hating the sea, " she said, her voice husky with emotion.
"If I ever marry a sailor I shall never leave him out of my sight for even a minute,
and I shall insist on him taking me on every voyage he makes. "

"My mother felt the same way about it before she was married, " rejoined
Danny, sheepishly wiping the moisture away from his own eyes with his bare arm.
"But when the time came for her to go she couldn't do it, for she was afraid. I guess
if she had gone though things would have been different. I don't hold it against
her however, for it is the will of God that someone who is near and dear to a
sailor shall always be waiting for his return. "

"Mother's always do a lot of things which do not seem fair at the
beginning, " observed Priscilla thoughtfully. "Mine brought me down here this summer
because she ~~thought~~ was afraid that I would run away too. "

"Where would you run? A girl like you with everything you want. "
queried Danny extremely puzzled.

"You wouldn't understand, " answered Priscilla. "I really shouldn't have
said anything about it at all it sounds so silly, now that I have had a chance to
think it over. I guess mother was right when she said a summer here in Eastham would
make me forget all about it. I'm beginning to and I have been down here less than a
week. It was very romantic while it lasted though, " she concluded with a deep sigh.

"It's all Greek to me, " remarked Danny. "I can hardly figure how a week in Eastham could make you change your mind about anything. "

"That's because you have never been away from Eastham and have had no experience with other places or people, " replied Priscilla. "Perhaps you would understand what I mean better if you should pay a visit to Boston. "

"Maybe I'd feel the way Old Eben Strout did after his first visit, " smilingly rejoined Danny. "When somebody asked him how he liked Boston, he was silent for quite a spell his brows wrinkled in deep thought, trying to think up something to say about what he saw up there.... "I couldn't see the dodgasted place fer houses", he finally answered. "

"I guess that you would have more of an understanding about a big city than Eben Strout would , " said Priscilla. "Father would probably say it was like 'comparing a clipper ship to a pinky', for he uses that expression to compare almost everything. I am quite sure there were a lot of things Eben Strout missed that you wouldn't. "

"You are probably right, Miss McKane, " agreed Danny. "I'm quite sure that I should be well-satisfied with Boston if the majority of people up there were like you. "

"I wish that you wouldn't call me Miss. McKane," said Priscilla frowning. "There is no necessity for our being so formal. I 'm going to call you Danny from now on. "

"And you won't ever hear me object to it, " replied Danny. "Didn't I say that I liked to hear you use my first name. But perhaps your mother would object to my calling you Priscilla on such a short acquaintance. It would sound too familiar. "

"She probably would think nothing of it in your case, " Priscilla rejoined hastily. "It would be different if Captain Panchez called me by my first name for he is a man of the world. "

"If you call him, a man of the world, I don't want to be one,"
replied Danny with a look of disgust. "And if seeing the world will
fill a fellow so full of conceit as it did him , I don't want any
part of it. Why that fellow has a fair wind with every woman and girl
in Eastham, and next to going out in the Red Jacket I should like to
give him the licking of his life. "

  "I really believe that you are jealous of him, Danny, " taunted
Priscilla. "It is only natural that Captain Sanchez would be a ladies
man ,for he entertains them with very interesting stories. I have proof
of t at for he has been very attentive to me since I came down on his
vessel. He has even asked mother if he can call on me next Saturday night
while the Firefly is in port. "

  Danny remaind silent for quite a while before he replied... " I
guess in t at case there wouldn't be any use of me asking you to go to a
dance at the Town Hall on that night, " he said finally.

  "I'm not so sure of that, " returned Priscilla. "I didn't say
that mother had given her consent for him to call on me. I only said that
he had asked for it. "

  "Well what are you going to do? " questioned Danny. "Entertain
this masher or go with me to the dance. "

  "Go with you, " smilingly answered Priscilla. "Mother told Sanchez
that she was down here for a rest and not to entertain visitors, and he would
have to wait until we returned home in the fall. Now are you satisfied? "

  The frown on Danny's face quickly changed to a smile of relief,
I certainly am, " he returned happily. "It didn't take your mother long to
get the cut of that fellow's jib. "

"Mother will be very pleased when I tell her how complimentary you were, " returned Priscilla. "Personally I think it was mean of mother to discourage the gallant captain. It makes me all the more anxious to be in his company , and I can hardly wait for an opportunity to meet him again, " she teased.

Danny smiled happily. "I know that you don't mean that, " he said. I wonder if your mother would go with us to the dance? " he queried changing the subject."We could take my mother along too for company. "

" I am quite sure that she would like to go very much. She has never been to a dance before down here on the Cape, nor have I for that matter, and both of us will enjoy it. " replied Priscilla.

"Then it is settled, " said Danny very much relieved. "Only please don't say anything about it to the Widow Dennison or she will want to go with us and that will spoil everything. "

"I won't say a word, " promised Priscilla.

"Then I'll be along about eight O'clock with Old Moses Trott and his calash," volunteered Danny happily. "Moses Trott is about the laziest man in town ,but he has a pretty good rig and the back seat will hold the three of you pretty comfortable. One afternoon while I was standing out in front of Ezra Coffin's store Moses Trout drives up in his calash and sings out ' Danny, I wish you would pull Ebenezers tail out from under the britchin' fer me. I've been waiting almost an hour for the dad-blamed critter to switch it out. ' All he had to do was reach out his hand and lift up the horses tail, but he was too lazy to make the move, " concluded Danny.

"I think that I am going to like it down here, " observed Priscilla when Danny had finished. "The things that you hear and see are more amusing than going to a circus. "

" I guess Eastham is as good as any other place, " replied Danny.
"You'll probably find people that will amuse you, and people who will
make you sad wherever you go. If anything I guess that they are more
honest and reliable in the small towns than they are in the big ones, "
Lots of people come down here from Boston just to laugh at the way we
do things. On the other hand we go up there to laugh at what they do,
so it sort of evens it up, " ..... he concluded thoughtfully.

"I wonder if Captain Sanchez will go to the dance Saturday night?"
mused Priscilla in a low voice. "I hope so for they say he is a fine
dancer. "

Danny made no reply, instead he gazed out towards the harbor where
long, straggling whisps of fog were rolling in from the sea... "Old Maushope's
smoking his pipe again, " he observed as his eye followed the drifting clouds
of fog.

"Who did you say was smoking, Danny? " asked Priscilla, looking all
around her for signs of someone smoking a pipe.

" All the old-timers here on the Cape say that when they first see
the fog start to drift in from offshore, " smiled Danny. "The expression came
from an old Cape Cod fable. Would you like to hear it?

"I should like to very much, " answered Priscilla eagerly. "I had no
idea when I first met you that story-telling was one of your accomplishments,
and here I've been bragging about what Captain Sanchez could do. It certainly
would not be a feather in my cap if it turned out that you could beat him. "

"All my stories are pretty commonplace compared with the ones men
like Sanchez tell " rejoined Danny modestly. "Most of them have to do with the
people here in Eastham and probably would not be very interesting to an outsider. "

" I probably should not have compared the people here in Eastham to circus performers, Danny, " Priscilla observed in an apologetic tone of voice. "They laugh and play like everyone else does I guess, but their fun seems to be cleaner than ours in the city - cleaner and more on the surface. The more I see of the people here the better I like them in every way. "

Danny waited until she had finished, and then taking a deep breath, related the fable of Maushope. "Once upon a time thousands of years ago there was an enormous eagle that used to hover over the South Shore, and whenever it saw little children playing it would pounce down upon them and carry one away in its tallons. Maushope was an Indian giant,gentle and huge,who unlike most giants of folk-lore, liked children very much, and the onslaughts of the eagle enraged him.. So one day when the eagle flapped away with a child in his claws Maushope started to chase him.. The bird flew out to sea and the giant strode after him... Farther and farther flew the bird - deeper and deeper waded the giant - but of course,since he was a giant he could wade into the very depths of the ocean... By and by he came to Nantucket ,which up to that time had never been known to the inhabitants of the mainland.. And there under a tree he found the bones of all the children the eagle had devoured... He sat down beside them and grieved for a long time... Finally he thought he would feel better if he had a smoke. So he filled his pipe with poke - a weed that ever since that time the Indians have used as a substitute for tobacco... He smoked and he smoked, and the smoke drifted back across the sound to the mainland... That was the beginning of the fogs on Cape Cod, and that is what the Indians meant when they used to say 'Old Maushope is smoking his pipe' " Danny smilingly concluded.

"I think that I like your stories far better than those of Captan Sanchez," observed Priscilla after Danny had finished, "Sometimes I think that his stories are made out of whole cloth like those fables.Yes , I like yours very much better. "

"The fog's coming in thick and you'd better scurry for home, " warned Danny, his whole being vibrant with pleasure at the compliment she had given him.

"You want to get rid of me and the fog is only an excuse, " rejoined Priscilla as she arose from the bucket and deftly arranged her wide skirt. "I think that you are as mean as you can be sending me home at this hour. "

"If you were down here every day there wouldn't be much work done, " replied Danny as he gazed ruefully at the unfinished traps before him. "It's almost noon, and the fog is coming in much earlier than usual. Why it only only seems an hour ago that the sun had cleared it all away, and now the wind is driving it back again. "

"I think that just to pay you back for sending me home so early, I will take a walk over in the direction of the wharf where the Firefly is moored, " threatened Priscilla. " I am sure that if I should meet Captain Sanchez he would not send me away. "

"If you will take a look out there in the harbor you will see the Firefly heading out by the Point. " grinned Danny. "I made sure she was well-away from the wharf before I said anything to you about going home. "

"I think I know now which way the wind is blowing, Danny, " said Priscilla as she started to leave. "And I feel rather pleased about it."

"Be sure and don't eat any supper at home Saturday night, Priscilla, " Danny called after her. "You will need all the room for baked beans and brown bread when it comes time for supper at the dance. "

. . . .

Moses Trott by a process of jerking the reins, flourishing his whip, and a series of loud clucks, was urging his faithful horse along the highway in the direction of the Widow Dennison's home, and by his side rode Danny dressed in his Sunday-best. "I ain't been to a shindig like this for a month of Sundays, " said Moses between clucks. "Melissa thinks that dancing is worse than the Old Nick himself, and she wouldn't have let me fetch you if I hadn't promised to stay out in the calash until it was all over. "

"There's no harm in dancing or sitting around the hall watching them, as far as I can see. The harm is in getting friendly with those fellows from the Cove that always carry a bottle of whisky in their pockets and get pretty generous with it, " replied Danny.

"A promise is a promise, but I ain't goin' to keep it this time, no surree Bob an' Taylor I ain't , " Moses exploded. " I'm goin' in there to see the fun an' get some of those vittels or my name ain't Moses Trott. "

"That's the spirit, " replied Danny. " We probably won't stay very late , and you might as well make the best of it while you're there. It's not every day you get a chance to break =lose from Melissa. "

"I don't care if the roosters is crowing when we get home, "rejoined Moses recklessly. " I ain't had a real spree since Martin Van Buren was elected, an' maybe I'll cut a pigeon wing or two myself before the night's over. Giddap there, you shif'less critter" he called out sharply to his horse. "Can't you travel faster then a walk anyways but towards home? " Ebenezer, sensing more or less the spirit of the occasion, raised his head, and relieving himself of a shrill whinny, much to the surprise of Moses, started into a jog-trot.

As the distance between them and the Widow Dennison's home grew shorter Danny began to experience a feeling of trepidation. His mother had not been able to go with him owing to a bad headache which had developed late that afternoon, and it was the source of a considerable disappointment, for he had counted on her holding Mrs. McKane's interest while he devoted his time to Priscilla..

And now as the pounding hoofs of Ebenezer sounded in his ears, bearing him to his fate, he trembled like an aspen leaf in the wind, and in this disturbed state of mind he even envied Moses Trott, seated there beside him slapping and clucking at his hores as if he didn't have a care in the world. "I wonder how he would feel if he was in my boots, " he pondered, running his fingers under his stock to loosen it.. "I'll bet that he wouldn't be crazy enough to get himself into a mess like this."

Then came a loud "Whoa" from Moses Trott, and a sudden tightening of the reins as the calash came to a halt in front of the Widow Dennisons, and Danny saw two shadowy figures hurrying down the path to meet him... With his heart in his mouth Danny climbed down from his high seat and stood hesitating beside the road... Priscilla came up to him first, and he could see in the twilight shadows that she was nearly out of breath.. "I didn't want to be late, Danny, " she greeted him, a vision of sparkling youth in her summery attire. "So I hurried like all possessed. "

"You shouldn't have done that, Priscilla, " said Danny as he removed his hat and courtised politely. "Moses and I could have waited. "

"I thought you said your mother was going with us, " observed Priscilla peering in at the empty seat.

"She wasn't feeling very well and couldn't make it, " replied Danny. "But it was only a headache. I wouldn't have left her alone if it had been anyt ing more serious, " he added quickly.

" I am quite sure of that " voiced Mrs. McKane.. "Perhaps it would be a good idea if you dropped me off at your mother's, Danny, and the two of you went on to the dance alone. I know that you could get along without me, and I could keep your mother company, " she added smilingly.

"Thank you Mrs. McKane, but mother will be all right," responded Danny reassuringly, as he helped the ladies into the calash....

. . . .

Once more Moses Trott pulled up sharply on the reins bringing
Ebenezer to a full stop, this time in front of the Town Hall. "Well
here we are at the scene of the festivities, Danny," he cheerfully
remarked ,giving Danny a nudge with his elbow. "Don't you go an' let any
of them slick fellers from the Cove cut you out. "

Danny ignoring the remark descended from his high perch and
gallantly helped his guests to alight..... The building which served as a
schoolhouse in winter, was crowded with people, while from its windows
a welcoming light shown forth upon a strange assortment of vehicles ranged
along the sides ,the propelling power of which snorted, stamped their hoofs,
and pulled fretfully at their halters, anxious as a horse usually is when
away from the barn, for the comfortable feel of the stall and the smell of
a well-filled crib.... The same light brought in to prominence a number of
young men and boys standing on either side of the steps ogling the people
as they entered, some talking and laughing boisterously,their eyes peeled
for newcomers,especially girl s.

It was a gauntlet which required a great deal of nerve to run, and
nobody knew it better than Danny did that night as he walked past the gaping
crowd of Eastham cut-ups,with a lady clinging to each arm.

"There goes the Griswold boy with the Widow Dennison's two boarders
in tow, " someone on the edge of the crowd remarked. "Danny, does your mother
know you're out? " voiced another,taking good care to keep his voice and
identity a secret. "She's as trim a Boston packet as I've ever laid eyes on"
added another. "Heh there you landlubber let Jack take the wheel, " another
deep-throated voice called out.

This final sally was rewarded with laughs from everyone within ear-shot and Danny's face turned the color of a boiled lobster. "I shouldn't have brought you here, " he said when the vestibule of the hall was finally reached. "I had no idea that they would make all those remarks. I'm awfully sorry. "

"You shouldn't be so self- conscious Danny, " smilingly rejoined Mrs. McKane. "We were not in the least put out by their comments. When you get to know women better, you will have a much clearer idea of what I mean. Compliments always please them no matter from whom they come. "

"None of them are fit to be in the same room with you and Priscilla, " returned Danny angrily. "This is the first time I ever brought any ladies to the hall other than my mother, and I had no idea that it was going to turn out like this. "

"Never you mind, Danny. We are not going to let a little thing like that spoil our evening. We not only like to hear nice things said about us, but we like to be shown-off too." observed Priscilla consolingly.

"If you will excuse us Danny we will go into the ladies room and primp up a bit, " smilingly interrupted Mrs. McKane. "We shall only be a minute. "

Left alone Danny lounged in the anteroom paying scant attention to to the ones who knew him.. His mind was almost wholly absorbed in trying to figure out this problem which had materialized so unexpectedly. "Hello, Danny!" boomed a familiar voice in his rear, arousing him from his reverie. "I thought you said that your ma was coming with you tonight. "

"She had a headache and couldn't come, " replied Danny, the frown leaving his face at the sight of his friend.

"That's too bad," said Captain Bowden, gazing disappointedly around
at the people passing in and out. "I had sort of figured on her being
here... You ain't alone?" he inquired after a brief pause.

"No," replied Danny. "I brought Mrs. McKane and Priscilla with me."

"Well, that's a hoss of another color," observed Captain Bowden.
"I guess in that case you'll want someone to give you a hand, won't you
Danny?"

"I sure would appreciate your help in entertaining them," rejoined
Danny in a relieved tone of voice. "I was pretty disappointed when I found
that mother couldn't come."

"I ain't excatly what one might call a ladies man, but I guess
I can give you a hand, Danny," cheerfuly replied the captain. "I'd try
almost anything once to help a friend."

They were soon joined by Priscilla and her mother, and Captain
Bowden was introduced.. "It's like runnin' into a spell of fair weather
after bein' bounced around for a month off Cape Horn, meeting you folks,"
remarked the captain as he shook hands with Mrs. McKane. "I used to know
your husband, ma'am, and no better man ever built a ship."

"Thank you," acknowledged Mrs. McKane with an engaging smile.
We are very fortunate in meeting you, Captain Bowden, for it is going to
take some of the load off Danny's shoulders. I was just beginning to wonder
how he was going to manage it, with his mother not being able to come. I hope
that you will not think me presumptuous if I ask you to be my escort to save
me from being a wallflower," she concluded laughingly.

"Danny and I have been talking it over an' come to the same conclusion.
ma'am . It will be a pleasure and an honor for me to help with the entertaining
if you ladies will allow me to. " responded the captain gallantly. "I was master
of a ship your husband built once, and a finer clipper never rode the ways. "

"We are the ones to be honored, Captain Bowden. I have heard my husband
mention you many times, but I never thought that I should ever have the pleasure
of meeting you. It pleases me beyond expression to find a man so loyal to Donald
as you are, and I am very grateful." answered Mrs. McKane graciously.

"I hear that he is going to build a new clipper and call her the "Flying
Cloud, " Mrs. McKane. Have you any idea who he has in mind to take her out when
she is finished?" asked Captain Bowden. "I wish that I was young enough to do
it, " he added in a wistful tone of voice.

"There is some talk of Captain Bacon getting the appointment, after he
has made one more voyage in the "Red Jacket",volunteered Mrs. McKane."They have
only just started on the Flying Cloud's keel, and it will be at least a year
before she is ready for launching. "

"At the mention of Captain Bacon and the Red Jacket Danny pricked up his
ears. "They couldn't find a better man for the job,Mrs. McKane, " he said loyally.
"We all think down here that he is one of the finest sailors on the Cape. "

"Of course what I have said about Captain Bacon is confidential, "
cautioned Mrs. McKane. " My husbands choice of captain's bears considerable weight
with the owners,but as yet he has only mentioned this particular preference in
the privacy of his family. "

"Speaking of Captain Bacon,they say he is going to get married to
Naomi Rutledge next week, " observed Captain Bowden. "I've known Naomi ever
since she was a little girl, and he couldn't get a better wife any place on
the Cape. "

Priscilla looked at her mother questioningly when Captain Bacon's name was mentioned but made no comment. "Yes, we have heard about it, and I am quite sure that Miss. Rutledge will make him a good wife, " said Mrs. McKane, seemingly for the moment slightly embarrassed by the subject they were on.

They were standing in the anteroom. "Hadn't we better go inside, ma'am, " suggested Captain Bowden. He had sensed that the mention of Captain Bacon's coming marriage had not met with a very warm reception.

"Why of course, " rejoined Mrs. McKane. "What are we standing here for when there is so much fun going on inside? "With that she attached herself to the arm of Captain Bowden and they entered the hall.

. . . .

The twanging strings of a fiddle sounded as they made their entrance, which was followed by an announcement from the orchestra leader that the Grand March was about to begin, and the room became suddenly alive with people scurrying every which way for partners. Captain Bowden with Mrs. McKane in tow, followed by Danny and Priscilla, traversed the full length of the dance-floor, finally coming to a halt near the platform where the musicians were seated... "Well I guess this is about as good a place to anchor as any, " said the captain indicating several vacant chairs.

Priscilla seated herself and began arranging her skirts, while her mother followed suit. "Aren't you completely thrilled with all of this, mother?" she smilingly asked.

"I feel quite sure that I am going to enjoy myself, " answered Mrs. McKane. "I wouldn't have missed it for anything. I guess you have forgotton that I was born here on Cape Cod, Priscilla, and this reminds me very much of old times."

By this time a long line of couples were marching around the hall, and in the lead was Captain Ezra Coffin,performing antics which would have done credit to a dancing-master, with a very pretty girl clutching laughingly to his arm.

"That old loon of an Ezra Coffin's been leading the Grand March for more'n forty years, an' cuttin' up like that," remarked Captain Bowden."It's a wonder to me he don't take someone like Old Mrs Lufkin to dance with, and leave the pretty girls to young fellers like Danny here. "

"You are not jealous of him by any chance,are you Captain Bowden? " teased Priscilla.

"What me jealous of that old flapdangler! " exclaimed the captain. "Why it wasn't so long ago that I danced down him and Abner Harrison in this very hall, and won one of the biggest turkeys in Eastham for doin' it. "

"Then why don't you go on with mother, " suggested Priscilla. "Can't you see that she is dying to go on the floor. Look at the way she is tapping her foot. "

The captain without a moments hesitation arose from his chair with the agility of a squarrel, and bowing low before Mrs. McKane, said, " Will you do me the honor,ma'am. "

"Why of course,Captain Bowden, " smiled Mrs. Mckane. " I was only waiting for you to ask me. "

"Wouldn't it be a good idea if we followed the example of our elders,Danny, " remarked Priscilla, eyeing him quizzically . "I hate to think of all this good music going to waste. "

" I should like to well-enough but I hate to make a fool out of you,Priscilla. I'm not the best dancer that ever was and I am afraid you won't have the patience to put up with my mistakes, " Danny rejoined,

"Oh, you can dance all right, only you are too modest to acknowledge it, " replied Priscilla. "Come on, Danny, let's not miss a minute of it. "

"All hands around... Salute your pardners;...... Grand right and left, " called out the fiddler as he swiftly bowed his violin, his lean body swaying to the rhythm of the music... Back of him the man at the organ, with his face turned smilingly towards the dancers, was making the stumps of four fingers on his right hand, fairly fly over the keys in a series of harmonious chords.. The tips of those fingers by the way had been neatly amputated by a whale-line some years before in the South Atlantic.... The popularity of this organ-player was evidenced by the salutations of the men as they danced by.. "Give her a fair wind, Hud .... Blow the man down.... Give her the skys'ls, Hud, we want to go faster, " and many other expressions that only a deep-water sailor knew and could make use of to enhance an evening of pleasure dancing with his sweetheart or wife. A slide trombone completed the three piece orchestra, and this was manipulated by a man with a huge walrus-mustache, whose face greatly resembled that of a fish. Long and loudly he blew it while the dance was in progress, only stopping long enough to free the valve of water and wipe the sweat from his forehaed.

Captain Bowden, filled with the spirit of gaiety surrounding him, balanced his partner with a whirl that would have done credit to a dancing-dervish.... "Oh! " exclaimed Mrs, McKane, as she felt herself being spun around like a top... "You have the strength of a grizzly bear, Captain Bowden. "

"Ma'am, this ain't nothin' to what I could do when I was younger," was the modest response. "Why, ma'am I could lift 'em right up off their feet an' hold 'em there for perhaps a minute before I let 'em down. "

"It would certainly thrill a person to be handled that way,but
you are doing it quite fast enough for me, " returned Mrs. McKane,
who was very much out of breath..... Down the center they went,each
laughing heartily as they stooped to evade the outstretched arms...
"It's been years since I have enjoyed a dance like this, Captain Bowden,"
said Mrs. McKane after the music had stopped and they were once more
seated. "You have made me feel like a girl again and I am deeply grateful. "

"I wish that Annie Griswold thought the same way about it," remarked
Captain Bowden thoughtfully. "I've been trying to get her to dance with me
for a month of Sunday's but she won't do it. "

"Perhaps you weren't persuasive enough, " smiled Mrs. McKane. "Women
like to be taken off their feet,not literally of course,the way you used to
do, but in an imaginative way. "

"I'm quite sure that you are right,ma'am, " agreed the captain quickly.
"And I'm going to try it out the next time she comes here to a dance with
Danny. I don't know how she's going to take it though. She thinks that I am
pretty much of a fly-by-night as it is. "

"Did you enjoy the dance,mother? " asked Priscilla as she and Danny
joined them.

"Every minute of it,my dear, " replied Mrs. McKane,her face aglow
with pleasure. "You must dance the next one with Captain Bowden and find out
for yourself. How did you and Danny get along? "

"We were enjoying it so much that I was sorry when it ended. I guess
everyone did for that matter, mother. I have never been to a dance before where
there was so much real pleasure shown by the people on the floor. "

"Priscilla certainly worked her passage when she was dancing with
me, and she's only saying that she enjoyed it just to be sociable, "
voiced Danny with a grin.

"Don't you believe him mother. He is a good dancer and knows it.
He's only telling you that just to be contrary. You wait until you have
had a dance with him and then you will find out that I am right, "

" I am sure that you are, " returned Mrs. McKane quickly."You will
agree with me after you have danced with Captain Bowden that he is a good
dancer, too. The only fault I can find with him, Priscilla, is that he's
a trifle shy when it comes to matching wits with the opposite sex. I think
you know what I mean, Captain Bowden, " she added, glancing smilingly in his
direction.

" I sure do, ma'am, and I ain't goin' to contradict it either," said
the captain. "But I guess after it's all said and done, that I had much rather
be on a lee shore with no room to tack, than try to make a woman do somethin'
she didn't want to. "

"Captain Bowden doesn't know very much about women, " volunteered Danny.
"He's a bachelor and lives alone with Barnacle, his cat. I have no idea why he
didn't get married when he was younger, for he would have made a far better
husband than a lot of men I know here on the Cape. If I made a guess, though
I would say that he was too bashful to ask any good women to marry him. "

"Choose your pardners for Boston Fancy, " called out the fiddler...
Captain Bowden sensing that the conversation might get him into hot water,
rose quickly to his feet and executing something akin to a double shuffle,
offered his arm to Priscilla saying and said, "Will you step this one out with me,
young lady? ". She complied readily and soon they were part and parcel of
the good-natured crowd on the floor.

Danny, left alone with Mrs. McKane, for a time remained bashfully

silent... She could have quickly put him at ease with a word or two,

but for the moment she preferred watching him out of the corner of

her eye. He was such an interesting boy and so conventional.......

"That's Captain Ed. Jordan over there dancing with that little girl,"

Danny remarked finally, indicating a nearby couple.

"I couldn't help but notice the little girl, for she seems to be

having such a good time, " replied Mrs. McKane.

"She's Captain Ed's only child, and two years ago nobody would have

ever thought she would xxxx be on the floor dancing like that. She had a

crippled foot and there didn't seem to be any cure for it, "returned Danny.

"How unfortunate! " exclaimed Mrs. McKane.

"It's funny how people always seem to want the things which are so far

out of their reach," observed Danny thoughtfully.. "Lola, that little girl

over there, wanted to dance more than anything else in the world. "

With added interest Mrs. McKane watched the movements of the pretty,

golden-haired girl. "How did this miracle happen Danny? " she asked.

"Lola's mother died the day her baby was born, and when Captain Jordan

returned from a long voyage which took almost three years, he found Lola there

in his wife's place. She couldn't play around with other children as she grew

older, and her greatest pleasure was to watch people dance; so when Captain Ed was

home between voyages he never missed a dance here in Eastham. Winter nights when

a blizzard was blowing and the snow waist-deep, he would come stamping into the

hall here with Lola perched on his shoulder all wrapped in blankets, and they

would sit up here on this platfrom, holding hands and laughing at the antics of

the dancers until the last gun was fired. Captain Ed called in every doctor for

miles around to treat her foot,but none of them seemed to do any good,
until one summer a big one came down here from Boston for his health.
I guess Captain Ed.had him in tow the minute he stepped off the packet.
"I think that I can fix your little girl's foot so that she can walk on it!"
said the doctor cheerfully. "'I'm down here for a rest,but I guess I won't
feel any worse if I give your daughter some of my time'." She suffered
terribly while the doctor was working on it, but Captain Ed kept her cheered
up by talking about the dances they would have together when she got well,
and I guess every right-minded person here in Eastham prayed that she would.
I don't have to tell you how the operation turned out for you can see for
yourself, Mrs. McKane, " Danny concluded.

"How happy that little girl must be, and how fortunate as well in the
possession of such an unselfish father, " remarked Mrs. McKane when Danny had
finished.

"I guess you will think it very strange,Mrs. McKane, that I am not a
sailor,when every man or boy here in Eastham is either one or expects to be,
with the exception of myself. " said Danny after a long silence. "I am what
you might call a part of the sea but still as far away from it as the moon.
I have never been more than a mile or two outside of Billingsgate Point in my
whole life,but still I feel quite sure that I could sail a ship to almost any
part of the world,thanks to the kindly teaching of Captain Bowden. "

" I am quite sure that your not going was from lack of opportunity,"
Mrs. McKane rejoined quickly. "I cannot imagine your not having had many offers. "

"I could have gone long before this if it had not been for mother, " was
the reply. "As it is I have to be satisfied with watching all the other young men
in Eastham go and come, and to say that I envy them would hardly express it. "

" I heard about your father, Danny, and considering what happened to him I can hardly blame your mother for not caring to have you follow in his footsteps, " replied Mrs. McKane. "If I had a son I am quite sure that I should feel the same way about it. "

"It would be no more than natural for all mother's to feel that way about their sons, " was the quick rejoinder. "But if there were no exceptions where would men be found to man the ships? "

"You have me there, Danny, " smiled Mrs. McKane. "I shall have to try and talk your mother into letting you go. "

"I wish you would, but I doubt very much if you meet with any success. I have begged and pleaded with her to let me go, ever since I was knee high to a grasshopper, and you can see that I'm still here. I'll thank you for trying t ough, from the bottom of my heart..... Boyd Frost, that young man over there by the organ, was born on his father's ship off Cape Horn, " Danny went on, changing the subject. "The day after, while the ship was running under goose-winged topsails, a heavy sea boarded her smashing in one of the after cabin deadlights, washing Boyd right out of the soap box he was laying in. He's eighteen now and mate of the Golden Horn. His father tells everyone there's no wonder that Boyd's a good sailor, having been baptized by a Cape Horn twister. "

"Isn't he rather young to be the mate of a big ship Danny," remarked Mrs. McKane, eyeing the young man referred to closely.

"No " rejoined Danny. "All the boys here on the Cape are grown-ups at his age. I'm eighteen myself, and if I had been born on a ship as Boyd was I should probably have been mate or master of one by now. "

"But where did Boyd get his schooling, Danny? " queried Mrs. McKane.

"On the ship, " was the reply. "His mother taught him the three R's and his schoolhouse was there, and in the busy ports of the world, where, as Captain Bowden says 'a man has to put on his thinking-cap. "

"I think that I can understand now quite well why it was they made him a mate, and perhaps given him command of a ship just as well," said Mrs. McKane thoughtfully. "I'm quite sure that he would have earned his promotion either way."

"There's little doubt of that, " returned Danny. "But when he gets to be master the people who envy him will say that he 'went in through the cabin window', meaning that he never served any time in the forecastle."

"I guess that very few people realize just what it takes to be the mate or master of a ship," murmured Mrs. McKane, partly to herself and partly to Danny. " I wonder if a woman will ever command one? "

"There's one right over there, " grinned Danny calling her attention to a sweet-faced woman with snow-white hair, seated alone with hands folded in her lap, smiling appreciatively at the dancers. "She took command of the bark "Neptune" off the Horn, several years ago when Captain Manly, her husband come down with brain fever, and brought the ship into port."

"What a remarkable thing for a woman like her to do, " exclaimed Mrs. McKane. "I could hardly imagine a woman of her type taking command of a big ship."

"And she done a good job of it, too, " Danny went on. "The first mate was in irons at the time for insurbodination, while the second mate did not know a thing about navigation, so the responsibility of navagating the ship fell on her shoulders. All her married days had been spent on the sea with Captain Manly, and he had taught her navigation, so she promptly took command of the Neptune, and tending her husband, meanwhile brought the ship into Yerba Buena without an accident forty-three days from Cape Horn, a record run in those days."

"Did Captain Manly die?" queried Mrs. McKane.

"No",replied Danny. "Captain Manly is very much alive, and his ship is in Boston loading general cargo for Capetown. Mrs. Manly is only here on a visit. "

. . . .

And then it came time for supper,and as they climbed the stairs to the raftered room above,where it was to be served, the odor of well-cooked food,and steaming hot coffee greeted their nostrils, and entering the room they beheld a long,board table,draped with a turkey-red cloth, and fairly groaning with the food heaped upon it. There were cakes, pies and doughnuts,dishes of piping-hot baked beans, loaves of brownbread, plates heaped with delicately-browned biscuits,and large thin slices of yeast-bread,platters of ham,beef, and pork,sliced thin,golden pats of butter ornamented with acorn, cloverleaf,and strawberry designs,dishes of chow-chow, and pickled cucumbers,pitchers of milk, and steaming coffee, all shouldering each other for room and giving off a never-to-be-forgotten odor. Sounds of happy voices and laughter echoed from the raftered ceiling,while above the odor of food one could occasionally smell the fragrance of lavender or the cloying sweetness of some Oriental perfume.

Young and old men alike vied with each other in being polite, as they helped their partners squeeze into the narrow space between table and seat and a great deal of merriment ensued when some of the more portly failed to accomplish this rather difficult operation.. They took it all in good part however,for the humorous side of their nature had been well-stimulated by the sight and smell of the food. The only casualty was when Serifina Perkins ,the most corpulant of all,while seeking a more comfortable position,raised a portion of the table thereby projecting all the food in her immediate vicinity into her lap... She was rescued from this very embarrassing predicament by Captain Ezra and

Moses Trott, who afterwards escorted her to a more commodious at the end,

leaving a trail of baked beans, custard pie, and coffee, in her wake.

Captain Bowden beaming with good cheer crowded in beside Mrs. McKane,

and stroking his fringe of whiskers remarked. "I come here tonight, ma'am,

with a well-swept hold, and I'm sure goin' to enjoy these vittels. "

And then came a season of passing the salt, pepper, mustard, and vinegar,

a period when everyone reached and said "Excuse Me", and the anxious swain watched

his lady-love's plate with the eye of a hawk to anticipate her slightest wish.

While she, with an appetite perhaps satiated by an early visit to the buttery

before leaving home, dallied with her food and studied the costumes worn by the

other girls, comparing them with her own.

It was a general reunion of the villagers, all talking, laughing,

gesticulating, eating, and listening, knives, forks, and dishes rattling, spoons

stirring, feet scraping.. All satisfying the inner-man or woman, and happy in

the companionship of wife, friend, or best girl.

Grizzled seamen with leathery faces, young men just home from a long voyage,

riggers, sailmakers, coopers, whalemen and carpenters. Here a lad of ten trying

hard to smile and show a brave face, for tomorrow the one ambition of his life is

about to be realized . He will be outward bound as a cabin-boy, and near him is

the master of the ship that he will be sailing in, a stern-faced man with greying

beard, a man whom he has looked upon as a god and worships with all the fervor

of a boyish heart... His eyes fill with tears as he looks at the happy throng

around him, and the lump in his throat grows bigger, for in his youthful mind is

the thought that he may be looking at them for the last time. He chokes down the lump however and smiles bravely,for in that small body of his lies the makings of a good sailor.

And there sits another lad somewhat older than the first,his small, round face, browned by the kiss of the sun in the trades. He is smiling happily,for only that morning he had clambered down the gangplank of a Boston packet with his small sea-chest in tow,home from a two years voyage.

......

"There will be a lot of black cats put under buckets next week, " obsereved Captain Bowden,laying down his knife and fork with the air of a man whose task had been well-done. The conversation had lagged a little owing to the confusion going on around them.

"What do you mean by that,Captain Bowden? " asked Priscilla and her mother in one breath.

"I mean that a lot of ships have been cleared for California, and are only waiting for a fair wind to sail. " replied the captain. "Years ago over on Nantucket,the day a ship was due to sail the wimen folks would put a black cat under a bucket and pray for a head wind to keep her in port. "

"Please don't tell me that it worked,Captain Bowden, for I wouldn't believe you, " remarked Priscilla with a smile.

"It must have workrd sometimes, for there was a lot of people over there who believed in it, " was the reply. "There was a women over there once,so they say, by the name of Susan Dexter,who used to make quite a lot of money out of letting her neighbors have her black cat when they wanted to hold a ship up with a head wind, " concluded the captain with a chuckle.

"I have heard a lot about Nantucket and always wanted to pay it a
visit, " observed Mrs. McKane. "They tell me it is very quaint, and
well-worth seeing. "

"I was born over there, ma'am, and if I do say it there ain't many
places that can beat it for neighborly kindness,and honest-to-goodness
hospitality, " replied the captain proudly. " Some day when I don't have
to go up to Boston ,Danny can get his mother and we will all go over
in the Hornet. "

"That will be fine, " responded Mrs. McKane. "We will take advantage
of your invitation,Captain Bowden,and make a regular picnic out of it. "

. . . .

"If you don't mind,Priscilla, I am going to sit this one out with
Captain Bowden, " said Mrs. McKane, as they again seated themselves in
the hall below,just as the fidler was announcing that the next dance would
be Soldiers Joy.

"Come on,Danny, " urged Priscilla springing to her feet. "They want to
get rid of us, and I shall have to put a flea in father's ear when he visits
us this summer, " she added laughingly. "You had better be careful,Captain
Bowden,for he is a very jealous man. "

"I'll take a chance. He ain't goin' to lose any sleep over an old coot
like me, " rejoined the captain with a chuckle... And then after she was out
of ear-shot he said to Mrs. McKane. " She's a mighty fine girl an' I wish that
I had a daughter like her. "

"You wouldn't find her very easy to handle, " rejoined Mrs. McKane with
a smile. "She has more beau's than you can shake a stick at ,and flits from
one to the other like a bee gathering honey. My one wish is that she will find
some young man who is worthy of her and eventually marry him. "

"I guess all young people have to sample first what they have around them to pick and choose from, " replied the captain thoughtfully. "They wouldn't be human if they didn't. "

"It seems a pity that Mrs. Griswold won't let Danny follow the sea for a living, " observed Mrs. McKane. "I don't know as I can hardly blame her, but with all the other young men going, it seems hardly fair that he should have to stay at home. "

"Most of us took the matter into our own hands when we was young and run away if our folks wouldn't let us go, " was the reply. "Danny is the only young man here on the Cape that I know of who has stood by his mother an' I admire him for doin' it. It wasn't easy, ma'am, for they don't have any more respect for a landlubber here on the Cape than they do a skunk. He might might just as well be the fifth wheel on a calash as far as they are concerned. They only have eyes for people who go down to the sea in ships, ma'am. "

"To think that one could be so narrow minded in this day and age, " rejoined Mrs. McKane indignantly. "Why it all sounds perfectly ridiculous, Captain Bowden. "

"It's the gospel truth though, " returned the captain. "But you let a young man make one or two voyages, and then stay at home, and it's a different matter. " the captain continued. "After that he is taken right into the fold an' he has a say in everything. He can raise cranberries, plant potatoes or do anything after that an' nobody ever says a word. "

"You don't suppose we could persuade Mrs. Griswold in some way to let Danny go, do you, Captain Bowden? " suggested Mrs. McKane.

"You might, but she wouldn't listen to me any more than she would to the Old Nick himself. She blames me for putting all these notions of the sea into Danny's head. "

"I can't see for the life of me why she should blame you any more than many other people here in Eastham, " returned Mrs. McKane. "In a village where almost all the population are sea-minded I do not see where any one person can be blamed . "

" She blames me because I have taught him nearly everything he knows about ships and the sea, " was the reply. "He took to it like a duck takes to water, and right now I figure that he is a better navigator than I am. But it ain't goin' to do him a bit of good if he don't take advantage of it, " the captain concluded with a frown.

"I suppose under the circumstances I would do the same thing, " replied Mrs. McKane thoughtfully. "It seems a shame though that all his talent in that direction should be wasted however."

"Annie Griswold is a very sensible woman, ma'am, and she can hardly be blamed for feeling the was she does about it, " remarked Captain Bowden loyally. "Danny is all she has left, so perhaps if she had someone to sort of take his place it might be different. "

"I am quite sure that I understand just what you mean, Captain Bowden, and I feel quite certain that Priscilla and I can help in some way if you will leave the matter in our hands, "replied Mrs. McKane.... "I wonder if you would mind telling me something about Nantucket? " she asked after quite a long silence.

"I sure would be glad to, ma'am, " was the quick reply. "I had a high old time over there when I was a boy, especially when we would go out stealing grapes, " the captain went on with a chuckle. "And how we used to bedevil them night-watchmen! They each carried a three foot pole with a hook on the end of it, and they would slip the hook around a feller's leg an' trip him up.. We used to sing out 'Hooker, Hooker' Catch us if you can, and then run like all possessed... Sometimes they would catch a boy and give him a good spankin' on his set-down , and then turn him loose with a 'Scat you dogratted grape —stealer'. I can hear as plain as if he was singing out right now, Jonathan Bunker. He would call 'Nine o'clock and all is well,Jabez Arey has beans to sell.' Sometimes I wish that I could turn back the days and be a boy again, " the captain ended thoughtfully.

"Girls did not go in for that sort of thing in my day,but I believe had it been possible I should have gloried in it, " smilingly remarked Mrs. McKane. "We did things that were equally annoying I am quite sure,but they were usually confined to the premise's of our parents. I too, have wished many times that I could turn back the years. "

"I guess it ain't written in the scripture that we can do much about it though, sighed the captain as he gazed thoughtfully out over the dance floor."We can't have our cake an' eat it too. Can we,ma'am? "

"There are times when we,who are in the winter of our lives envy youth, " rejoined Mrs. McKane with a slight catch in her voice. "It is very wrong,though, and when I find myself doing it I feel heartily ashamed of myself. When I see old people trying to place themselves on the level with youth, and making every effort to appear much younger than they really are, I always feel very sorry for them.We have had our youth Captain Bowden, and it would hardly be fair to envy others that privilege. "

"You are perfectly right,ma'am, " agreed the captain.. then after a short pause he changed the subject. "Captain Bacon has offered Danny a berth in the Red Jacket, and I wish that he could take it. I wonder if the whole three of us,you, Priscilla and I could talk Mrs. Griswald in to letting him go. I have already promised Danny that I would help out, but I never had much hopes until you came along. "

"The three of us should be able to win her over," replied Mrs. McKane hopefully.

In the wee small hours of the morning when Danny,tired but happy,
assisted the ladies into Moses Trott's calash , Captain Bowden standing
close by to see them off,whispered hoarsely in his ear." I'm coming over to
see your ma tonight about your going out in the Red Jacket, but don't you
say anything to her about it. "

Ebenezer, the horse,legs stiff from long-standing,pricked up his ears
at the sleepy commands of his driver and sensing that he was heading toward
the barn and oats,started off at a rapid gallop,drawing behind him a wagon
in which were seated a quartet of weary but well-satisfied people.

. . . .

Captain Bowden while on his way to the home of Mrs. Griswold the
following evening,turned slowly over in his mind various ways of broaching
the subject of her son's going out in the Red Jacket,but the more his mind
dwelt upon the matter the more confusing it became. He couldn't say to her
in so many words, "You should let Danny go down to the sea in ships for that
is the only calling he is suited for." If he did that he had every reason to
believe that she would tell him to mind his own business. For reasons best
known to himself he valued her friendship exceedingly,and harbored no desire
to weaken the already flimsy structure upon which it was built. On the other
hand, he wished to remain loyal to Danny and either by word or deed assist in
the furtherance of his ambition.. He was positive that there would be no relenting
on the part of Mrs.Griswold, so summing it up he found himself between what might
have been called 'the devil and the deep blue sea' .

In his hand Captain Bowden carried a bouquet of flowers picked from his
garden, and his ruddy face fairly glowed from the effect of a vigorous scrubbing
with soap and water. The large brass buttons on his pilot-jacket were polished
to a degree of brillancy rivaling the stars,while upon his head rode a wide-brimmed
sailor-hat of straw perched at a rakish angle.

Arriving at Mrs. Griswold's kitchen door he hesitated for a moment in
an effort to overcome the persistant urge to right-about-face and go home..
Then he knocked boldly... It might have been two minutes he stood there
after that but to him it seemed hours, and he was just on the point of
turning away when he heard footsteps approaching and the door swung slowly
open.. "Why, Captain Bowden! " exclaimed the widow ,blushing modestly as she
viewed his round,shining face,framed in the doorway. "I didn't expect a call
from you this evening. Won't you come in. "

"Thank you,ma'am, " said the captain,removing his hat with a flourish
and tucking it under his arm."I figured that you might be a little bit surprised."

The widow with a puzzled look on her face closed the door behind him and
then led the way into the sitting-room.. "Won't you take that chair over there, "
she offered politely. "My husband used to say that it was the most comfortable
one in the room. "

"I've brought you some of my peonies.ma'am, " said the captain,handing
her the bouquet. "There ain't no others like 'em on the Cape, and I thought
you might like to have some. "

"It was very thoughtful of you.Captain Bowden, " returned the widow,
taking the huge bunch of red and white flowers from him with a smile. "My peonies
haven't done so well the past two or three years, but even at their best they
couldn't compare with these. "

"You can have all the bulbs you want from my flowers, " offered the
captain generously. "I'll dig up a lot this fall and you can have Danny plant
them for you. "

While the widow carefully arranged the peonies in a pitcher on the
table,the captain leaned comfortably back in proffered chair and followed her
every movement. "They certainly look nice, " she said , as with the last stem
tucked and tilted at the proper angle she stepped back to view her work.

"There ain't nothin' more interesting in this whole world than flowers,when you come to think of it," remarked the captain thoughtfully. "Some of them is just like human beings they need coaxing,while others just grow out of nothin' you might say. When Jed Stover's cow hooks down the bars of his fence and tramples down the flowers in my beds, I just say to myself that's the last of 'em,but it ain't, not by a long shot,ma'am, for the next day I find 'em standing up stiff and straight as soldiers. All they need ma'am,is a hand-hold like most of us human beings,a little bit of dirt,the sun, and some fussing over. "

The widow smilingly approved of what the captain had said,and seating herself opposite him carefully arranged the knitting.-work in her lap. " I am positive that I never could trust anyone who dislikes flowers, " she observed. Then as she reached for her needles the ball of yarn in her lap rolled off and disappeared under the table.. With the agility of a squarrel the captain retrieved it , and before one could have taken a second breath he was back in his chair again.

"My but you are spry Captain Bowden, " remarked the widow.

"I can move pretty quick when there's a distress signal flying, " replied tha captain,drawing a bandanna handkerchief from one of his capacious pockets and applying it to his face.

"I should say you could, " returned the widow, and then after a short silence "I am afraid that you find it too warm here. Shall I open another window? "

"No,thank you ma'am, " hurridly answered the captain. "I always get spells like this when I'm off my bearings. "

"Oh! " exclaimed the widow a bit perturbed by the announcement."I
hope that it is nothing serious, Captain Bowden. "

"It is an' it ain't, " was the evasive reply.. "It might be worse
if it was allowed to run its course though. " He was thinking of the
widow's objections to Danny following the sea.

Mrs. Griswold on the other hand thinking that there was something the matter
with his internal organs, advised the taking of anodyne liniment, a few drops
on a teaspoon of sugar just before going to bed. "I am sure that would help, "
she said consolingly.

The captain meekly agreed to follow here instructions, and then went
about on another tack with the conversation. "Do you know ma'am that people
are more safe at sea than they are ashore, " he solemnly remarked.

"You could never make me believe it no matter what you might say, "
returned the widow skeptically. "And what's more I wouldn't believe it,
if it was sworn to on a stack of bibles, " she concluded.

"I've known a lot of cases where if a man had stayed on his ship he
would have lived to be ninety, " rejoined the captain. "I guess I could think
of more'n a hundred of 'em without having to stretch my imagination a bit, "
he added warming up to his subject.

"I guess that you had better go right home and take that anodyne, "
suggested the widow with a smile. "I am quite sure that something has gone
wrong with your head. "

The captain overlooking the widow's sarcasm, stubbornly continued his
theme. "You take the case of Captain Lige Bunker over in Harwich, " he went on.
"He had been going to sea for more'n forty years , and then one day while he was
home tinkerin' around in his yard he fell out of an apple tree and broke his neck. "

The widow remained silent.

"And then there was Cap'n Witherspoon over Yarmouth-way. He probably would have lived to be ninety-five or more, if when he was home one voyage, the bale of a bucket he was washing his face in hadn't caught him around the neck and strangled him... Then there was.... "

The captain was interrupted at this point by a giggle from the widow. "Excuse me," she said, trying hard to keep her face straight. "I couldn't help laughing. Captain Bowden, you have such a forcable way of arguing a point. Tell me please, just how it is that you have escaped some dire calamity? Is it because the Creator spares those of us who cherish flowers? "

"A sailor ain't safe on shore no matter what he's doin', " rejoined the captain doggedly. "I've been lucky, ma'am. "

"If you can tell me of a case where someone has been harmed working in a flower garden I may come around to your way of thinking, " smilingly observed the widow.

The captain's jaw dropped and for ~~and for~~ several minutes he scratched his head in deep thought... " I can do it, ma'am, " he said finally. "In the spring of 1830 Cap'n Alonzo Bartlett of Brewster brought home with him a species of newfangled cactus from the West Indies. He was a great lover of flowers like I am, ma'am, and he would go miles out of his way to find a new one. Well he got this cactus home and while planting it one of the thorns pricked him in the finger.. He didn't think much about it at the time, but the next day his finger began to swell up and pain him somethin' awful!... Here the captain paused to let the facts of the story seep into the widow's brain...

"Go on, " said the widow breathlessly.

"He only lived a week after that, ma'am... Blood pizening from the prick of a thorn from that ferrin cactus, " concluded the captain dramatically.

" Even at that I guess that we are much safer here on dry land" remarked the widow, still unconvinced.

The captain sensed that he was not making any headway so he abruptly changed the subject. "I guess you know Sofroney Parker that lives over on the other side of the township, ma'am. Well she's got a boarder from Boston who's about as tall and thin as a beanpole. He's a professor of somethin' or other and goes around catchin' all sorts of things in a contraption that looks like a fish-net. "

"Why that's Professor Hangerbottom, " interrupted the widow. "They say he is going to teach over at the Truro Academy this winter. "

"Then it will be about fish, " grinned the captain. "Sofroney says he wants them served to him three times a day, and it keeps her jumping like a pea on a hot skillet thinking up ways to cook 'em. She said that soon fish-bones will be growing out of his ears if he keeps on eating them the way he does. "

"They say that fish is a great brain food, " remarked the widow.

"Maybe that is why we're so smart down here on the Cape, " rejoined the captain with a chuckle. "If fish will give us brains we ought to be the smartest people in the whole United States. "

"I must have Danny meet Professor Hangerbottom, " observed the widow. "He may be able to advise him about his studies at the Academy this fall. "

" Danny might learn somethin' if he could get near enough to the feller without bein' caught in that net of his, " sniffed the captain. "Sofroney says he's the most absent minded man she ever heard tell of, and nearsighted to boot. The other day she put that stuffed owl of hers that she keeps on the whatnot, out on her back porch for an airing, an' along about three o'clock ,when she

happened to be looking out of the window,she sees the professor creeping
towards the house on all fours. She thought at first that he had gone plumb
crazy,until she spied the owl settin' there on the rail as large as life,
then she knew right away what he was after. After that,Sofroney said he
got down flat on his stomach and began inching along like a caterpillar,
pushing the net ahead of him. She said it was as good as a circus to watch
the maneuvers he was goin' through,so she let him go right ahead with it."
Here the captain paused for a moment to catch his breath...

Mrs. Griswold was all smiles. "That's about the funniest thing I have
ever heard of happening here in Eastham, " she remarked. "What happened
after that Captain Bowden? "

"Sofroney said it took the professor quite a while to get within striking
distance ,but when he did he swooped down on that stuffed owl like a flash and
scooped it into his net. It took Sofroney quite a spell to stop laughing,but
when she did, she went out and said to the professor. 'Thank you for catching
my owl,' she says hardly able to keep her face straight. 'I'll put it right
back on my whatnot where it belongs ' The professor didn't answer her for almost
a minute,and all the time he just stood there looking at that owl as if it was
one of the seven wonders of the world...'Mrs Parker where did you get this specimen?'
he finally asks, and Sofroney said his voice sounded just like a judge in court, and
she felt just like a prisoner before a bar of justice... 'I didn't steal it,'Safroney
says,her dander roused. 'As far as I know it used to belong to my grandfather
Obediah Parker' .Mrs..Parker says the professor that bird is an excellent specimen of the Hornibus
Rusticatowlus, from the Platosopian age, and worth its weight in gold. It looks
like an ordinary owl to me, and all the gold you could get from it wouldn't fill
a flea's ear, ' says Sofroney. Would you part with it for a hundred dollars', 'says

the professor, drawing out a long leather wallet an' beginning to count out the money. He was a man of action an' didn't believe in lettin' any grass grow under his feet when he wanted somethin'. Sofroney says she felt one of her heart spells coming on, so she grabs the money an' goin' into the house flops down in a rocking-chair,an' it was almost supper time be ore she got up,feeling as limp as a dish-rag. "

"It must have been a great surprise to Sofroney,receiving all that money for just an ordinary stuffed owl, " smiled Mrs. Griswold. "No wonder she was so upset. "

"She says she'll never get over it, and I figure they'll be ransacking every attic here on the Cape for more of them birds just as soon as the people get wind of it, " chuckled the captain.

A long silence followed broken only by the ticking of the clock on the mantel.. "Everybody and his grandmother is heading towards California these days , " finally observed Captain Bowden reflectively. "I could sell my schooner for twice what I paid for her any day. These'Argonauts'as they call 'em, would take passage in a wash-tub ,if it was fitted with a sail and bound around Cape Horn. "

"Wouldn't it be a good idea to sell her then,if you can make such a good profit, Captain Bowden, " rejoined Mrs. Griswold. "I am quite sure that I should. "

"I've got quite a spell to think it over, ma'am, " replied the captain. "In less than two years from now we'll be hearin' the train tootin' through here on its way to Provincetown, and then there ain't goin' to be any more Boston packets. "

"In that case I should think that it would be better for you to sell now while you have a chance, " returned Mrs. Griswold.

"There's just one fly in the ointment, " replied the captain. "If
everybody sells their vessels and they are put into the California trade,
there ain't goin' to be any left to carry freight between here and Boston,
nor passengers either, before the railroad comes through here. "

"But they can build more, can't they Captain Bowden. "

"They can, but none to run between here and Boston, " was the reply.
"They're all looking Westward, where pretty soon another railroad is goin' to
be put through, and they all want to make hay while the sun shines, totin'
freight and passengers around the Horn. That's why Donald McKane is building
all them clippers, ma'am. They will be the only means of transport outside of
the wagon-trains to California for a good many years, and so the clipper is
goin' to have her day, ma'am. If I was a young man like Danny I'd rather aim to
go out master of one than be President of these United States. "

"Didn't you ever consider going out there yourself in the Hornet? "
queried Mrs. Griswold. "I have an idea that you are about the only man here
in Eastham with a fine, seaworty vessel, that is not getting ready to go. "

"More times than you have fingers an' toes, " was the quick reply. "But
goin' to sea is not for me any more, ma'am. I'm getting too old. I've seen the time
though when I would have been off like a streak of greased lightnin' at the first
call. As it stands now, ma'am, I'm probably the only seafaring man here on the Cape
who hasn't a California bee in his bonnet. "

"I can't see for the life of me how you manage to resist the temptation,
with all this hue and cry going on for ships and sailors. " remarked Mrs. Griswold.
"You must be very strong-minded, Captain Bowden. "

"I ain't so strong-minded as you might imagine," returned the captain,
stroking his whiskers thoughtfully. "I wallow around like a ship without a rudder
when it comes to some things, but when I once get my bearings I figure there is
a promised land right here in Eastham, so why should I go out to California lookin'

for it? "

"I guess by that you mean your home and flower garden, " rejoined
Mrs. Griswold. "You certainly have the right idea,Captain Bowden. "

"An' someone in it to help stand the watches, " replied tha captain
hurridly.

Mrs. Griswold blushed. "I guess you won't have any trouble in that
respect, " she said. "There seems to be plenty of widows here in Eastham to
fill the bill. "

"There's widows - and then there's more widows, " observed the
captain reflectively. "They are as thick here in Eastham as an April fog comin'
in off Georges. "

"That should make it all the more easy for you to select one, "
returned Mrs. Griswold. "It's not every man who can find himself in a position
to pick and choose. "

"If you will pardon my sayin' so ma'am,I ain't in no position like
that, " responded the captain ,growing quite red in the face. "I couldn't just
tag the one I wanted and say you're it, " he went on. "She would have somethin'
to say about that herself. "

"Do you know whom I should recommend if I were asked to decide? "
queried Mrs. Griswold with a twinkle in her eye. "Sofroney Parker? "

The captain squirmed in his chair uneasily.. "Sofroney ain't a bad woman
at heart, but she's an awful gossip an' makes a mountain out of a mole hill. With
all due respect to your judgment ma'am, I wouldn't want to marry her. "

"It seems common knowledge,however, that you are a regular visitor to her
house , and that she is setting her cap for you. " smilingly returned Mrs. Griswold.
"That is why I suggested that it would be a good match. "

The captain while the widow was speaking, stared vacantly into space
with an expression which might have equaled if not surpassed Sofroney
Parker's stuffed owl. "It's just as Mrs. McKane says," he reflected. "You
can hint about things to a woman until doomsday, an' she will understand
what you mean, but just out of pure cussedness she will shift to another
point of the compass, and tangle you up tighter than a ship's running rigging
in the doldrums."... And then aloud. "Sofroney Parker's an old maid. If I ever
marry anybody it's goin' to be a widder. "

"Have you ever told Sofroney Parker? " asked the widow teasingly. "She's
been hinting all over town that you have been sitting up with her. "

"By Tophet! " exclaimed the captain, very much perturbed. "I wouldn't
be here calling on you if I was courtin' Sofroney Parker. Not if I had any
sense. Why she'd scalp me alive. "

"Oh, I guess you would be able to take a night off occasionally without
her finding it out, " teased the widow.

The captain scratched his head, stroked his chin, fumbled with a button
on his coat, and squirmed some more in his chair.... "I wish that womyn was in
Halifax, " he mumbled. "I ain't goin' over to her part of the town again,
not if I live to be a hundred. "

"Then she will be suing you for breach of promise, " rejoined the
widow, trying hard to supress a smile. "After telling nearly everyone in town
that you've been sparking her, she's not going to relish the idea of being
dropped like a hot potato. "

"She's a sly, designing, two-faced Belzebub, " stormed the captain.
"If you should give her an inch she would take an ell. Why I haven't been in her
house more'n twice in my whole life. "

"I guess once would be enough, " replied the widow dryly. " I am
quite sure that she wouldn't need any more encouragement than that. "

"If you'll give me a minute, ma'am, I'll tell you just how that
desiging female lured me into her house, an' then if you can call it
sparkin' I'm a grampus whale, " rejoined the captain.

"Oh pshaw! " exclaimed the widow. "I've run out of yarn and I shant be able
to knit any more until Danny finds time to hold the skein for me. "

"Let me help you, ma'am, " offered the captain. "I ain't held a skein
of yarn for windin' since I was a boy, but I used to do it slick as a whistle.
You get the yarn, ma'am, an' let me give you a hand. "

"It is very nice of you to offer, Captain Bowden; but won't Sofroney
be jealous? " smiled the widow.

"I might as well be hung for a lamb as an old sheep, ma'am, " tactfully
replied the captain, reversing the old saying so that it would sound complimentary.
"I ain't goin' to lose any sleep over her. "

Blushing, the widow handed him the skein of yarn and watched with keen
enjoyment his clumsy attempts to arrange it in his hands. "You look awfully
warm, Captain Bowden. Wouldn't it be more comfortable if you removed your coat, "
she suggested.

"Thank you, ma'am, I do feel a bit moist, " was the reply. Then suiting
action to the word he removed his coat and placed it on the sofa. "Now we can
get down to business, " he remarked, once more taking up the skein of yarn. At
this point they were interrupted by a loud knock on the kitchen door. "Who in
tarnation do you suppose that is? " queried the captain nervously.

"It's probably Mrs. Dennison," replied the widow, rising from her
chair. "Did she see you when you turned in here tonight, Captain Bowden? "

"Yes, she did, " replied the captain. "She was out front watering her flowers when I come by. "

"Well that settles it, "remarked the widow. "She is coming here under the pretext of borrowing something so that she can find out what's going on."

The captain's jaw dropped and he remained motionless in his chair.. Entirely inocent of philandering, he suddenly found himself entangled in a net of circumstantial evidence , which seemed destined to cause him a great deal of embarrassment, through no fault of his own. It was bad enough that he had been accused of sparking Sofroney Parker, but now with the Widow Griswold added to it , the tongues of the village gossips would have something to chatter about for months. With the skein of yarn still on his wrists he sat there bolt upright in his chair, his face the picture of uncertainty... Again the knock sounded on the door and the widow-not a little agitated by the turn of events-hastened to answer it.

"With the house all lit up this way I was quite sure that you wasn't out, " came the sound of the Widow Dennison's voice as soon as the door was opened. She held a cup in her hand and her eyes were centered on the sitting-room door.

"Won't you take a chair? " invited Mrs. Griswold, motioning to one well-out of range of the door which was wide-open.

"No, thank you, I'll only be staying a minute, " replied the Widow Dennison, edging close to the door in order to get a better view... "I said to myself Mrs. Griswold's got company or she wouldn't be wasting so much oil, and it would be a shame to disturb her. I only come over to borrow a liitle cream-a-tarter until I can get some from the store. My boarders just dote on cream-a-tarter biscuits, but I can't ever make them twice alike. I was telling Mrs. McKane and her daughter only yesterday that you made the best biscuits in Eastham. "

While the Widow Dennison was speaking, her eyes had been centered upon the red face of Captain Bowden, shining like a beacon on a rock-bound shore, and squirming uneasily as their eyes met, he could have blessed the floor with all his heart, if it had suddenly opened up and projected him into the cellar beneath.

"I guess you don't make such bad biscuits yourself from what I hear, " replied Mrs. Griswold charitably, as she took the cup from her neighbor's hand and started toward the cupboard. "Won't you sit down for just a minute, Mrs. Dennison" she called back over her shoulder.

The Widow Dennison with another sharp glance in the direction of the sitting-room, placed a chair where she could obtain an unobstructed view of Captain Bowden, and then seated herself... "It seems to me that all Eastham has gone topsyturvy," she remarked in a loud voice, as she settled down in her chair comfortably and folded her hands in her lap.

"Do you mean all of this excitement about going out to California to mine for gold? " queried Mrs. Griswold, handing her the cream-a-tartar with a movement meant to hasten her departure.

"No, it ain't the gold, " replied the widow, resting the cup in her lap and settling still further back in her chair as if prepairing for a long visit. "It's the philandering that's goin' on here in the village. Why only this afternoon Mrs. Crabtree was tellin' me she heard that Elija Crocket, who is old enough to be my grandfather , took his housekeeper, Lulu Marsh, over to Wellfleet yesterday, an' married her there. Lulu ain't more than twenty if she's a day. I know it because Abigill Marsh, a second cousin on her father's side who lives over in Chatham, when I was over there visiting cousin Rebecca Morton last winter. " After imparting this bit of information the widow paused for breath and glanced balefully in the direction of the sitting-room, as if its occupant should have been held responsible for the happening.

"After all it was she who married him, and being twenty she ought to know her own mind, " commented Mrs. Griswold. "I don't see any reason for an outsider getting upset over it. "

"She married him because he has a lobster pound an' one foot in the grave, " replied the widow .

"It's her own business not ours, " rejoined Mrs. Griswold in a tone which was meant to convey the impression that the subject was closed as far as she was concerned. "We've been having nice weather lately, " she went on, changing the topic of conversation.

The widow ignoring the hint completely,kept on going. "It seems to me that there's no end to the scandal goin' on in these parts, " she continued, casting another look in the direction of the sitting-room. "I blush for shame when I think of what fools people can make of themselves. "

"Well,I wouldn't think of it then,if I were you, " advised Mrs. Griswold, arriving at a point where patience seemed no longer a virtue. "We have troubles enough of our own without shouldering those of our neighbors."

But there was no stopping the Widow Dennison once she got started, and off on another tack she went with her yards braced up sharp to catch the wind. "Malvina Pruden run away with that Portugee barber over at the Cove this morning an' her folks are all stirred up over it. They say that she has been hanging around his shop for month's, an' everybody prophesied that no good would come from it. They went up to Boston on the ~~Firefly~~ HORNET, an' Mel Pruden,that's her brother ,followed them in his sloop to bring her back. He says he ain't goin' to let any sister of his marry a furriner. "

"Yes,I heard about it this afternoon, " answered Mrs. Griswold resignedly ."Danny tells me that he is a good mate for the captain of the Firefly, for he had all the girls down at the Cove chasing after him. If I had a daughter I shouldn't want her to run off with a man like that either. "

"They say it's goin' to be a big surprise to both of them when they find Mel Pruden waitin' for them on Commercial Wharf. His sloop can outsail the Hornet any day,especially when that no account mate of Captain Bowden's has charge of her, " finished the widow with a sly glance in the direction of the sitting-room door. Her baiting was rewarded by a loud snort,seemingly of derision,followed by a strange hissing noise ,not unlike the sound of steam escaping from a pent-up boiler... The widow,somewhat startled by the sound,rose hurridly to her feet and started toward the door. "I guess that I had better be goin' " she remarked as Mrs. Griswold let her out. "It's time for all night-hawks to be in bed, " she concluded in a loud voice just before the door closed behind her.

"Well that's over with, " breathed Mrs. Griswold with a sigh of relief, as seated herself and reached for the ball of yarn. "That woman can think of more gossip in ten minutes than the whole of Eastham can in a month of Sundays. "

" She's a regular Polly-scatter-the-news, " commented the captain. "An' she ain't goin' to let any grass grow under her feet tellin' everybody that I was calling on you either. She'll be out tomorrow morning bright an' early, under full sail, and there won't be a house in town that don't know about it. "

"I don't mind her as far as I am concerned, Captain Bowden, " said Mrs. Griswold. "It is your reputation I have in mind. What will Sofroney Parker say when she hears of it? "

" I don't care a tinker mackerel what she thinks, " exploded the captain wrathfully. "That old sandpeep ain't got any more reason to be talking about me than she has about the Bunker Hill Monument. I'll explain to you,ma'am,just how it was I happened to be at her home the night she's cackling about, and then go on home about my business."

"I'm quite sure that it is no affair of mine, and you don't have to tell me about it, Captain Bowden, " voiced Mrs. Griswold hurridly. "As far as I can see you have a perfect right to call on anyone you choose. "

"That's just the point, ma'am. I thought that I could until I heard Sofroney was tongue-wagging, " rejoined the captain very red in the face. "I always figured on mindin' my own business, but I guess I've slipped up on my calculations. "

"You shouldn't allow it to disturb you so much, Captain Bowden. It comes natural for most people to talk about their neighbors," replied Mrs. Griswold soothingly. "Everything I hear I take with a grain of salt, and most of it goes in one ear and out the other. I have all I can do to keep my own house in order. "

"You're right, ma'am, " agreed the captain, settling back in his chair more comfortably. "Most of us have a skeleton in our own closet and if we talk too much it's liable to get out. "

"I'm sure of it, " was the reply. "And now if you will tell me what happened at Sofroney's I shall be all ears, " Mrs. Griswold concluded with a smile.

And so the captain, very much relieved, cleared his throat, and taking a firmer hold on the skein of yarn, described the evening he spent with the Widow Parker.

"Wash Pangs, who lives just a house or two south of Sofroney on the Orleans road, had been owing me a freight bill for more'n a year, so the other night I figured I would go over there and try to collect it. Well, when I got abreast of Sofroney's house she hails me and says 'Cap'n Bowden, I wish that you would come in for a minute and lissen to the new organette I just got from Boston' ".

"I would be very pleased to," I says, not wishing to hurt her feelings any by refusing. So she takes me into her parlor..... " Here the captain was interrupted by Mrs. Griswold quoting 'Will you step into my parlor said the spider to the fly'. The captain blushed a fiery-red, and clearing his throat once more,continued. " Well,she showed me into her parlor as I said before chattering away like a magpie about the weather,her neuralgia, and the new organette of hers, 'That's it over there' she says when we got into the room, pointing to a box on a stand in the middle. 'It's the only one in Eastham and cost almost as much as a horse an' wagon'.

"I've heard of 'em,ma'am,but this is the first one I ever got real close to, I says. "

"You set right down in this easy-chair, Cap'n Bowden,an' I'll play it for you!,she simpers. "

"Thank you,ma'am, I says. It will be a real treat to hear one of them newfangled things played. "

"You may not believe it,Cap'n Bowden,she says,but it was nothin' short of fate that brought you along this way tonight. I don't know of a single soul in Eastham that I would rather play it for than you.' "

"That's mighty nice of you,Safroney,to say that,an' I'm glad that I happened along, I says, bearing in mind that she always traveled with me on the Hornet,and not wantin' to ruffle her feathers with a short answer."

"'I invited Professor Hangerbottom in to hear it last night,' she went on to say. 'But I might as well have been playin' it in a deaf and dumb asylum for all the attention he paid to it. He was too busy lookin' around the parlor for more of them stuffed owls.' "

"'He probably didn't know that you was in the land of the livin' I says. Professors are all like that.''

"' I wouldn't marry one if he was the last man on earth' she says,turnin' up her nose. 'Give me a man who sails the deep-blue sea an' fights the elements. ' "

"It's six of one and a half dozen of the other, I says jokingly. A sailor is away from home most of the time,while a professor might as well be for all the company he is,I've heard say. "

"'Just the same I would prefer a sailor,'she says,taking a roll of music from a shelf under the table."

"It's a matter of opinion, I says.'Everybody for their own taste' as the woman said when she kissed the cow. "

" 'Could you ever imagine,Cap'n Bowden, a person gettin' heavenly music out of a roll of paper cut full of holes,' she says,holding the roll out for me to look at. "

"No,ma'am,I couldn't, I says. But there's fellers all over the world setting up day an' night figuring out thingamajigs for our entertainment, an' I wouldn't be surprised at anything... "

"' I want you to hear this one, ' she says, pickin' out another roll. 'It's called the Wildflower Waltz, and just too sweet for anything. ' Then she put it into the machine an' plays it over twice... 'Don't you wish that we had someone here who could turn the crank while we danced it together. ' she said finally. 'If the professor was here I would ask him to do it,but he's out huntin' night-birds. ' "

"I don't dance nothin' but square dances,ma'am, I says, hoping to get away before the professor put in his appearance. I never did learn how to waltz. "

"' Oh what a shame' she says.'You have missed half of your life,Cap'n Bowden. Here you take the handle an' I'll show you the steps. ' Well just to pacify her I took it an' she began skipping around countin',one two three, one two three,one two three, until she didn't have wind enough left to blow a feather off the palm of her hand... Finally I said ,'Sofroney it's almost ten o'clock an' I've got to be movin' along. I shan't be able to see Wash Bangs for he's gone to bed long before this. I'll have to come over again next Saturday night when I get back from Boston. ' I was almost home before it dawned on me that Sofroney took it that I was comin' over especially to see her, an' that was why she simpered an' giggled so much when I was leavin' . That's the whole of it in a nutshell, ma'am, " the captain concluded after a long pause. But I guess it was enough to make her think that I was sparkin' her, " he added sheepishly.

"I should say it was, " agreed Mrs. Griswold,who could hardly keep her her face straight. I remember a case over in Barnstable,where a woman sued for breach of promise,who didn't have any more reason for doing it than Sofroney Parker. "

" You don't say, " replied the captain, trying hard to appear at ease. And then after a long pause,during which he wrinkled his forehead reflectively, "I'm not so sure but what Sofroney would be man-crazy enough to do it at that. "

As the last thread of yarn slipped from the captain's wrist and was deftly wound on the ball held in the capable hands of Mrs. Griswold,he rose from the chair,reached for his coat ,and putting it on started for the door. "I come over here tonight,ma'am,with a lot of things on my mind to say which I didn't , " he remarked as he turned half-way around with his hand on the knob. "I'm a plumb failure where helping a friend is concerned. I take up too much time with my own affairs. "

"I'm not quite sure that I understand you captin, " replied Mrs. Griswold, looking a bit surprised. "Was it a favor you wished to ask in behalf of a friend? "

"It was, ma'am, but I didn't know just how to go about it, " rejoined the captain sheepishly. "I drifted clear off my course when the Widow Dennison come in ,an' I ain't got back on it yet. "

"In that case hadn't you better stay a little longer and tell me what is on your mind. " suggested Mrs. Griswold. "I shall be glad to help you if I can. "

"I know that you would, ma'am, " replied the captain gratefully. "But I will have to go home an' adjust my compass. I couldn't steer a straight course tonight no matter what I said. "

"You know best, Captain Bowden, " smiled Mrs. Griswold.. "Good night and don't forget the latch string will always be out, " she added.

"I won't, ma'am, " he called back cheerfully over his shoulder. "Good night and pleasant dreams. "

On the captain's arrival home that night Barnacle, his cat, greeted him by rubbing against his legs and purring loudly. "I was pretty much off my course tonight, old fellow, " he muttered as he reached down to stroke its back. " I guess that if Danny gets any help from anyone after this it will have to be God. "

. . . .

The friendship of Danny and Priscilla progressed smoothly for a week or more, and then one evening while they were standing in front of Ezra Coffin's store, waiting for the mail, the storm broke. "Oh Danny, there's the Firefly coming into the wharf now! " exclaimed Priscilla. "Let's go down and watch the passengers land. "

"All right, " agreed Danny reluctantly. "But if Sanchez starts anything I won't be responsible for the outcome. "

"Oh why do you have to be so jealous of that man, " rejoined Priscilla angrily. Is it because you envy him his position? If it is, why don't you get away from your mother's apron strings and do some of the things that he has done.? " She spoke hastily and the minute the words were out of her mouth she regretted them.

Danny flushed a deep-red. "I guess that you did me a favor by saying what you did just now, Priscilla, " he replied evenly. "I have been thinking of getting clear of my mother's apron strings for a long time, and your remark has made me more determined than ever to do it. "

"You are capable of doing much bigger things on the sea. Danny, " Priscilla returned earnestly. "I only said what I did to shame you. I have heard father say many times that they are in need of good men to captain their ships, and that is where you belong. "

"You are right, Priscilla, " agreed Danny thoughtfully. "I'll go up to Boston in the morning and ship out on the Red Jacket. I probably won't see you again after tonight until I have made something more than a lobster fisherman out of myself. "

A long silence followed.... "Here comes Sanchez," Danny finally observed, his face breaking into a grim smile. "I hope that he gives me an excuse to tan his hide. "

"Why, how do you do my pretty friend, " saluted Sanchez, coming close and peering into Priscilla's face with an insolent smile. "I hope that your mother has changed her mind about my calling on you. It would be a sin to separate such good friends. " He paid no attention to Danny, who stood back of Priscilla angrily gazing in his direction.

Priscilla stepped back, her face flushed with embarrassment.. "I am quite sure that Mother is still of the same mind, Captain Sanchez; and I should appreciate it very much if you would consider the matter closed, " she replied in a low voice.

The captain of the Firefly had been drinking and was in a very quarrelsome frame of mind. "Your mother objects to me,but otherwise she is not very particular in the choice of company her daughter keeps, " he rejoined sneeringly.

"It is not a matter which concerns you, " was Priscilla's angry retort. "We are quite capable of choosing our own friends, Captain Sanchez. "

"So that's the way the goose hangs, " returned Sanchez with a drunken leer. "You would prefer a beardless fellow who lacks the courage to become a sailor,to a man who owns one of the fastest packets sailing out of Cape Cod. "

"It matters little whom I prefer as far as you are concerned " was the the reply. "I beg of you to go on about your own affairs,Captain Sanchez. You are acting anything but the part of a gentleman. "

"I think that it is about time that I took a hand in this,Priscilla, " remarked Danny stepping forward. "Go on about your business,Sanchez,and leave this young lady alone. "

Sanchez with a scowl quickly turned his attention to Danny. "So the half-grown rooster has found his tongue at last, " he jeered. "Come on then if you want to get your sails trimmed,my gallant sparrow . I should like nothing better than to clip your wings before this high and mighty woman. "

"Defend yourself,Sanchez! " warned Danny,squaring off belligerently. "There won't be any Captain Bowden around this time to stop us , so we can make the best of it. "

"Please don't fight him, Danny, " begged Priscilla, laying hold of his arm in an effort to stop him. "The man is drunk and has no idea of what he is saying. "

"He's sober enough to be taught a lesson, Priscilla, " replied Danny, pushing her gently to one side. "In about a minute he is going to feel the fist of a fellow who has really cut loose from his mother's apron strings. "

Attracted by the argument, idlers came hurrying from every direction. "Danny Griswold is having a fight with the captain of the Firefly, " was passed from mouth to mouth.

Moses Trott, whom nothing short of an earthquake could have previously aroused, on hearing it methodically wound the reins around his whip and clambered gingerly down from the high seat of his calash, where for more than two hours he had been patiently waiting for someone to bring him out his mail. "Give that dude sailor what he's got comin' to him, Danny, " he voiced excitedly.

Captain Ezra Coffin, deep in the bowels of a sugar barrel filling an order, bobbed up out of it like a Jack-in-the-box to hurry out the door. "Lick the tar out of him, Danny, " he shouted, waving his sugar-scoop in the air.

Danny leaped forward, and the impact of his fist on the captain's jaw sent the latter reeling backward. "There's something for you to think over, " taunted Danny.

Sanchez recovered quickly, and with a well-directed blow sent Danny to the ground with a dull thud. "And now you clam-digging bantam, here is something for good measure, " he snarled, kicking Danny savagely in the side before he could rise to his feet.

A chorus of protest follewed the act. "Don't you do that any more,you dodratted son of a sea-cook, " shouted Old Obediah Bacon,shaking his fist at Sanchez. "I ain't quite so young as I used to be, but I'm not goin' to stand by an' see Danny kicked when he's down. " Priscilla also intervened but her efforts were fruitless.

It seemed for a moment that Danny was out for the count,but such was not the case. In less time than it takes to tell it he struggled slowly to his feet, and pushing Priscilla away closed in on Sanchez. "Now you damned harbor-sailor, I'm goin' to show you what a Griswold can do in the way of fighting, " he exclaimed.

Sanchez gamely met him half-way,and for several minutes they aimed blows at each other thick and fast... Suddenly Danny's fist flashed by the others guard and a blow on the chin sent him staggering. Danny then followed quickly with a right and left to the jaw which made Sanchez spin around like a top. Still the man, a glutton for punishment, faced Danny,his once handsome face bruised and smeared with blood.. "I hate to do this,Sanchez, for you are a pretty game fighter;but you kicked me when I was down,and you've got it comin' to you."With that he struck Sanchez a blow between the eyes that floored him like an ox, with all the fight taken out of him.... You could have heard a pin drop after that the silence was so intense. Then it was broken by the cracked high-pitched voice of Old Obediah Bacon, "It's the first time that boy has had a fight since I 've knowed him, " remarked the old man, a gleam of satisfaction lighting up his faded-blue eyes. "He's a Griswold sure as shootin' an' tonight he's found himself. "

Danny,overhearing the remark,squared his shoulders, and throwing back his head with the light of battle in his eyes, answered, "Yes, I've found myself,Obediah, and from now on I'm going to follow my rightful calling..."

"Will you look at him,Ezra, " observed Obediah Bacon,nudging Captain Coffin with his elbow. "It's the spirit of Ephram Griswold come back to life. I know it for I sailed with him on many a voyage, an' there never was a more ripsnortin' man for a fight,nor a better sailor.

Sanchez raised his shoulders from the ground and resting on one elbow,stared vacantly at the faces of the men gathered around him... "I've had enough,Griswold, " he muttered catching Danny's eye. " I made a mistake when I started to run you,thinking that I was the better man. "

"We'll forget it, " returned Danny gruffly, as he helped the beaten man to his feet. "All I ask of you in the future is to give Miss. McKane a wide berth when you've been drinking. "

"You need have no worry about that part of it after next week, " replied Sanchez with a shrug of his shoulders."I'm sailing for California in the Firefly with a load of passengers. "

"In that case I wish you luck and a quick voyage , " rejoined Danny holding out his hand. "I am willing to forget everything if you will keep a civil tongue in your head from now on.

Sanchez grasped the outstretched hand and shook it gratefully. "I misjudged you,Griswold,and I am sorry,"he replied simply, and then he turned and walked slowly down the path leading to the wharf,never once looking back.

For a minute or two after that Danny stood where Sanchez had left him, his brows wrinkled thoughtfully... "I had to do it, " he said finally, turning to Priscilla with a sheepish look on his battle-scarred face. "He was getting too high and mighty. "

"A nd to think,Danny,your first real fight was over me," rejoined Priscilla proudly. "I hardly know whether I should feel glad or sorry. "

"It makes little difference now that it is over, " was the reply. "I had to get it off my chest sooner or later,and now I feel better. "

"And you intend leaving home in the morning,Danny? " queried Priscilla trying hard to keep back her tears.

"Yes, I have made up my mind to go, and nothing will change it as far as I am concerned, " was the answer. " I am going up to Boston in the morning, and if Captain Bacon won't take me on the Red Jacket I will find a berth in another. "

"Your mother will never forgive me when she hears that I was the cause of your leaving home, " observed Priscilla contritely. "I wish now that I had been more tactful, Danny. Wouldn't it be better for you to wait a while? " she added wistfully.

Danny eyed her with a smile. "You are as changable as the wind," he said. "One minute you taunt a fellow into doing a thing, and the next minute you are trying to talk him out of it. "

Priscilla smiled in turn. "I guess I did make a mess of it, Danny, " she replied thougtfully. "Will you ever forgive me for making such a fool out of myself? "

"Why, of course, I will, " was his quick reply. "Would you mind going in after the mail, Priscilla, while I sneak out back and wash some of this blood off my face? " he went on, eyeing the crowd collected in front of the store with a look of disgust.

Before turning away Priscilla handed Danny a dainty square of cambric freshly laundried and perfumed. "You may need this to dry your face with, " she suggested with a smile. "

"What, use a pretty thing like this on my face!" he exclaimed smilingly as he held the dainty creation between his thumb and forefinger. "I know a better use for it than that, Priscilla. Will you let me keep it to remember you by? "

"If you wish it, " she answered. "I have something else, though, which would be far more appropriate, that I will get for you on our way home, " she added.

The remark of Priscilla's made Danny's face light up with pleasure.
"I'll be satisfied with anything that would remind me of you, " he replied.

They separated then, Danny hurridly washing his face at the pump and
drying it as best he could with his own handkerchief,after which he joined
Priscilla,who was waiting for him by the side of the road. "Here's your
mail,Danny,"she said, handing him one letter and a newspaper. He took them
with little interest, thrusting the letter in a pocket of his shirt,then
nervously twisting the paper,he silently took his place beside Priscilla
and they began their homeward journey,each for the time-being engrossed in
his or her own thoughts..... "I guess you would never be satisfied with
marrying anyone but a sailor,or give up your liking for ships and the sea, "
Danny remarked breaking the silence.

"It wouldn't be easy, " rejoined Priscilla quickly. "At home that is all
I hear from one days end to the other, and the majority of people whom I meet
talk of nothing else. Can you blame me,Danny? "

"No" replied Danny."It's the same down here. The sound of the surf is
in our ears all the time we are awake,and it forever keeps reminding us of the
sea. It is before our eyes every day except when we have a thick fog, and then
the bell out there on the Point tells us that it is still there. Here on the
Cape we couldn't help having "Sailor Eyes " even if we wanted to. "

" At home the sound is left more to our imagination, " returned Priscilla
thoughtfully. "But we are continually stirred by its thoughts, for hardly an
evening finds us without some captain or owner seated at our dining-table discussing
trade winds, or record-breaking ocean voyages. My father has taught me to look
upon ships and the sea as gods to be worshipped with the fullness of ones heart. "

"I guess that father would have taught me the same if mother had not put her foot down right from the start. " returned Danny. "As it was ,Captain Bowden took his place, and taught me every thing I know about the sea. And he didn't do a bad job of it either, " he added proudly."Mother disliked him for it and done everything she could to discourage our friendship,but to no avail, for I still think that he is the salt of the earth, and some day she will be of the same mind. "

They had come to a road leading off the main highway. "I don't want to go home yet,Danny, " sighed Priscilla."It's too early. Let's go out along this road. It looks so beautiful in the moonlight. "

The thoughts of parting with Priscilla were uppermost in Danny's mind when she made the suggestion, and he eagerly assented. " I am very much afraid that it will be a long time before we see each other again after tonight, " he remarked in a voice which sounded strangely subdued and worried. "It makes a fellow have an all-gone feeling in the pit of his stomach to think of going away from home like this,Priscilla. It all seems so uncertain - so difficult to understand - so hard to do. "

They had turned their backs on the moon and were walking hand-in-hand along a marsh-lined country road. In the distance, almost at its very end, glimmered and sparkled the waters of Great Pond. "I wish with all my heart that you were not going, " said Priscilla with a sob in her voice. "I shall never forgive myself for what I said to you back there at the post office. It was the most thoughtless remark I ever made in all my life, and I am so ashamed of it that I do not know what to say or do. "

"You are not to blame,Priscilla, " replied Danny soothingly. "I have had the idea in mind for weeks. Even before Captain Bacon asked me to go out with him on the Red Jacket. I needed something like what you said tonight to wake me up. "

"I feel responsible for your going,nevertheless; and wish that I had never said what I did, " rejoined Priscilla, her eyes filling with tears.

"Captain Bowden is going to have the surprise of his life when he sees me coming on board the Hornet tomorrow bag and baggage, " smiled Danny. "He knows that Captain Bacon has offered me a berth on the Red Jacket, but he hasn't any idea that I'm going to take it.. "

At the mention of Captain Bacon's name Priscilla's face flushed a deep-red, and the hand Danny held grew suddenly limp in his grasp."I thought that I was in love with Captain Bacon last summer, Danny, " she confessed in a low voice.

Danny,very much surprised at the declaration,relaxed his hold on her hand and looked at her inquiringly. "That's news to me, " he said,his thoughts disturbed by a swift pang of jealousy. "When you came out of the church that Sunday with Sanchez . Captain Bacon acted as if you were a perfect stranger. "

"It was nothing more than I deserved, " returned Priscilla quickly. "I just threw myself at him while he was in port last summer, and acted like a perfect little fool. He was too much of a gentleman,however, to take advantage of it, and told my father all about his engagement to Naomi Rutledge. It made me quite angry at first for I could not understand how a country girl could hold the attention of a man like Captain Bacon. I found out,though,after I met Naomi, and I don't blame him one bit for his loyalty. "

"Captain Bacon will never be disloyal to Naomi,you can be sure of that, " rejoined Danny. "And Naomi can handle herself in any kind of weather, and won't let any city-girl take the wind out of her sails, " he concluded with a smile.

By this time they had reached Great Pond, and in a grove of pines
beside it where a number of tables and benches had been left for the use
of picnic parties, they once more came to a halt. "Let's sit down here
for a while, Danny, " suggested Priscilla.

Danny quickly agreed and they seated themselves on one of the
benches. "This place seems to be made just for you and I, " he remarked,
and then for quite a while they gazed in silence out through the openings in the
~~openingsxinxthe~~ trees onto the shining surface of the pond.

A gentle breeze stirred the branches of the trees, and filled their
nostrils with the scent of pine. Night-hawks circled about in the shadows,
voicing at intervals loud croaks of seeming displeasure over being disturbed
in their quest for mice and bats. Occasionally the call of a loon greeted
their ears, brought to them on the wings of the wind, followed by the resonant
sound of the surf, for the sea was not far away, only just over a narrow strip
of land connecting it with the pond. Instinctively they moved closer to each
other, awed perhaps by their surroundings, and the thoughts of what the future
might have in store... Danny was the first to break the silence. "I can think
of nothing but how I shall miss you when we part tonight, Priscilla, " he
observed falteringly.

Priscilla sighed deeply. "My own mind is racked by the same thought,
Danny, " she replied choking back a sob. "I have never in all my life been possessed
with such a feeling of sadness at the thought of someone leaving me. "

"This is the first time I have ever thought seriously of saying
good bye to anyone, " rejoined Danny, reaching for Priscilla's hand and holding
it tightly within his own. "It will be bad enough leaving mother behind, but with
you added I shall feel like a cat in a strange garret.' "

"If I could only be going with you,I would be the happiest girl in all the world..As it is, I feel that same world has turned upside down and projected me into space, " observed Priscilla .

"It would be a cowardly thing for me to back out now that I have decided upon going,but just the same I feel very much like it, " confessed Danny.

"No,you can never do that,Danny," returned Priscilla quickly. "If you did our romance would soon be ended. " With that she snuggled closer, and Danny after a moment's hesitation,released her hand and placed his arm around her waist. She moved still closer and raised her head, and Danny unable to resist the temptation reverently bent his head and kissed her on the lips,then he straightened up and gazed blindly off into space,his face and body glowing with warm pulsating blood. "Priscilla darling! " he exclaimed,just as soon as he could pull himself together. "That was the first time I ever kissed a girl before in my life. "

"Did you like it, Danny' " murmured Priscilla,relaxing in his arms, her flushed face turned upward toward his.

His answer was another kiss,longer this time and filled with all the power of his being.... "Priscilla! " he exclaimed, hugging her warm yielding body close to his own. "I love you. "

Priscilla closed her eyes, and her whole body vibrated with ecstasy. "I love you too, Danny, " she replied , modestly screening her face on his shoulder. "I have, ever since the first day we met on the gangway of the Firefly. "

Bewildered by this, his first romance, Danny lapsed into a profound silence. "She would only be a memory in the morning" he thought. "But now she was real flesh and blood. Something tangable which for the time being was his to have and to hold. He gloried in this for a while until it was replaced by a feeling of awe at their intimacy... Then with the thought came the feeling of responsibility. It was as Priscilla had said,there was no turning back. He must go on with

it and become the master of a ship in the shortest possible time.. And
so with this thought settled firmly in his mind,he said with all the
sincerity and confidence of youth . "I'm going to make you proud of me,
Priscilla. I am also going to make everyone understand,if I can,that the
sea is my rightful heritage. "

"I am sure that you will, Danny, " Priscilla rejoined confidently.
"And I shall pray every night for your safety while you are absent, " she
added,smiling bravely through her tears.

They remained seated on the bench for a long time after that,
discussing as lovers will their future happiness... Then a thick blanket
of fog came creeping in over the marshes from the sea,and as it slowly
blotted out the pond the pine trees looked like ghostly shadows in the
moonlight... A thin film of moisture settled on their clothing, and feeling
the chill of it they drew more closely together.... Suddenly the fog-bell
on the Point boomed out a long, vibrating note, and its ominous sound brought
them quickly back to the reality of their surroundings."It is late,Priscilla,
and we must be going, " said Danny rising to his feet.. "I shall miss the sound
of that bell , " he added thoughtfully, as another deep-toned stroke echoed
through the fog. "Along with everything else here at home it has become a part
of me. " And so in the fog which hung heavily over the land they retraced
their steps homeward, both strangely awed by the mystery of this newly created
paradise which had so suddenly come into their lives.

When they reached the Widow Dennison's gate Priscilla was suddenly
reminded of the keepsake she had promised Danny and excused herself to fetch
it. "I'll only be a minute, " she called back over her shoulder.

Danny watched her slim figure hurrying up the walk until it was lost
in the fog,and then he listened with a beating heart to the sound of
her footsteps on the gravel... A lump rose in his throat as he thought
of how uncertain everything was that lay ahead of him, and for the first
time that night he realized how hard it was going to be to part with this
girl who had come so unexpectedly into his life. "I'll work my fingers
to the bone,if it will give her what she wants , " he reflected..

With his ears strained to catch the slightest sound of her approach,he
leaned against the gate wishing that he might turn back the hours and live
the evening over again....

He was rewarded at last by the sound of a softly-closed door and the
click of a latch, then like a wraith she appeared out of the mist. "It's
after midnight,Danny, " she exclaimed . "I tried very hard not to awaken
mother but I couldn't find what I wanted without a light. "

"Did you wake her up,Priscilla? "

"Yes,I knocked over a vase on the bureau looking for a match, and
the noise startled her out of a sound sleep. You needn't worry though,Danny.
She likes you and I'm going to tell her everything in the morning. "

"You will write to me,Priscilla, " said Danny eagerly. "Captain
Bowden or your father will tell you where to send the letters, for they will
know where the Red Jacket is bound and to whom she is consigned. "

"Father will keep me posted on where you are, for it will only be
natural that he would be interested in the movements of his future son-in-law, "
repiled Priscilla.

"I am sure that Captain Bacon will speed my promotion,if I prove
myself capable,"remarked Danny confidently."I really know a great deal about
a ship even if I have never sailed in one,thanks to Captain Bowden. "

"I shall have to go now, Danny, " voiced Priscilla reluctantly.
"Mother will be annoyed if I stay out here too long. " With that she
handed Danny a small package ,and with a sob threw herself into his
arms.... Their parting words we shall hold scared and not repeat.
Needless to say they were of love, fidelity, and encouragement,mixed
with pangs of sorrow, which are always so characteristic of all lovers
in a like position. The outpouring of youthful hearts which are about to be
separated by distance and cannot foretell the future......

Once more Danny watched the girl he loved hurry up the walk and
disappear in the mist,and like a statue he stood there, his whole being
numb with the agony of parting... Again the sound of the clicking latch,
but this time she was going in to stay ,and it might be a sign that she
was passing out of his life forever.

....

Slowly,with his mind bent on thoughts of leaving Priscilla,
Danny Griswold walked homeward along the country road, and as he drew abreast
of Captain Bowden's house,standing out dark and ghostly in the fog,he felt
like going in,late as it was, for counsel,at this,the turning-point in his
life. He kept on,however,deciding that nothing the captain might say regarding
the matter would induce him to change his mind.... A little farther on the
outlines of his own home came into view , and strange as it may seem,for the
first time that night he considered seriously what effect his going away would have
on his mother. She always left a lamp buring in the kitchen window for him, and
it was there now,shining out on the lilac bush by the back porch..It was then
he recalled other nights when returning late from the store,that very same lamp,
placed there by her loving hands,had given him a feeling of security... But
tonight it was different,the hitherto friendly beam seemed to awaken within
him a sense of disloyality - in other words it seemed to be chiding him for the

step he was about to take.. Could it have spoken it might have said,
"Danny,your mother placed me here to guide you home. Your well-being is her
first consideration,and has been ever since you were born. Think of how
empty her life will be with you away. Think of the sorrow that will be hers
when she enters your room tomorrow morning and finds you gone..."

Danny's steps faltered as the shadows of old, familiar objects rose
up to greet him out of the fog... The figure-head of his grandfather's ship,
a never-ending source of curiosity and inspiration from childhood,faced him
on the front lawn,brought into prominence by a silvery ray of moonlight shining
through the scattered fog overhead.. From the syringa bushes which lined the
 walk the subtle fragrance of their moisture-laden blossoms filled his nostrils,
and in his ears echoed the night-sounds of insects snugly hidden away among
their branches.... Somewhere off in the distance,a rooster, roused perhaps from its
slumber by the nearness of a prowling fox,and mistaking the moonlight for the
harbinger of a coming day,flapped its wings and crowed lustily.... Danny choking
back a sob,entered the kitchen and taking the lamp from the window passed on
into the sitting-room. The silence there was only broken by the steady tick-tock,
tick-tock, of the clock on the mantel.... In a listening attitude he paused before
it,silently paying homage to an old friend ,whose metallic voice had registered
the passing of time to three generations of Griswold's.... Then ascending the
stairs he came to a halt before the door of his mother's bedroom, and obeying an
impulse, directed the rays of his lamp so that they fell upon her pillow... She
stirred uneasily and then opened her eyes... "Is that you,Danny? " she called out
sleepily . "Yes,mother, " he answered,advancing toward the bed.

"Did you get the baking-soda I wanted, Danny? " she asked, rising to a sitting posture in bed to greet him. "I'll need it for biscuits in the morning. "

"No, Mother. It went clean out of my head with everything else, after my fight with Sanchez, " he confessed sheepishly.

"Oh, Danny! " his mother exclaimed in deep concern, "Your face is all bruised. "

"I guess it is a little bit scratched up, Mother, " acknowledged Danny sheepishly. "I had quite a fight with Sanchez, and it was pretty tough while it lasted. He almost gave me a licking. "

"What was the reason this time, Son? Was it because he said something that you did not like? " his mother asked gently.

"Yes, " replied Danny flushing a deep-red. "He called me a clam-digger, and said that I was tied to my mother's apron strings. "

Mrs. Griswold sighed deeply and for a time remained silent.... "Would it make you happy, Son, if I objected no longer to your going away to sea, " she said finally, with a look of resignation.

Danny taken completely by surprise, gazed at his mother questioningly. "To be honest with you Mother, I had planned on going up to Boston in the morning. Captain Bacon has offered me a berth in the Red Jacket," was his reply.

Mrs. Griswold smiled knowingly. "I know Son, and I have resigned myself to your going, " she said gently. I have even gone so far as to pack your father's old sea-chest, and have it ready. You can go Danny, whenever you wish, and with my blessing. "

Danny,greatly surprised at his mother's change of heart,hesitated with his reply.. "I was almost sure that you would never consent to let me go.. So sure of it that I had made up my mind to run away," he said finally.

"I guess you would have been justified in doing it,Danny," his mother replied gently. "It was only yesterday that I began to fully realize just how much this going down to the sea in ships really means to you. In common with everyone else here on the Cape, I too have sailor eyes,Danny; otherwise I wouldn't have married your father.. But they were not far-seeing enough, those sailor eyes of mine, for had they been I would have gone with him on his voyages.... If I had done that perhaps he would have been alive today, for I kept nagging at him to leave off going deep-water. It is for that reason ~~that~~ I have decided not to put a single obstacle in the way of your going, Danny, "

Danny breathed a deep sigh of relief.. "It has taken a big load off my shoulders, " he remarked happily. "I couldn't get it straight in my head just how I could go away without talking it over with you beforehand. I guess in the end, I couldn't have done it. "

"Well it's all over now,son, " said Mrs. Griswold,as she reached for his hand and patted it gently... "Why your knuckles are all skinned and bleeding! " he exclaimed. "Hurry and fetch me the arnica bottle on the bureau and a handker-chief from the right hand,top-drawer. "

"I had so many things on my mind mother,that I didn't even give a thought to my hand, " rejoined Danny as he hastened to do her bidding. Mrs. Griswold tenderly applied the arnica,and carefully bandaged the injured hand.. "My hands will be a great deal worse than that after I have been on the Red Jacket a month or two, " he added when she had finished.

"Don't be like those 'bucko mates' Captain Bowden is forever talking about," cautioned Mrs. Griswold.

"Don't you worry, Mother, I'll be careful, " smiled Danny.

"Naomi called this afternoon and said that Captain Bacon was anxious for you to go out with him as third mate, " observed Mrs. Griswold after a long silence. "I told her that your sea-chest was all packed and that you were all ready to make a 'pier-head' jump. It wasn't, of course, Danny, but after she left I dragged it down from the attic and made sure that it was. She says the Red Jacket is sailing just as soon as the tide starts to ebb tomorrow night, and that she will be going up with you in the morning on the Hornet. "

"It all seemed easy, this going away, until on my way home I sighted that light in the kitchen window, " observed Danny thoughtfully. "It was then I began to have a real feeling of homesickness, when I began to think of leaving you, Mother. It takes more courage than one has any idea of, to leave home, and a mother like you. "

"I shall always love that light, Danny, for it was really the means of bringing us closer together, and to understand each other better. While you are away I shall look upon it as a dear friend, and sometimes I shall put it in the window just to make myself think that you are at the store and will be coming home any minute." replied Mrs. Griswold.

"You are the best mother a fellow ever had, " rejoined Danny, resting her head on his shoulder and gently smoothing the gray hair back from her temples..... "I'll be walking in on you before you know it. They say the Red Jacket is going out to California, and from there to China for a cargo of tea and silk. Captain Bacon's a driver, and it wouldn't surprise me any if we were back home by this time next summer. "

"It will seem an eternity, " sighed Mrs. Griswold. "I shall be living all over again those almost endless days and nights before I knew the happiness of having a son,when alone in this house,I checked one by one, the days from the calendar which stood between me and your father's return. It's hard, awfully hard, for the one left behind,Danny. But I'm going to grin and bear it for your sake. "

"Captain Bowden will stand by in case you need help or advice of any kind mother, " Danny returned comfortingly. "He never was in favor of my going without your consent,so please don't blame him for putting the idea into my head. If anyone is to blame for my having sailor eyes,it's the Griswold who planted the first seed. "

"You are your father all over again,Danny, " sighed Mrs. Griswold. "He used to say practically the same thing when I accused him of being a slave to the sea. 'Annie, he used to say, 'Don't blame me for having the sea in my blood. Blame my grandfather or his grandfather before him. I'm only reaping the harvest that was sown by my forefathers'. "

"And I guess he was right, " rejoined Danny with a smile."I am very proud of being a Griswold mother, and I shall do my very best not to disgrace the name. They were all good sailors, and if I can be half as good a one as Father or Captain Bowden, I shall be well-satisfied. "

"There will be no fear of that Danny, " his mother replied confidently.

"Here's something that Priscilla gave me tonight for a remembrance, observed Danny, taking the parcel from his pocket and quickly removing the wrapper.. "Why it's her picture! " he exclaimed,eyeing the person in the small oval frame with a pleased expression on his face. "She's a mighty fine girl and I'm going to marry her one of these days when I become master of a ship, " he added proudly.

Mrs. Griswold took the picture from Danny, and a mist swam before her eyes as she looked down on it. "It is the beginning of the end," she kept repeating to herself... And then out loud she said. "I am sure that Priscilla is a fine girl, and all that you could ask for in a woman, Danny, and I hope if you marry her that she will make you happy. "

....

"Who's that coming down the wharf in Moses Trott's calash? " queried Captain Bowden of his mate, just as they were getting ready to cast off the mooring lines of the Hornet.

"It's Danny Griswold and his mother," answered the mate, after taking a long squint in the direction of the approaching carriage. "I guess they are going up to Boston with us. "

The object of their scrutiny came rumbling along over the loose planking of the wharf, and with a loud "whoa" from the driver drew to a sudden halt close to the gangway.

"I'll be dodgasted if they ain't getting a sea-chest off the back of that wagon, " observed the captain, now very much interested. And then, raising his voice he called out. "Are you an' your mother goin' up to Boston, Danny? "

"I'm going but mother's not, " was the reply. "Didn't Naomi tell you that I was going out in the Red Jacket? "

"I haven't seen her since she come on board. She's down in the cabin, " was the answer. "You've taken the wind completely out of my sails Danny. You never said anything about your goin' to me yesterday. "

"I didn't know that I was going myself until last night, Cap'n Bowden," Danny rejoined, as he up-ended his sea-chest on the capsill of the wharf so that the mate could reach the becket in the end and haul it on board.

By this time the news of Danny's going had spread like wildfire throughout the village. "They say Danny Griswold is going out in the Red Jacket," echoed and reechoed from house to house, borne on the swiftly-moving wings of gossip, while singly and in pairs his friends gathered on the wharf to see him off..

"Good by, Danny", shouted Old Silas Bacon. "Don't you let any of them Jezebels out in the Feejees' put a spider in your dumplin'. "

"Give my regards to that old bull whale that sawed my fingers off, if you happen to see him down Madagascar-way, " called out Hud Keeley.

"Don't you go gettin' tangled up in the Sargaso Sea, so you won't be able to find your way home," cautioned Cap'n Ezra Coffin.

"When you come back home next summer I'll take you to the dance for two bits, " proclaimed Moses Trott, ever mindful of business where no real exertion was required.

Danny's eyes filled with tears as he listened to the friendly banter, for only now he was beginning to realize the strength of the tie which bound him to the village of his birth. He understood now in a concrete way, how sincere their feelings were for him, and like the water in the proverbial well, he was going to miss them very much.

"You'll get Danny up there in time to catch the Red Jacket, won't you Captain Bowden? " inquired Mrs. Griswold anxiously. "I should hate awfully to have him miss her, now that he has made up his mind to go."

"You needn't worry about that ma'am, " returned the captain confidently. "The winds southeast and we're sure to have a spanking breeze all the way up. Besides, they ain't goin' to sail without Naomi here, " he added turning to Mrs. Bacon who had just come on deck and joined them near the rail.

"You'll keep your eye on him won't you Naomi? " said Mrs. Griswold turning to her friend with tears in her eyes. "I don't know what I should do if he never came back. Danny and I have never been separated before, even for one night. "

"Don't worry about Danny, " smiled Naomi. "I think that he is quite capable of taking care of himself. It is I who will need looking after. "

"He's strong physically, but when it comes to sewing on buttons and taking care of his clothes, I am very much afraid that he will wish many times before the voyage is over that he had me along, " rejoined Mrs. Griswold, trying bravely to smile.

"Captain Bowden's anxious to get away mother," interrupted Danny with an effort to appear unconcerned. Priscilla and her mother have gone ashore and are waiting for us there. I'll go down with you and say my last good-byes there. "

"Ma'am, it was the bravest thing you ever done, lettin' Danny go this way, " said Captain Bowden to Mrs. Griswold as she was leaving. "The good Lord has entered it in his log-book, an' you can be sure ma'am, that it ain't goin' to be forgotton. "

. . . .

Out across the Bay whipped into whitecaps by a fresh southeast wind , sailed the Hornet, her sheets taut, her booms and blocks creaking the chorus so familiar to the ears of a sailor, as she surged along, throwing a green shower of spray over her bows. On her poop with his feet braced far - apart to steady himself when she rolled, stood Danny, gazing longingly at the dim, receding coast-line, which marked the boundry of the place where he was born.

In retrospect he could picture the favorite boyhood haunts he was leaving fast behind. .. Once more he was back on the shores of the Salt Pond,sailing the boats which Captain Bowden had so painstakingly built for him.. He could see through the moisture which dimmed his eyes,. a puff of wind from an April-day squall,ripple the waters of the pond , filling the sails of his miniture ship until she heeled far over,almost to the point of capsizing,and then suddenly righting,would flash up into the wind,her sails,small squares of cotton cloth, fluttering helplessly,as taken aback she drifted astern.... And as he stood there on the quarter deck of the Hornet watching the land that he had known so well become nothing but a blur on the horizon,the sudden transition frightened him, for like the frail craft he had sent out from the shore of the pond,on that April morning so long ago, he needed a guiding hand. And then his thoughts centered on the nights, when in company of other boys and girls he went out hanging May-baskets. What fun they had going from house-to-house , hanging on the knobs of the doors, gaudily designed baskets of tinsel and tissue,filled with Mayflowers,candy, and the bright-red checkerberry. How thrilled he had been,when after a loud rap on the door,they had all scuttled away,to hide behind lilac, syringa or hedge,there to await with beating heart ,discovery by the recipient of the basket. He could almost smell the warm fragrance of the earth,in the clearings where he had picked the Mayflowers,and visualize their pink blossoms peering up at him from amongst the green foliage,as he cleared away the underbrush. This thought brought on another, his nightly visit to the apple barrel in winter. Once again in his minds-eye he was descending the cellar stairs,lamp in hand, and as he reached the bottom step the musty odor of vegetables greeted his nostrils, and a breath of cold air brushed his face.. The rays of the lamp soon separated the apple barrel from the surrounding darkness, and in a moment he was leaning over it inhaling a never-to-be-forgotton odor..... And then he was upstairs once more, seated near the sitting-room stove, the bowl of apples within easy reach... At this point his reverie was interrupted by the voice of Captain Bowden. "Well Danny", he said. "How about goin' back home with me tomorrow, and not goin' out in the Red Jacket? "

"Right now I feel homesick enough to do it, Cap'n Silas, " Danny answered a trifle sheepishly. "But I guess if others can leave home, I should be able to."

"That's the spirit, " rejoined Captain Bowden. "It takes stout-hearted men to brave the dangers of the sea, Danny, an' it's no place for weaklings. "

"I felt pretty scared a few minutes ago when I got to thinking of what I had left behind, and if I should ever see Mother and Priscilla again, " acknowledged Danny . "I guess being brave means taking things as they come, and making each day speak for itself. "

"Most of us get scared into fits over nothin' at all, " replied Captain Bowden thoughtfully. "I've known people to crawl into bed and cover their heads up with a quilt during a thunder-storm, but the Lord only knows what they done it for. They would have been just as safe sittin' in a chair with their eyes open. Being scared is a disease worse than the smallpox. "

Danny turned and faced toward Boston, his shoulders thrown far-back. "I feel better already, Cap'n Silas, " he said cheerfully. "What time do you think we'll get in? "

"About two o'clock if this wind holds out, " was the reply.

"Now that I am almost over being scared, I feel more anxious to get there, and feel the decks of a clipper under me, " remarked Danny. "I am sure that I shall be too busy after we get clear of Highland Light to feel homesick. "

"Speaking of being scared, reminds me of somethin' that happened to me back there on the Cape, while I was home between voyages in one of the Black Ball packets, " observed Captain Bowden reminiscently. "In those days I used to take

in every dance within a radius of thirty miles in a hoss an' buggy.
I was bashful as a potato-bug an' most of the time I rode alone. Well
on the night I'm tellin' about, I was comin' home from a dance in Brewster,
an' half-way through a long stretch of woods known as the 'Pines' I must
have dozed off, for the next thing I knew the horse was rarin' back in the
britchin' snortin' like all possessed...." Here the captain paused to
methodically fill and light his pipe... "Well, why don't you go on, Cap'n Silas",
questioned Naomi Bacon who was standing close by. "You are as long-winded as
~~winded as~~ a devil-diver. "

"As I was saying, " the captain continued with a grin. "I was taken
aback in a stretch of woods darker than a stack of black cats, with the hoss
layin' back in the britchin' an' snortin' like a steam-engine. Then all of a
sudden, just as I was reachin' for the whip, I heard the most God-awful screech
on my starboard bow ... Then I heard a crashing noise in the bushes an' the
sound of a heavy body landin' in the road alongside the buggy.." Here the
captain came to another halt, during which he gazed appraisingly up at the
weathercock on the maintopmast, down at the bulging foresail and mainsail, and
then out at the land marking the entrance to the Narrows, now plainly visible
under the Hornet's bows. The mate at the wheel, following a motion from the
captain's hand, changed the course a point or two, the sheets were hauled taught
and the captain continued with his story. "I thought the Old Nick himself was after
me when I heard that thud alongside the buggy, an' I let out a holler fit to wake
the dead. Whatever the critter was it must have stopped for a minute trying to
figure out what to do next after that yell of mine, for it didn't jump at me,
Then the hoss sensing the critter was behind him started off on a gallop, and
I heard whatever it was following behind screeching at the top of its lungs......
Pretty soon we come to the edge of the woods, an' a little farther on we sighted
a light in the window of a farmhouse, an' I dont't remember of havin' seen a light

before or since that made me feel so comfortable as that one did.
I managed to stop the hoss an' a farmer who was just getting ready
to milk his cows come out to see what was the matter. I told him about
the scare I got back there in the woods, an' added in a joking sort of
way,that it must have been the devil ... The farmer held his lantern up
so that he could get a good look at my face and says. 'You're right,neighbor,
it was a devil, an Injun Devil with his belly full of meat from my back-pasture.'
He was all riled up about that critter,the farmer was. It seems that he an'
his hired man had tied a calf out in the pasture the night before, and then
hid in the bushes,waiting for the critter to show up,with their guns all
cocked an' primed,ready to shoot... He said the critter had strayed down on
the Cape from the Lord knows where,an' was raising particular Cain with the
cattle.... They hadn't been waitin' long in the bushes when they heard twigs
snapping . It hadn't taken the critter long to locate the calf,for it kept
up a continual mooing for its mother.. The farmer said he didn't wait a
second after he heard the critter land near the calf,but let go both barrels
of his gun, and the hired man did the same... The guns made so much noise an'
the smoke was so thick ,that it took 'em quite sometime to get their bearings,
and besides they were afraid that the critter might not be dead... The farmer
said it was quiet as a church after the sound of the guns had died away. The
calf had stopped mooing and all the other night sounds with it. It was dark
as a pocket an' the farmer said it took 'em sometime to light the lantern,after
which they moved over to where they expected to find the critter stretched out
dead... "Did they kill the animal? " asked Naomi and Danny in one breath.

"No, " grinned the captain. "The farmer said they did a pretty good job on
the calf, but the Injun Devil got away as slick as a weasel. "

. . . .

To Danny his first glimpse of Boston Harbor was a never-to-be-forgotton sight. In by emerald-green islands bathed in the warm glow of a noon-day sun. Sailing close to lofty China clippers,tugging at their ground tackle like race-horses awaiting the command to "Go"... Shearing off just in time to clear a full-rigger beating out to her anchorage in the Roads, her sails beating a thunderous tattoo as she goes about on another tack, deep-voiced sailors chantying as they haul away on sheets and braces.

> "Oh don't you see that black
> cloud rising over yonder?
> Away,haul away! Haul away Joe! "

In by Nicks Mate, The Graves, and Castle Island,they sailed ,skirting East Boston Flats,where a score of small vessels lay at anchor waiting the turn of the tide. "I usually tie up over there , " said Captain Bowden, pointing to the East Boston shore,where from Jefferies Point to Chelsea Bridge , the wharves were lined with pinkies, clipper ships, Mediterannean Fruiters, and packet schooners. "But today I am goin' to take you right over alongside the Red Jacket. "

"You don't have to do that,Captain Bowden, " remonstrated Naomi. "Danny and I can get a drayman to take our baggage over to India Wharf, and then take a hansom ouselves. It will be something new for Danny,riding in a cab. "

"I think that is a good idea Cap'n Silas, " voiced Danny. Why don't you do it, and save yourself a lot of time."

"I'll be back in East Boston before you know it, after I have landed you folks, " replied the captain . "They'll have a Jacob's-ladder over the side , and in two shakes of a lambs tail you an' all your dunnage will be on board. "

"We may as well let him have his own way, Danny, " said Naomi
with a smile. "You know how stubborn he is. "

Hauling more to the south they shaped their course across the
Flats in the direction of India Wharf, skillfully keeping clear of
the shipping, which at times threatened to completely surround them.

"Them dodgasted fishin' schooners are as thick as fleas on a
porcupine, out here this afternoon, " exclaimed Captain Bowden
peevishly as he put his wheel hard-down to clear one which had tacked
unexpectedly across his bows. "Don't you know, you mackerel -chaser ,
that you can't cross the bows of a vessel with her starboard tacks aboard,"
he shouted, shaking his fist at the offender. "You almost run me down. "

The man at the wheel of the fisherman, thumbed his nose at Captain
Bowden defiantly, and flung back some unintelligible retort which was
drowned out by the Hornet's flapping sails and pounding blocks.

Off on another tack the Hornet soon came in sight of India Wharf,
which at a distance appeared to be a veritable forest of spars and rigging.
Some of the ships were moored bow-on to the ~~sting~~ STRING -piece, with a cage anchor
out astern, while others were snugly berthed alongside the bulkhead.

"Can you smell the tar, Danny? " queried Captain Bowden with a
twinkle in his eye. "You are lookin' at the prettiest fleet of clippers
that ever sailed the seven seas, " he continued proudly. "An' the best of
'em all is the one that lays the futherest out there with her bows headin'
this way, the Red Jacket. "

Now that Danny had arrived within sight of this ship that was to
take him down to the sea, his first impression was that of dismay. Theoretically
he was familiar with every inch of this majestic creation of wood and iron, but
the sight of it awed him - made him feel small and unimportant, but as they

drew nearer and his eyes discerned more clearly her tall, tapering spars, and well-trimmed yards, the feeling vanished and in its place he felt a glow of pride in the fact that he was about to become a part of her. A warm summer breeze fanned his face, bringing with it the smell of oakum and tar, and like a hound scenting its quarry he raised his head and sniffed, for to those who were sailor-minded it was an odor much to their liking.

The slanting rays of an afternoon sun shown down upon the Red Jacket , bringing more clearly to view her white deck-houses and long, black hull, tipped with a rakishly up-tilted bowsprit, harnessed with a tangle of stays and foot-ropes. And as she sagged fretfully at her moorings, that same sun danced and sparkled on the eddy made by the tide under her sharp bows. Loaded and like a thing alive she was ready to spread her wings, and once more feel the kiss of the trade winds on her snowy canvas.

"That husband of yours sure knows his business, Naomi, " remarked Captain Bowden, as he eyed the Red Jacket critically. "There's goin' to be a slant of wind an' he smells it. He's got his ship in just the right position to haul in his cage an' put to sea at a minutes notice. We're goin' to have a 'smoky sou'wester' that will probably last two or three days, but he's goin' right out an' buck it just as soon as the tide turns. "

"Arnold never lets any grass grow under his feet when he's ready for sea, " rejoined Naomi proudly. " He says any wind's a fair wind as long as you can keep going. "

In a matter of minutes the Hornet had rounded up into the wind and was fast to the big ship. "Hello down there, Naomi. You are coming on board in grand style, " called down Captain Bacon from his stand by the rail near the Jacob's ladder.

"He insisted on doing it, Arnold, and there's no denying him, " returned Naomi, flashing Captain Bowden an appreciative smile.

"Thank you, Cap'n Silas, I'll do as much for you sometime. " replied the captain of the Red Jacket.

"That's all right, Arnold, " said Captain Bowden. "I'll call it square if you will keep your weather eye on Danny here this voyage, and see that he don't get into any trouble. "

"Why of course I will. was the reply. "I wasn't sure at first that he intended going out with me, and was only up here with you for the day. "

"No sir, I'm ready to turn-to just as soon as I change my clothes, " volunteered Danny cheerfully.

"In that case, Mr. Griswold, step lively and see to it that all the dunnage is taken on board, " called down Captain Bacon sharply. And then with a friendly grin and a change of voice, he added. "It isn't every day that I find a young man so anxious for work. "

"Did you hear that, Danny? He's calling you Mr. Griswold already, " said Captain Bowden in an undertone. "Just remember son, that he won't be showing you any favors unless you earn 'em. "

"And I won't be asking for any, not if I can help it, " was Danny's quick rejoinder. "All I ask is an equal chance with the rest of the men. "

"You'll get that all right, " replied Captain Bowden. "His bark is worse than his bite. He'll probably run you some at the start, but you just hold your temper, Danny, an' don't answer back. You don't have to be too meek though, for no captain likes to have his mates agree to everything he says. "

"Don't worry, Cap'n Silas. I shall always stick up for my rights and ideas, no matter what happens, " was Danny's smiling rejoinder.

"Cap'n Bacon is like a man I used to sail with, Danny. On shore he was one of the most easy-going fellers that you ever set eyes on, smilin' an' jokin' all the time, " observed the captain of the Hornet with a chuckle. "But when he come on board sailin' day he would call for a bucket of salt water the first thing, an' putting it on the hatch he would give his face a good washing in it.. Then when he had finished he would call all the men together in the waist of the ship, an' yell at the top of his voice. 'Now you bullies, I've washed the land off my face an' the first man who speaks out of turn, or lags in his work will feel the weight of my fist.' After that he used to shut up like a clam at high water an' never smile or crack a joke for the whole voyage. "

"Well, there goes my sea-chest, and I may as well follow, " said Danny choking back a lump in his throat. "You'll keep an eye on Mother, won't you Cap'n Silas? Tell her that I will send her a letter by the first homeward bound ship we meet. "

"Don't worry about your ma, Danny, " the captain replied cheerfully. "I'll see to it that she don't get snowed under this winter, or want for anything."

"Good-bye Cap'n Silas, " said Danny, giving his old friend a long and hearty hand-shake. "I'm going to make you proud of being my teacher. " With that he turned and began his climb up the Jacob's-ladder, his eyes misty with tears.

. . . .

The remaining months of summer were slow in passing, at least so it seemed to Mrs. Griswold, for she missed Danny's cheerful voice, and the confident feeling which his presence around the house always imparted.

Mrs. McKane and Priscilla called the day after Danny went away, and their words of cheer went a long way toward relieving the dull ache that was in her heart. The ache was nothing new to her, for she had felt it many times before, always after Danny's father had packed his sea-chest and sailed away on a voyage. In the years which followed, after that fatful morning when she stood on the headland, watching with anxious eyes what was left of John's vessel come drifting into port, a seed of contentment had taken root and flourished within her soul, for the pleasure of having Danny with her had eclipsed everything else. Like in ancient Gaul, her small world was /divided into three parts, and in order of consequence Danny came first, which was only natural, and then followed her kitchen and garden.

The decision to send Danny away with her blessing, had not been formed on the impulse of the moment, for 'coming events had cast their shadows before', and in the days preceding Danny's departure, Mrs. Griswold's motherly instinct had warned her of an impending crisis. She had sensed what was uppermost in her son's mind, and that no argument of hers would ever prove strong enough to efface it. And to make Danny's case stronger the words of her husband came drifting back to her out of the past. " The sea is in his blood, Annie, and you never would be able to change him, even if you lived to be as old as Methuselah." She knew now just how true that prediction had been, so with a sigh of resignation she folded her hands and gave up the struggle. "The Lord so loved the world that he gave his only begotton son, " she repeated over and over again to herself. So why shouldn't I? "

Arriving at this decision, her procedure become clearly outlined, and almost as if the gods were conspiring in Danny's favor, Naomi Bacon called on her the very afternoon she had made the decision. "Arnold would like to have Danny go out with him as third mate, " Naomi had said, coming right to the point, the minute she entered the door. "Of course he wouldn't think of shipping Danny without your consent, Annie, but we are sailing tomorrow night, and he is quite anxious to find out if you will let him go. "

It seemed to Mrs. Griswold at the time as if God had put the
answer right into her mouth. "Of course I will, Naomi. Danny is old enough
to know his own mind, and if he wants to go I shall never stand in his way."
she had replied... Then after Naomi had taken her leave, she had gone up to
the attic and dragged her husband's old sea-chest down to Danny's room, where,
after dusting it carefully, she began to pack it with the things that Danny
would stand the most in need of... She had packed that same chest many times
before, always with a feeling of desolation, and today as she bent over it the
feeling was more intense, and tears of sorrow gathered in her eyes as she
emptied the bureau drawers of Danny's shirts, which only a day or two before
she had so carefully ironed and placed there, little thinking at the time that
she would ever be called upon to remove them for the purpose in mind.

Danny had come home late for supper that evening, and had been in such
a hurry to meet Priscilla, that he had not even gone upstairs to his bedroom. "I
guess this shirt is clean enough Mother. I only put it on this morning, " he had
remarked, after he had finished washing his face at the kitchen sink.

Mrs. Griswold made no reply, but went right on removing the dishes
from the stove she had been keeping hot pending his arrival. Danny had been over
to Nauset Harbor that afternoon to see David Hatch about a lobster-car, the latter
had expressed a willingness to sell at a very low price; consequently he looked
quite presentable. It was Mrs. Griswold's intention to first let Danny go to his
room and discover the sea-chest, after which she would deliver Naomi's message and
sanction his going, but as he made no move to do it, the plan from necessity had
to be abandoned.

Danny had eaten his supper hurridly that night, and if his mind had
harbored any thought other than that of meeting Priscilla, he never
expressed it by word or look. His mother seated opposite made a brave show
of being hungry, but every morsel of food had to be choked down, and every
drop of tea seemed to strangle her. She couldn't even find the courage to
give him Naomi's message, or tell him what she had done that afternoon in
preparataion for his departure on the Red Jacket.. As she watched every move he
made, the thought came to her that it would be the last time but one that she
would have him with her, eating his meals, for many a long weary month, perhaps
never. It was then a film of moisture obscured her vision, and she had all she
could do to keep from crying out "Danny! Danny! Please don't go away and leave
me all alone..".... After a time the paroxysm of grief died away and her mind
become more at ease. She would give him Naomi's message when he came home that
night, and the postponement of this ordeal, even for so short a time, brought
with it a modicum of comfort. Her eyes cleared and she asked Danny how he had
made out that afternoon.

"I didn't buy his old lobster pound, " was his reply. "I could make a better
one myself for half the money. "

She was going to say that he wouldn't need one after tomorrow, but caught
herself just in time. " I guess no one ever gains much by buying things second
hand, " she said instead.

"You are right, Mother, " he returned, pushing his chair back from
the table. "I will have plenty of time to make one this winter. "

His words brought the color back to her cheeks, and with it the
hope that he might not care to go out in the Red Jacket after all. She
must tell him, though, of Captain Bacon's offer, and of her own change of
heart. She couldn't keep that from him. It wouldn't be right.

"Well, I'll have to be running along now, " he said, rising to his
feet. "I'm going to have a big day tomorrow. " (Tomorrow never comes, but
the new day which was about to dawn for Danny, although he knew it not at
the time, was destined to be the most eventful one of his whole life.)
He crossed over to the other side of the table and kissed his mother on the
cheek... She raised her eyes to his and said chokingly. "Danny, you are the
best son a mother ever had. " He stood for sometime after that, looking down
at her with a thoughtful expression on his face.... "You won't forget to
bring me home some baking-soda, will you, Danny? " she asked in a matter of
fact way, although her heart was breaking. "I won't, " he said turning toward
toward the door. Then as he went out he called back over his shoulder, "Good
night, Mother. Don't sit up for me. "

Mrs. Griswold hurried to the door, and standing in it, watched his
tall form go swinging down the road until it was lost to view.... "He's my
son, " she murmured. "My own flesh and blood. A mother has no right to bring
an eagle into the world and then clip its wings. " Then she returned to the
kitchen , washed and dried the dishes, put some beans to soak for it was Friday,
laid a clean cloth and set the table in readiness for a quick breakfast, filled
a kettle with water and set it on the stove; and as a final arrangement, reached
for a lamp on the shelf back of it, and removing the chimney blew into it
several times, after wich she polished it carefully with a dry cloth.. This
completed to her satisfaction, she placed the lamp on a stand by the window, and
lighting it turned down the wick. These movements were a daily part of her routine

She would have done them regardless of any overhanging calamity. And
now they were finished, she removed her apron, and hanging it on a hook
back of the kitchen-door, moved on into the parlor... Why she had chosen it
in this, her hour of grief, she did not know. The parlor was seldom used, and
the air hung heavy with the odor of dried rose-leaves, and musty furnishings.
Feeling her way along carefully in the dark, she reached one of the front
windows, and raising it, opened the blind.... A current of fresh air quickly
entered, followed by a silvery ray of moonlight.. She drew a rocker close to
the window and seated herself.... For a long time after that, with her hands
folded in her lap, she rocked back and forth, reviewing the days of her youth,
and the events leading to her marriage.. There was no denying that she possessed
Sailor Eyes in those days, otherwise she would not have been attracted to John
Griswold. She went back in memory to a time when he, about Danny's age, had
courted her with all the fervor of youth. How manly and self-reliant he had
appeared to her. How she had dwelt upon his every word as if it were a pearl
of great price. The sea had given him to her, for he was born on a ship somewhere
in the Indian Ocean... And the sea had taken him away..... The sea had taken his
mother, too. .. Away down where the waters of the Atlantic and Pacific meet, in
the vicinity of Cape Pillar, God had called her, and in a shroud of canvas
weighted down with pieces of iron, her body had been sent to its last resting place,
while circling about in the spindrift, Cape Horn Pigeons chanted her requiem.....

And then there was the day out of the never-to-be-forgotton past, when John
Griswold had asked her to be his wife. "They have given me command of a ship,
Annie, and all we have to do is get married and go on board. "

She had demurred at first, pleading that it was too short a notice, and that
she would be unable to get ready in time. She hadn't the heart to tell him that
she was deathly afraid of the water. But if she had only told him the truth

in the first place,how different her life would have been from that time on, for
believing in him as she did,it would have been an easy matter for him to
have convinced her,how groundless her fear of the sea was. She had married him
shortly after and taken up her abode in the Old Griswold Home,and having been the
only child of a Baptist minister, and orphaned at an early age, her ~~early~~ environment
had had very little to do with the sea,in consequence of which there was nothing
strange in her having formed a dislike for it. Living in a village like Eastham,however,
where every family boasted of at least one nautical ancestor, and in the majority
of cases three or four, and having none herself,hindered her in a great many ways
from making friends among her neighbors. But could she have boasted of even one sailor
hanging on her family tree, her position as a substantial citizen of the village
would have been assured.

John had never urged her to go,after that day. What disappointment he felt
after her first refusal he kept to himself,thinking perhaps as time wore on she
might change her mind. But regularly as clock-work on the day he ~~would sail~~ away
on a voyage he would say wistfully. "Well,I'm leaving today,Annie. If you should care
to pack up and come along, I should like very much to have you. "

And now she fully realized just how much her going would have meant to him --
how much he wanted her,just as she wanted Danny tonight... A ray of moonlight stole
in through the open window and focussed on a picture of John hanging on the wall,one
that had been taken shortly after they were married. Instinctively,she raised her
head and saw his face smiling down at her... It almost seemed as if he knew her
decision regarding Danny and was giving his approval.... For a long time after that
she rocked gently back and forth,thinking over the events of the past.. and then
she fell fast-asleep... The moon sunk lower and lower in the western-sky, and the
parlor become once more wrapped in darkness.... A light breeze rustled the vines
outside the window, and gently swayed the curtains ....

A thin whisp of fog separated itself from the heavy bank that was rolling in over the lawn, and hurrying ahead entered the open window and brushed coldly against her cheek... It awakened her with a start. "I must have dozed off",she thought, rising from her chair. "In a minute this house would have been full of fog.". Then she hurridly closed the window and groped her way back to the kitchen.. The light still burned brightly in the window, a sign that Danny had not as yet returned. "I wonder what's keeping him", she thought as she noted the time. It was nearly midnight.It was never Mrs. Grsiwold's habit to stand idle while in the kitchen, nor in any other part of the house for that matter; so she busied herself putting a clean face-towel on the roller,then she filled the stove with kindling ,first placing a layer of shavings whittled by Danny that morning at the bottom to give it a quick start. This accomplished she reluctantly abandoned the idea of waiting up for him and made ready for bed, "He won't know what to make of it when he sees his father's chest all packed and ready, " she thought as she blew out the lamp. "I must get up bright and early tomorrow and let him know that I am in favor of his going. "

....

No person in the world could have been more attentive to the well-being of Mrs. Griswold,than Captain Bowden,after the departure of the Red Jacket. The very first thing he did after his arrival home from Boston,was to dig down deep under the papers which littered his sitting-room table and bring to light several of his old charts,from which with a great deal of humming and grunts of satisfaction he selected one of the North Atlantic, and one of the South Atlantic. He also rummaged around until he found sailing directions for the waters referred to, and a book entitled Ocean Currents. "I'll tack the charts on the kitchen table,and when

I eat, cover them over with the cloth. After that he made one more trip
to the sitting-room returning with compasses and a parallel ruler. "I guess
that will hold me for a spell, " he remarked as he seated himself at the table.
"Now let me see, " he mused, scratching his head thoughtfully. "If she holds that
breeze she started out with up to now, she'll probably average about twelve
knots per hour, but I'll make it ten to be on the safe side. He then carefully
measured off a distance on the chart ,and with the stub of a pencil made a cross
on the spot ,where in his imagination the Red Jacket was supposed to be. "Danny's
mother will be surrised when she finds out about this, " he chuckled. "I'll take
it over right after supper, an' it will be just like hearin' from him. "

Early that evening Mrs. Griswold was agreeably surprised when she answered
a knock on the back door to find Captain Bowden standing there on th step. His
round bewhiskered face was shining like a full moon, while under his arm he carried
a roll of something wrapped in a newspaper. "Come in, Captain Silas, and make
yourself right at home, " the widow greeted him cheerfully. "I'm awfully glad to
see you. "

The captain stepped inside, doffed his cap, placed the parcel he was carrying
on the kitchen table, and then removed his coat. It was quite evident by his actions
that he was making preparations to take the widow at her word, and make himself
at home.

"Won't you come into the sitting-room, " invited the widow.

"No, thank you, ma'am, " was the polite reply. "I've brought over a new
game that both of us can play. out here on the kitchen table. "

"How thoughtful of you Captain Silas! " exclaimed the widow. "Did you
bring it down from Boston? "

"No, I invented it myself, ma'am, " the captain replied. "It's a game
that will keep you in touch with Danny all the way 'round Cape Horn and up to
Frisco. "

"Well I never! " exclaimed the widow in astonishment. "I think that you are the most thoughtful and ingenious man that ever lived, Captain Silas. How do we play it? "

"Why that's easy, ma'am, " was the reply. "You just clear off the table an' I'll show you how it's done in two shakes of a lamb's tail. "

The widow hastily complied , and Captain Bowden unrolling the chart, spread it out at full-length on the table, carefully anchoring the corners with two flatirons, the sugar bowl, and a cruet. Then he cleared his throat with a loud 'hem' and pointed with his index finger to the cross he had made that afternoon. "That is where he is tonight, ma'am, about two hundred miles southeast of Highland Light. "

The widow, interested beyond words, gazed down upon the spot indicated, as if she expected at any minute Danny would emerge from it and speak to her...

"He's probably pacing the quarter deck right now listening to the creaking of her timbers, and the singing of the wind in her riggin', " the captain went on , warming up to his subject. "She's probably steering a southeast course with everything on her includin' the studdin' s'ls, an' out behind her is a wake of phosphorescent water that in Danny's eyes reaches clear back here to Cape Cod. There's a blanket of stars winkin' down at him too, ma'am, but he'll be only interested in one and that is Polaris, the pole-star ma'am, for that is the one that helps him to get his latitude. It's a bright star hanging onto the tail of Ursa Minor, an' in line with the pointers Merak an' Dubhe. Then after a while the pole-star will get nearer the northern horizan, and the Southern Cross will began to show itself in the south, an' keep on risin' until you can't see any more of Polaris. " Here the captain came to a full stop, completely out of breath.

The widow, completely carried away by the captain's eloquence, seated herself in a chair near the table, and with hands folded in her lap, waited patiently for him to continue...

Captain Bowden in the meantime reached for his handkerchief, and after mopping his brow, replaced it in a pocket of his coat which was hanging on the back of a chair, Then he thrust his hand into another pocket withdrawing a pipe, his eyes sheepishly fixed on the widow.

"If you would like to smoke, Captain Silas, go right ahead, " smiled the widow. "It will seem like old times smelling tobacco-smoke around the house. John used to get a great deal of comfort out of his pipe. "

"Thank you ma'am, " replied the captain, very much relieved. " A smoke sort of puts me on an even- keel, an' clears away the cobwebs. Goin' without smoking reminds me of a time when I was on a ship called the Golden Arrow, " he observed thoughtfully. "We was about ninety days out of Soreabaja, a port in the East Indies, when the cap'n come forrard one morning and says to us. 'Lads we've run out of smokin' tobacco. There ain't enough in the slop-chest to fill a hen's tooth. Either I was plumb off my reckonin' when I stocked up this voyage, or you've smoked a great deal more'n usual.' "

"It must be very annoying to run short of tobacco a long distance from any port, " remarked the widow. "I have heard John speak of doing it a number of times. "

"It sure is, ma'am, " agreed Captain Bowden. Then he continued with his story. "It happened one morning, when a sailor rummaging around in the forepeak found somethin' that looked like tobacco leaves, an' brought 'em into the fo'cas'l. 'Here's somethin' I'll bet we can smoke, ' " he says, an' everyone but me got ready to sample it."

"Didn't you smoke in those days, Captain Silas " queried the widow.

"Yes ma'am. I've smoked ever since I was knee high to a potato bug,
but the day was Sunday, an' I was just about to go aft to take my trick at
the wheel"

"What a shame," commented the widow.

"It didn't turn out so bad after all for me," chuckled the captain.
"I had a pretty good view of the fo'cas'l from where I was at the wheel,an'
pretty soon I saw smoke comin' out of it in all directions. Them fellers is
havin' a regular picnic, I says to myself... Pretty soon it got to be noon an'
I made eight bells loud enough to wake the dead, an' then stood on pins an'
needles waitin' for my relief......" ' What's the matter with them fellers
forrard, ain't any of them coming aft to relieve you, ' says Mr. Hatch the mate,
after I had stood there for quite a spell. I guess they're too busy smokin'
them leaves they found in the forepeak this morning, I replies, madder than a
wet hen. "

"What sort of stuff was it? " inquired the mate, pricking up his ears.
"I didn't know there was anything down there fit to smoke or I would have had
a hand in it myself. "

"It looked like tobacco I says, but I didn't get a chance to try it
before I took the wheel. "

"I guess I had better go forrard an' see what those fellers are
up to,'" he says. 'Maybe they've gone an' pizzened themselves. '"

"Well he was gone about five minutes,an' when he come back he looked
as if he'd seen a ghost.. 'I've ordered the cook to relieve you at the wheel,
Silas, ' he says sort of frightened like. I'm goin' down to get the Old Man
an' when we come up I want you to go forrard with us. ' "

"It wasn't more than two minutes before he was back with Cap'n Nickerson in tow, an' the three of us started forrard...." here the captain paused to light his pipe.

"What happned then, Captain Silas? " inquired the widow breathlessly. "Did they find all the crew dead? "

"Pretty near it, grinned the captain. "When we got inside the for'cas'l we found 'em all stretched out on the floor groanin' fit to kill. 'Phew! " exclaims Cap'n Nickerson.'This place smells like a ante-room in purgatory. What kind of stuff have these men been smoking? ".

"I don't know I says, but there's the bag over in the corner they got it from. "

"Haul it out on deck an' let's have a look at it, Silas, ' the captain orders, holding onto his nose.

"Glad to get a bit of fresh air I grabs hold of it, an' in a minute we was out on deck.

"The captain looked the bag over for a minute or two an' then his face broke into a broad grin. "Mr Hatch, would you mind goin' aft an' fetchin' me that bottle from the medicine chest marked 'Number Two' .... The mate was back in less time than it takes to tell it ,with the bottle an' a spoon which he hands over to the captain. Now you and Silas start dragging'em out on deck, an' I'll give 'em a dose of this, ' he says,uncorking the bottle.

"Well,me an' the mate started in, an' as soon as we got one out on the fore-hatch the captain would pry open his jaws and give him a dose out of the bottle,.an' pretty soon the whole nine of 'em was leanin' over the rail ,the sickest crowd of sailors you ever laid eyes on... "

"What was it they found in the bag, Captain Silas? " queried the widow,trying hard to curb her curiosity. "Was it some kind of poison? "

They was leaves from the cannibas plant that grows in India,ma'am. The natives call it Bhang over there, and they smoke it in their pipes. It's like opium an' if a feller ain't used to smokin' it,he passes out quick."

"And what was it the captain gave them from that bottle marked 'Number Two', Captain Silas? " asked the widow.

"Epicac, ma'am, " replied the captain with a chuckle. "The captain gave 'em enough to turn their stomach's wrong side out, and not want to smoke any more for the rest of their lives. "

"Were you ever sorry afterwards that you didn't smoke some of it ? " observed the widow smilingly.

"I was, an' then again I wasn't, " replied the captain evasively... The silence which followed was eventually interrupted by a knock on the kitchen door. The captain gave a nervous start. "By Jerusalem! I hope that ain't the Widow Dennison again, " he exclaimed.

"You won't have her to worry about tonight, Captain Silas, " replied the widow. "She's gone over to a meeting at the Cove with all her boarders. If I'm not mistaken,it's Wash Prebble's boy bringing the groceries. "

"Well,that's a cat of another color, " rejoined the captain,very much relieved. " I thought it might be her, coming over to borrow some more cream a tartar. "

"Come right in Freeman and put the groceries on the shelf by the sink," greeted the widow pleasantly, as she opened the door. The boy did as he was told, his densly freckled face a-glow with vitality and the pleasure of living,for he was only twelve. "I guess you remember me,don't you,Cap'n Silas, " he grinned as he passed the latter on his way out. "It was you who got me the chance to go out with Cap'n Red Grant in the Reindeer. "

"So it was, " replied the captain with a benevolent smile. "I had almost forgotten about it, Freeman. Why ain't you with him now? "

"The grin faded from the boy's face. "I didn't give it up on my own free-will ,sir, " the boy rejoined quickly, as if the captain might have mis-judged his reason for staying home. "Mother wouldn't let me go on account of father breaking his leg just before the Reindeer sailed this spring. But I'm goin' out with Cap'n Red next voyage. I ain't afraid of the sea,Cap'n Silas;an' I am goin' to stick until I'm made a captain. "

"That's the ticket! " exclaimed the old sailor approvingly. "I'm sure that you ain't stayin' home because you want to give it up. You just keep on minding your ma, Freeman, an' pretty soon you'll find yourself prancin' up and down your own quarter deck."

"Thank you, Cap'n Silas. I just wanted to let you know that I wasn't a quitter, " was the boy's manly reply.

After the boy had gone Captain Bowden stroked his chin and cleared his throat explosively,his face expressing deep emotion... "There goes a sample of what Cape Cod raises, " he commented. "Ain't you proud of bein' the mother of one, ma'am? "

"Yes,Captain Silas, I am, " replied the widow meekly. "You can't go against the will of God. I thought once that I could, but I found out before it was too late that I was mistaken. "

" I guess we've all had that same feelin' before now,ma'am, " replied the captain thoughtfully. "But I ain't ever heard of anybody yet who obeyed God's will that was sorry for it. "

For sometime after that there was silence,the widow busying herself
with putting away the groceries,while the captain smoked contentedly in the
chair... "Have you heard anything from Sofroney Parker lately? " the widow
asked suddenly.

At the mention of the Widow Parker,the captain squirmed uneasily,and
his face turned a bright red... "She's off on another tack now an' don't know
that I'm in the land of the livin', " he answered finally. "Cap'n Latham who
lives down the road a piece from her says she's settin' her cap for a pedler
that comes here from over Yarmouth-way. He's got Simeon Samuelli painted on his
his cart,but most of the people in these parts say his name is Samuels. Sofroney
says he's French an' comes from the nobility, an' raves about him to anybody
who'll listen to her. She puts him up every time he comes through Eastham,an'
keeps Professor Hangerbottom playin' the organette like a galley-slave while
they flit around the parlor like a pair of worn-out butterflies. "

"Aren't you terribly jealous of him, Captain Silas? " asked the widow,
trying hard to keep her face straight.

".hat me jealous of that feller, " snorted the captain. "Why you might
as well ask me if I was jealous of a skunk. "

"You seem so set against him,that it would lead one to believe that
you were, " rejoined the widow."Do you know him very well? "

"Not very well, " admitted the captain. "I only met him once, an' that
was the other day over in front of Mrs. Lufkin's house,when I stopped to gossip
with her for a spell. He's got a newfangled cart all filled with draws, an' in
them draws he's got everything under the sun. I must have stood there an' hour
watchin' him maneuver with Mrs. Lufkin. 'Have you any roo-shing Mr. Samuelli?'

she would ask.'Yes madam' he would say,bowing as if she was a queen..
Then open would go one of the draws an' he would pounce down on the
roo-shing like a chicken-hawk. 'Have you any needles?' she would go on,
an' out would come another draw an' out popped the needles. The reason I
waited around so long was to see if she would ask for somethin' he didn' have,
but I guess it wouldn't have been any use, for as I told you before he had
everything under the sun. "

"It is pretty handy having a man like that calling at your door, "
observed the widow. "He was here yesterday afternoon, and when I told him that
Danny had gone away on the Red Jacket,he was very sympathetic, and said that it
was a shame that I had to stay here all alone. He even asked me if I could put
him up for the night, and if Sofroney ever hears about it she will come right
over here and scalp me. "

As the widow volunteered the above information,the captain's jaw sagged
lower and lower, and in rapid succession his face reflected amazement, increduality,
and apprenhension... Then in a pitying tone of voice he said. "Ma'am,I didn't ever
think think that you would let a sweet-smelling feller like that fool yer. Sofroney's
different. She would set her cap for a walrus just because it had whiskers. The
only reason she didn't start shining-up to Professor Hangerbottom when he first
come to board with her, was because she was afraid if they got married,he would
cut her open an' stuff her like he does those birds of his. She told me that
herself. What all the old maids an' widders see in that waxed- mustached, pomaded,
clove-eatin' pedler to go crazy about is beyond me. " Having finished with his tirade,
and to a certain extent relieved himself of his pent-up feelings ,the captain
leaned back in the chair, and none too calmly awaited the widow's rebuttal.

"Why lands sakes alive,Captain Silas, " smiled the widow."Didn't you know that he has been coming through Eastham for more than twenty years? I can remember when he used to carry a pack on his back and sleep in folks' barns. "

"I guess I never did, " acknowledged the captain with a sheepish grin. "I just took it for granted from what Sofroney said, that he was new to these parts. "

"Well you mustn't take all you hear for the gospel-truth, " rejoined the widow. "As for Mr. Samuelli,he always pays strict attention to business, and naturally he caters to the women,for they are the ones who buy his wares. Sofroney knows all about him, you can be sure of that, and so does every other woman here in Eastham.".. Here the widow paused for a moment, and then with a twinkle in her eye observed. "And Sofroney also knows,Captain Silas, that this man has a wife and nine children over in Yarmouth. "

The frown which had hither-to lingered on Captain Bowden's face, disappeared as if by magic, and in its place blossomed a broad smile of satis-faction... "I was only jokin' about him, " he voiced finally. "Of course where it come to you puttin' him up that was different. There probably wouldn't be any harm in it, but the neighbors would have cackled louder than Mrs. Clement's flock of geese. "

"He volunteered with a Christian spirit,Captain Silas, knowing that it was my first night without Danny, " returned the widow."I think that it was very thoughtful of him. "

"So it was ma'am, " hurriedly replied the captain. "I guess my tongue is hung in the middle and wags at both ends. "

"It would be much more interesting to talk about Danny and the Red Jacket,wouldn't it,Captain Silas? " suggested the widow.

"It sure would ma'am, " was the reply. "I don't see why I had to go off on that tack anyhow. "

"'t was my fault , Captain Silas, " rejoined the widow. " I mentioned the subject first and I should be heartily ashamed of myself for doing it. How long do you think it will take them to sail the Red Jacket around Cape Horn to San Francisco? " she asked,changing the subject.

"I can only make a guess at it,ma'am," answered the captain thoughtfully. "It took Cap'n Bacon 115 days last voyage,but he said he was goin' to try an' better it this time. My guess would be about 110 days. It's a matter of taking advantage of every slant of wind that will blow you in the right direction, an' keepin' in the currents that flow in the direction you want to go. That's why Cap'n Bacon makes such quick voyages. he knows all about ocean currents an' prevailin' winds. I used to tell Danny all about tem , an' say the more he learned about 'em, the quicker he would make a voyage when he become master of a ship. You can almost always tell where you are,when you are on a ship, but what counts most is to know how to get to places where you ain't,the quickest way. What I don't know a lot about,ma'am,is how long it will take a letter to get here from Frisco, after Danny arrives there. They say there is a boat that takes the mail down to Panama and then overland to Colon,but I don't know how often they sail or how long it takes 'em. I'll try an' find out more about it before he gets out there. "

"Captain Silas,you are one of the most helpful men I have ever met, " observed the widow gratefully. "Why it won't seem any time at all before Danny will be home again,with you explaining everything the way you do. "

At this compliment the captain's honest face fairly beamed with pleasure. "I'll come over every Saturday night, ma'am, an' we'll make believe that we are sailin' with Danny on the Red Jacket, an' before you xx know it winter'll be over, " replied the captain cheerfully, as he rose from the chair and donned his coat in preparation for going home.

. . . .

As the month of August drew to a close Mrs. Griswold met with an accident. Being of thrifty habits and possessed with a great deal of energy, she had decided on keeping her cow, Spotty, and not selling her as Danny had advised. "I'm so used to having my own milk and butter that I hate to depend on my neighbors for it," she reflected. "Besides she is so gentle and we have had her so long, I don't want to part with her. "

Now cows, like human beings, have their frivolous moments, and Spotty proved no exception , as was demonstrated one afternoon while Mrs. Griswold was shifting her to a more succulent spot of grass near the barn.

Mrs. Griswold had gone about the process methodically, first getting a stake and driving it down deep-into the ground, after measuring with her eye the possible range of Spotty's rope... Then she went over and untied her from the other stake.. The cow looked at her inquiringly and then began to calmly ~~nonchalantly~~ brush the flies which had settled on her rump, off with her tail.. "Come on, Spotty, " coaxed Mrs. Griswold pulling away on the rope, but the cow braced her feet stubbornly and refused to move an inch.... Mrs. Griswold hauled away on the rope for a few minutes and achieving no results, in exasperation walked to the rear of the animal and hit her a sharp blow across the flanks with the slack.. The cow resenting this sort of treatment kicked up her heels

and started off with tail in air,Mrs. Griswold following after holding
onto the rope... Their course led past the stake where she wanted to
hitch Spotty,and reaching it she quickly started to wind the rope around
it, but the cow was going too fast,and as the coils rendered around the
stake they caught the forefinger of her right hand and for a moment she
felt a sharp twinge of pain in her forearm... Wrenching her hand free she
stood erect and watched the cow go scampering away,to eventually halt and
began feeding as if nothing had happened... Then she looked down at her
finger.. The tip of it had been almost completely pulled off, and was only
hanging by a ligament at the first joint... At first the sight of it made
her feel light-headed , and for a moment she thought she was going to faint,
but she set her jaws together firmly and hurried into the house, leaving a trail
of blood behind her... There she quickly dipped a basin of water from the
bucket and set it on the stove to heat,then she went into the sitting-room and
returned with her sharpest scissors... She found it a trifle awkward snipping
of the hanging tip with her left hand,but it was finally accomplished , and
then removing the basin from the stove she submerged her hand in the hot water...
she held it there for sometime thinking about what to do next... The water changed
from a sickly-yellow to a deep- scarlet... "I shan't be able to fix it myself, "
she decided. " I had better let Dr. Haggerty take care of it if I can find him
at home. " This settled in her mind, she rummaged in a kitchen-draw and finding
a piece of linen from one of Danny's old shirts, she clumsily bandaged her finger
with it... The finger pained her a lot now, especially when her arm hung down,
so from the same draw she found a piece of old sheet for a sling... These
arrangements eventually complete she bravely started of up the road in the
direction of Dr. Haggerty's.

When she arrived within sight of the doctor's house she saw his
old sorrel horse and ancient buggy fastened to the hitching-post,
and her reaction as she viewed it was not unlike countless others.
A strange mixture of fear, and confidence in his ability to do her good.
Through years of constant association with the kindly doctor, the ancient
turnout had become part and parcel of his personality, and at night when it
rumbled over the stony roads conveying the doctor to the bedside of some
patient, there was no mistaking the sound of its wheels, and those of the
villagers who were awake would exclaim. "There goes Dr. Haggerty. I wonder
whose been taken sick now? "

The doctor greeted her at the door, his kindly, spectacled eyes, taking
in at a glance, her improvised sling. "For the land sake, ~~Mrs. Griswold~~ Annie!
What have you been doing to yourself? "

"I've gone and lost a piece of my finger, doctor, " was her brave reply.
"But I guess it isn't anything to worry about, only inconvenient ,being on
my right hand. "

The doctor hurried her into his consulting-room and seated her in a chair,
humming meanwhile what he always smilingly termed his 'ten mile chorus'. It was
a small, stuffy back-parlor, smelling of iodine mixed with ether, and it required
every effort on Mrs. Griswold's part to keep from fainting. The doctor noticed
this and quickly opened a window, then he gave her some aromatic spirits of
amonia.. This done he sterilized the wound, and then applied a local anesthetic,
keeping up a running fire of converstaion while he worked. "Why I haven't treated
you for anything since Fanny was born , Annie, " he suddenly remarked . "If all
the people here in Eastham were like you I should have to take up digging clams
for a living. "

He was deftly suturing the ragged edges of the wound together, and it hurt quite a bit, so Mrs. Griswold made no immediate reply, but her mind traveled swiftly back over the eighteen years to that night when he had been summoned to deliver Danny. Then back again came to the morning when she had said good bye to him as he was leaving on the Hornet.. Unable to control herself she started to sob.

"What's the matter, Annie? Does it hurt? " the doctor enquired gently. "I must be getting rough in my old age. "

"It's not waht you are doing that hurts, doctor, " Mrs. Griswold replied, choking back her sobs. " I was thinking of Danny. "

"You couldn't have chosen a better subject , " the doctor rejoined. "If I were in your shoes I should be very proud of him. "Don't you remember that night when I brought him into the world, I said that he was going to be a chip off the old block. "

"Yes, and I didn't like it a bit," returned Mrs. Griswold, drying her eyes. "I thought that you were horrid for even suggesting such a thing . "

"Well ,how do you feel about it now? Wasn't I right? " smiled the doctor.

"I shall have to acknowledge that you were, doctor, " answered Mrs. Griswold, returning the smile. "But I only came to that conclusion a short time ago. I know now that you cannot cage young men like Danny up like birds and profit by it. "

"Of course you can't, Annie, " agreed the doctor patting her on the shoulder gently. "And one of these days when Danny becomes master of a clipper ship, you are going to be very proud of him, " concluded with a reassuring smile.

. . . .

Her finger dressed, Mrs. Griswold hurried out of the doctor's office
and directed her steps homeward. Moses Trott rattled by in his calash,
and from his lofty perch called out a friendly greeting, which she answered
in kind, at the same time stepping to one side and lowering her head to escape
the cloud of dust kicked up by the heels of his horse... When she raised it
again Priscilla McKane confronted her, very much out of breath. "What happened
Mrs. Griswold?" she asked. "Did you break your arm?"

"It was only the tip of my finger, Priscilla, and nothing to make a fuss
over. Spotty, my cow, went on a rampage, and I caught it in her rope."

Priscilla took her gently by the arm and eased her along the road.
"It may be a great deal worse than you would have me believe, only you are too
brave to admit it," she replied.

"It's the inconvienance more than anything, that will bother me,"
returned Mrs. Griswold. "It was awfully nice of you to come and meet me, Priscilla,
and I hope that it didn't put you out any."

"Of course it didn't," Priscilla rejoined quickly. "You can't do
any housework with your arm in a sling, so I am going home with you and take
charge of it myself."

"Well I guess that is what John would have called 'taking the wind
out of his sails,'" smiled Mrs. Griswold. "I had no idea that you would do
a thing like that for me, I feel almost certain that we can get along together,
but what will your mother say about it?"

"She won't mind," answered Priscilla. "Mother is very sensible
about things like that. Besides, father is coming down tomorrow and she will
be busy showing him around. We had planned on all going back together next week,
but now this has happened, I'm going to stay right here with you."

"I should like to have you very much, Priscilla; but you would find little pleasure in staying with me, " said Mrs. Griswold.

"I'll be the judge of that, " rejoined Priscilla. "You are Danny's mother and I know that he would want me to help you if I could. " They were now opposite the Widow Dennison's home. "I'll go in and get some of the things I need, and tell mother where I am going," said Priscilla. "Won't you come in and sit down while I am getting ready? "

"No thank you, Priscilla, " answered Mrs. Griswold with a wan smile. "I'll hurry right on home and be waiting for you there. If I once get set down in a chair it would take a yoke of oxen to pull me out of it again. "

Once more under her own roof Mrs. Griswold slumped down in one of her most comfortable chairs, and in something akin to a trance reviewd what had taken place... "It might have been a great deal worse," she thought. "I might have lost two fingers, instead of the tip of one. It beats all creation how God shapes our lives so that we can fit into the scheme of things. If I had never met with this accident ,I might have been a long time finding out what a really fine girl Priscilla is. I can hardly blame Danny for falling in love with her."... Mrs. Griswold's reverie was interrupted at this point by the entrance of Priscilla. "I didn't stop to rap for I thought that you might be asleep, " she said, as she deposited a small portmanteau on one of the chairs. "Don't you think that it would be a good idea for you to take a nap? " she went on before Mrs. Griswold could frame a reply.

"Why - yes - perhaps it would, " returned Mrs. Griswold hesitantly. "But I don't remember when I have ever done such a thing before at this time of the day. I'm very much afraid that you are going to spoil me. "

"You have never lost a part of your finger before, " smiled Priscilla. "I'll go right ahead and fix the sofa so that you can stretch out on it and be comfortable."

And then before Mrs. Griswold hardly realized what was going on , she found herself lying at full-length on the sofa, her shoulders covered with a light shawl.... For sometime after that she lay there watching Priscilla's movements out of half-closed eyes... Then she fell fast asleep.... Later when she awoke she found that the shades had been drawn,and the sitting-room thus darkened, very cool and refreshing. From a half-opened window came the distant hum of insects,so typical of the country on a late summer afternoon, broken at intervals by the metallic,long-drawn-out whir of a locust's wings... And then as she lay there drowsily listening to the sounds, Priscilla came tiptoeing into the room.. Mrs. Griswold opened her eyes and gazed at her admiringly.. The sleeves of Priscilla's blouse were rolled above her elbows,and she was wearing one of Mrs. Griswold's aprons.. Mrs. Griswold rose briskly from from the sofa and placed her free arm around Priscilla's shoulders. "I have never been fussed over this way since I was a very small child, " she remarked, drawing the girl tenderly against her breast.. "But I like it, and you too,dear," she added softly. "It almost seems as if you were sent to take Danny's place. "

"I am proud to hear you say that, Mrs. Griswold, " Priscilla replied, with a modest lowering of her eyes. "I want you to like me,if only for Danny's sake. "

"I should have no more feeling than a brass monkey,if I didn't like you for your own sake,Priscilla, " rejoined Mrs. Griswold quickly. "I am sure that you will make Danny a good wife, and that I'm a very lucky woman. "

"I guess if you knew that it was I who urged Danny to go,you
would think differently, " confessed Priscilla. " I should hate very
much to come to you sailing under false colors,Mrs. Griswold. "I told
Danny to let go of your apron strings and be a man,but after I said it
I could have pulled my tongue out by the roots I was so sorry. Can you ever
firgive me for that? "

Mrs. Griswold smiled. "There is nothing to forgive, dear, " she said
kissing Priscilla lightly on the cheek. "You and Captain Bowden have been
too much for me, and from now on I shall leave the shaping of Danny's career
entirely up to you. "

. . . .

Priscilla pitched in right after that,and under Mrs. Griswold's
direction, washed, baked, made the beds, and did everything but milk the
cow. She even tried that the first day much to Mrs. Griswold's amusement;
but Spotty switched her tail and moved about so much the attempt was reluctantly
abandoned. Later they arranged for Freeman Prebble to do it on his way to and
from the store.

That Priscilla, a rusticator and from a socially prominent Boston
family, could roll up her sleeves and engage in so menial a task as housework
proved a nine days wonder in the village. Donald McKane arrived on a week-end,
and the situation having been explained to him,decided on remaining a week or
two longer than he had planned. Mrs. McKane was now spending most of her
time at the Griswold home,so as to be with her daughter, only going back to
the Widow Dennison's when it was time to retire; so it was only natural that
Mr. McKane followed suit.

The Widow Dennison, with the aid of a spy-glass,which she had quite
often pressed into service,when the distance was too great for a satisfactory
observation with the naked eye, followed every movement of the people at
the Griswold home when they were out-of- doors,when her various household
duties would allow, with an interest worthy of a better cause. This exodus
of her boarders to what might have been termed a more attractive field had
not inconvienenced her financially;if anything it had proved an unexpected
grist, for their board and lodging had been paid well in advance. What
troubled the widow was jealousy,for previously she had been hailed as the
good -shepherd Of Eastham's most elite summer boarders,whom she had always
guarded from becoming too well acquainted with her neighbors, only introducing
them at such times as it would appear to her advantage socially, and more
often financially. Now owing to Mrs. Griswold's accident, and the friendly
visits of the McKanes, her prestige was on the wane,and the widow realized it
only too well.

As an added insult to injury, Mrs. Griswold had installed a croquet set
on her front lawn, and on afternoons when Captain Bowden was at home, she
could be seen playing with him as a partner,against Mr. and Mrs Mckane, or
Priscilla paired up with one or the other of them. Mrs. Griswold did very well,
too,considering her sore finger, and there was always a great deal of fun
when she come out ahead.

The taste this scene left in the mouth of the Widow Dennison was not
unlike bitter aloes, for as it so happened she was not the only observer.
Every afternoon on pleasant days the road leading past Mrs. Griswold's house

was filled with people from the village,hoping to catch a glimpse of the famous shipbuilder or some member of his family. Neighbors who previously had only a nodding acquaintance with Mrs.Griswold. now stopped to enquire about her health , and she was busy answering questions from morning until night. She modestly refrained from discussing her private affairs,however; and this attitude proved a never-ending source of annoyance to most of them,who had used every art known to their simple minds to gain their ends.

"I don't see for the life of me,Annie Griswold,why a girl with all her money and social position, (referring to Priscilla) would hire herself out to cook and scrub floors, " remarked Ellie Webster,a neighbor,who, with Dwinal her youngest offspring in tow, had descended upon her one afternoon while she was sprinkling her flower beds.

"I guess it's because she likes it, " returned Mrs. Griswold shortly.

"Likes it? " repeated Ellie sarcastically. "Whoever heard of anyone liking housework? ".

"Well,I do for one, " replied Mrs. Griswold evenly.

"What are you doing there?" inquired little Dwinal, looking up at her with a vacant expression.

"I'm helping Zeke, " she answered facetiously.

"Who's he? " asked the boy, now completely mystified.

"He's the brother of Hide. Didn't you ever hear of him? "

If Dwinal had ever heard of the above mentioned Hide .his face belied it,and if anything it was more vacant than ever. He was making ready in a lame-brained way,however, to ask another question when his mother interrupted.

"Now you run along, Dwinal, and play with your hoop and let your ma do the talking, " importuned Mrs. Webster,but as he seemed in no hurry to depart she gave him a push."Dwinal is a very bright boy for his age, and his pa says he takes after me, " observed Mrs. Webster,while at the same time she gave her offspring another push that nearly sent him headlong into a rose bush.

Mrs. Griswold agreed after a moment's hesitation,having in mind a certain answer given by Mrs. Webster to a neighbor who had mildly suggested that her wallpaper needed cleaning. "I'm not going to wear out my wallpaper by cleaning it, Mrs. Talbot, " she had made reply. "It cost too much money. "

"I suppose you'll be goin' up to Boston this winter on a visit, now that you are so friendly with the Widow Dennison's boarders, " hinted Mrs. Webster. "I was talking with Mrs. Prouty ,the dressmaker, about it only this morning , an' she says she's comin' right over to see you just as soon as she has finished Mrs. Willet's new black bombazine. "

"You can tell her when you see her again that I'll not be needing any new dresses this winter, " replied Mrs. Griswold good-naturedly."I have no more idea of visiting Boston right now than you have. "

"Now,Dwinal,you stop rolling your hoop into Mrs. Griswolds flower beds, or I'll shut you down the cellar when we get home, " admonished Mrs. Webster,rushing to extricate him from a bed of asters ,in which he appeared to be hopelessly entangled. "I never saw such a child in all my born days for gettin' into things. I can't take my eyes off him even for a minute. "

"We were all like that when we were young, " observed Mrs. Griswold charitably. "You know they say 'childish flesh is always on the move'. "

"I was quiet as a mouse an' awfully bashful when I was a little girl, " remarked Mrs. Webster after a moment's silence. "They used to call me 'Sunshine and Showers' for I was laughin' one minute an' cryin' the next. I don't know who Dwinal takes it from. "

Mrs. Griswold smiled. " Being bashful and minding one's own business, are two of God's richest blessings, and I am very thankful that I have always observed them. "

"That is what I keep telling Enoch, " sniffed Mrs. Webster righteously. "I said to him only the other night, 'If you want to get into trouble just stick your nose into other folks' business.' " Mrs. Webster by the way, had a large mole on the left side of her nose, from which protruded several long hairs, that were aptly termed by the wags of the village " Her smellers". She never practised what she preached, and could smell out a choice piece of gossip long before any of her neighbors; hence the appellation.

" I was never much for prying into other people's affairs, " observed Mrs. Griswold with an air of finality. I had all I could do looking after my home and Danny. "

"I guess you won't be seein' much of him after he gets married, " remarked Mrs. Webster, glancing at her inquiringly. Here she paused long enough to yank her son down with a savage jerk, from half-way up a trellis, he had climbed with the object in view, so he stated, 'of looking for whales. ' "When his ship's in Boston he'll be spendin' all his time with those highfalutin' friends of yours, " she concluded insinuatingly.

Mrs. Griswold held her temper and counted ten before she made reply... "I guess whatever he does will have my approval, " she answered finally.

Mrs. Webster raised her eyebrows and sniffed dersively; then catching sight of Priscilla and her mother coming down the road, she grabbed Little Dwinal by the hand and streaked it in the opposite direction, not forgetting to call back over her shoulder before she was out of ear-shot. "You had better hurry up an' marry Cap'n Bowden before Sofroney Parker gets him. "

"I know that it isn't Christian to harbor such a thought, but I could skin that woman alive, " muttered Mrs. Griswold. "She reminds me of a toad and that Little Dwinal of hers, a fat tadpole. "

. . . .

Donald McKane returned to Boston, leaving his wife to prolong her visit as long as she liked. "I don't mind if Priscilla stays down here all winter, but I hope that you come home before snow-fall, " he had remarked on the eve of his departure.

During the shipbuilder's stay in Eastham, there had been two Saturday evening visits to the home of Mrs. Griswold, where he and Captain Bowden had discussed at great length the probable course of the Red Jacket, and her whereabouts on that particular day, for the benefit of the ladies. Their imagery had followed her out over the blue waters of the Gulf Stream, where long, wavy lines of gulf-weed, broken loose from the Sargasso Sea, moved restlessly northward following the current. They had each in turn elaborated upon what they had found in clumps of that weed, yellowish-brown in color, from which hang berries greatly resembling gelatin capsules, tinged with pink. Carried back again to the days of their youth, in retrospect they again, on a Sunday when they were off watch, lowered a wire grapnel over the side of the ship and catching a lump of the weed, hauled it on deck, where they extracted from it jelly-fish, tiny crabs, sea-horses, and various forms of marine growth. Then off on a long tack they went in the direction of the Canary Islands, where in about 30 degrees north latitude, they picked up the Northeast Trades and squared away to the westward. They told of the relaxation in the second dog-watch,

and the days of fine weather in the trades,when they moved steadily onward
over the ocean,without having to touch a brace,tack, or sheet,only to 'sweat
them up' at the end of each watch; of the water all a-sparkle in tumbled white
and blue, and the fleecy,white clouds hanging low on the horizon.. Of dolphin
playing around the ship's bows,reflecting all the colors of the rainbow;but when
they were caught and landed on deck,the color quickly dimmed.. Of mollusks by
the thousand (Portuguese man-of-war)looking like tiny ships of pearl,with their
gauzy sails and delicate coloring, driving over the blue water before a gentle
breeze... On their last Saturday night together the two men,who were so deeply
wedded to the sea,had left the Red Jacket according to their calculations,somewhere
in the vicinity of St. Paul's Rocks,and presumably the next landfall would be the
Island of Fernando de Noronha. So it was there Captain Bowden began on the Saturday
night following Donald McKane's departure for Boston.

"He 's down about there now," said the captain,pointing his finger to a
spot just below the equator, and near the coast of Brazil. His listeners in turn
looked at the spot and then resumed their seats with exclamations of wonder....
"I can remember as if it was yesterday,the first time I ever set eyes on that
island, " the captain went on. "Night was just settin' in,an' our ship was justx
about a mile to the north of it,headin' a southwest course. Noronha ain't more'n
a mile wide an' about five miles long,with a big peak stickin' up in the middle
of it that looks like a tooth. It was almost dark when we first sighted the island,
and soon after a big thunderstorm come sweeping out of the west covering it up
completely... After that we only got a glimpse of it,when a big flash of lightnin'
would come, that looked as if it was goin' to tear the island to pieces."

All three women exclaimed "Oh"! in unison.

"The infernal regions ain't nothin' compared to that island, "
Captain Bowden went on after he had cleared his throat. "It belongs to
Brazil and lays about four hundered miles off a place called Pernambuco.
There's a convict settlement on it , an' I've heard it said that they send
out a boat loaded with murderer's every now and then. They call it the
"Night Boat"; for it always leaves at night ,an' only the high Mogul's knows
who's on it. "

"For all we know Danny may be looking at that terrible place right now, "
observed Mrs. Griswold nervously. "You don't suppose there is any chance of his
being wrecked on it, do you,Captain Bowden? "

"No ma'am,not a chance, " replied the captain quickly. "It's like a
sign-post on land, an' every captain keeps his eyes peeled for it. It's been
out there in the Atlantic a long time,ma'am, an' I ain't ever heard of any ship
being wrecked on it. "

. . . .

On another Saturday night Captain Bowden regaled them with tales of
the doldrums and the Sargasso Sea. On being asked what the doldrums were by
Priscilla,he replied. "They're what the sailors call 'hoss latitudes' and lay
about 5 degrees north and south of the equator, where the wind is mostly up an'
down if there's any at all. I've known ships to float around in 'em for weeks,
like chips in a washtub an' not get any place. You might sight a ship one mornin'
ten miles off to starboard, an' another the same distance off to port, an' when
it come afternoon they would be within' speakin' distance of each other. All the
the time edging closer as if they wanted to get acquainted an' swap a yarn or two
on their way to different ends of the earth. "

"How remarkable! " exclaimed the ladies in one breath.

"Over toward the African coast about twenty degrees north of the line, is where the Sargasso Sea starts in, " the captain went on, warming up to his subject. "There's miles an' miles of seaweed in it, an' old wrecks come together there just as the ships I was tellin' you about. It's a regular graveyard for 'em; an' they say that the souls of lost sailors come out of it in the shape of a ball of fire. an' go floatin' around in the air to eventually light on a ship's topmast or yard-arm for a friendly visit. The sailors call 'em corposants; an' if they sink down towards the deck after they light, the ship ain't ever goin' to reach port. "

"What a weird superstition! " exclaimed Mrs. McKane. "Did you ever see any of them, Captain Bowden? "

"Yes ma'am, I've seen quite a few of 'em in my day, but they always floated away peaceful-like an' never settled down on deck any place. They have to light on deck or on one of the houses before there's any use of worryin'," was the answer.

"You can't make me believe, though, that one of those things could be responsible for the loss of a ship, " Priscilla remarked skeptically. "It is only one of the many superstitions an old sailor's head is always filled with. "

"There's a lot of 'em that maybe wouldn't hold water, Miss McKane, such as turnin' over a hatch, the rats leavin' a ship, a bell falling off its standard, heavin' a cat overboard, killin' a albatross, or sightin' the Flyin' Dutchman," admitted the captain somewhat reluctantly. "But this here corpasant is a cat of another color. "

"By that remark I should judge that you believed in it, Captain
Bowden, " commented Mrs. McKane, smilingly. "Would you mind telling us why? "

"I don't exactly believe in it, ma'am, " answered the captain, scratcing
his head, as was his custom when perplexed. "But I saw somethin' once that
set me to thinkin'. "

"Won't you please tell us about it Captain Bowden, " urged Mrs. Mckane.
"Can't you see that we are practically eaten up with curiosity to hear what
it was. "

"All right, ma'am", replied the captain, clearing his throat. "It ain't
what you might call a pleasant story, but as far as I know it was true. I was
master of the ship"Leander" at the time, and on my way home from China by the
way of Good Hope, an' we had had a spankin' run down the Indian Ocean and around
the Cape; but when we got up into the Gulf of Guinea the wind left us entirely
an' we sloshed around in a dead calm for more'n two weeks. We was in them
doldrums that I told you about. Well one mornin' when I went up on deck with my
mouth all puckered to whistle for a wind, I saw a whaling brig off to starboard,
an' close enough to throw a biscuit on board; so I says to the mate 'you get
the gig ready an' after breakfast we'll pay her a visit'. "Well, we went on board
an' found out that she was the Peacock ,forty-nine days out of New Bedford,
captained by a man named Hathaway, and bound for the whaling-grounds in the
South Pacific... It sort of relieves the monotony ,havin' someone to talk to
besides the mates and crew of your own ship, after you've been out for quite
a spell, so we set ourselves down on the main-hatch an' started in to gossip
just like the women do at a quiltin' ... Finally after we was pretty well run
down an' gettin' ready to leave, the captain exclaims, 'By Judas, Cap'n Bowden,
I almost forgot to show you somethin' that you'll be mighty interested in.' "

"What's that, Cap'n Hathaway, a mess of dandelion greens? I says jokin'ly.
I ain't had a mess of 'em for two years. "

"I wish it was, " he says, smacking his lips.'But it ain't.'It's a log-book
I took off of a derilict we found floatin' around in the doldrums about two weeks
ago. You hold on a minute an' I'll go fetch it, ' he says..."... He was back again
in a jiffy an' takin' the log-book from him I began to read out loud. 'The official
log of the bark "Sea Witch",hailing from Pictou, Nova Scotia, Captain Lafayette
Cates, an' twenty-one days out of Benguela, Portuguese West Africa,an' bound for
Halifax with a cargo of palm oil.' " Here I was interruepted by Cap'n Hathaway. "

" 'Yes, an' she's been drifting around in the Gulf of Guinea for more'n ten
years, ' he says. 'Her spars and bowsprit had been carried away as slick as a whistle
an' there wasn't any signs of wreckage. It looked to me as if the crew had cleared
it all away right after she was dismasted. The boats was what puzzled me the most.
The dingy was lashed on top of the forrard house ,an' the yawl still hung over her
stern, lashed to the strongback with wire gripes. We looked high an' low for signs
of the crew but we couldn't find any. ' "

"They might have been taken off by some passin' ship" I says. "Did you find
any of their dunnage on board? "

" ' Yes,it was all there as far as I could tell, ' "says Cap'n Hathaway. "
"' A soggy mass of seabags an' beddin', all covered with mold, an' everything topsyturvy as if they had left it in a hurry, an' never come back. If you want my idea
of it,Cap'n Bowden,'" he says. "' The devil must have come on board an' taken 'em
all to purgatory, for when the mate an' I went into her cabin it still smelled of
brimstone.' "

"Do you mind if I take this book along with me? I says. "I see the wind
is coming up,an' I want to read it over when I have more time on my hands. I'll
send it to Mrs. Hathaway just as soon as we arrive in Salem. "

"' Go ahead' says Cap'n Hathaway. ' I don't want the thing around
any longer. It might bring me bad luck' '." Here Captain Bowden came to a
full stop, and leaning back in his chair gazed around the room thoughtfully...
His audience remained silent,each with an air of tense expectancy... Then with
a sly twinkle in his mild,blue eyes,he continued with his story....

"I don't remember what was written on the last pages of that book word
for word,but I can give you a good idea It was written in a scrawly hand,that
looked along towards the last as if a fly had crawled out of the inkwell and
an' wandered promiscuously over the pages . The entry began with the latitude
an' longitude, an' the date, July 13th 1830, an' the day was Friday. Their
position on the chart was about a hundred miles to the east'ard of Ascension
Island An' then it went on somethin' like this. "

"' Another day of stark calm is just drawin' to a close - a day that has
been the hottest in all my forty years of goin' to sea. The sun has raised
big blisters on the paint work,an' melted the tar in the deck-seams so that
you can see the planks spreadin' before your very eyes.. Big bubbles are rising
out of the water alongside the ship an' burstin' in the air, givin' forth a
strong smell of sulphur... All day the bark has been driftin' in a vast area of
boilin' water.' "

"' It is now six bells in the evening watch (seven o'clock) an' about
ten minutes ago a large ball of fire come down out of the heavens an' settled
on our fore t'gallant yard-arm, burnin' with a greenish-yellow light ... At
eight o'clock the thing floated down from the fore t'gallant yard and come
to rest on the starboard end of the fore-yard... The crew are now all huddled
near the break of the poop,frightened as only men can be who expect death at
any minute. I have reasoned with 'em, sayin' that it was only a corposant, and
would do them no harm, but they were in no mood to listen.' "

" ' It now lacks only a few minutes before midnight , an' I have just
come below to write what I believe will be my last entry in this log-book.
The thing has settled down on top of the galley,an' the crew are all praying
in the waist of the ship,for they are sure that we are all about to die. The
mate an' I are of the same opinion, so we have made our peace with God an'
prepared for the worst... As I write this the air in the cabin is blisterin'
hot, an' I can hear the crew on deck screamin' with fear... An' now the ship
feels as if she was slidin' down the side of a mountain stern first... I must
get on deck for the smell of sulphur is stranglin' me... I. ' " .... Here
Captain Bowden stopped and gazed at his audience thoughtfully.....

"Mercy on us! " exclaimed Mrs. Griswold, as pale as a ghost. "What
happened to those poor men after that , Captain Bowden? "

Getting up from his chair the captain went over to the water pail
resting on a shelf by the sink,and deliberately helped himself to a good, long
drink... "I don't know,for that was all there was in the log-book,ma'am, "he
answered finally

"But you have some idea don't you, Captain Bowden? " queried Mrs. McKane.
"I feel quite sure that object which some call St. Elmo's fire, had nothing to
do with it, " she added skeptically.

"I can agree with you there,ma'am, " quickly replied the captain. "They
was probably right over a submarine volcano when it erupted. That thing that
I have heard called a 'Igny Fattus' , had no more to do with it than my great
grandmother Abbott's wash-tub. "

"I think that Captain Bowden has thrilled me enough for one evening, "
said Mrs. McKane rising to her feet. "So if you folks will excuse me I shall be
going. "

"I'll see you home ma'am,if you haven't any objections, " offered the
captain gallantly.

"I shall feel honored, " replied Mrs. McKane,dropping him a courtesy.
"After that weird story of yours,Captain Bowden, I think that it is only
fitting that you should. "

....

Mrs. McKane returned to Boston a week or two later,while Priscilla
remained with Mrs. Griswold. She had graduated from a girl's seminary the
previous spring;so there was nothing imperative which would demand her presence
in the city. Her decision to stay on indefinitely was prompted primarily by her
regard for Mrs. Griswold, and the fact that she was the mother of Danny.

By the latter part of October Captain Bowden had imaginatively worked
the Red Jacket around Cape Horn and up into the Pacific, taking her through
a pamparo off the Rio de la Plata where,at certain times of the year, the wind
comes howling out of the high reaches of the Andes Mountains, and bringing with it
torrential down-pours of rain, blows out across the pampas of Argentina,to finally
spend itself in the South Atlantic Ocean. He told how, as the last lingering rays
of daylight slowly fade away, an impenetrable blanket of haze envelopes the sea and
ship, and the wind in her stays hums discordantly, as braced on the starboard tack
she races to meet the storm.. Aloft the men are furling the royals and topgallant'sls
and above the pounding of the leech-ropes you can hear their voices as they struggle
to smother the heavy canvas at the bunt. To the westward ragged flashes of lightning
rend for a moment the black curtain which obscures their view, and they see hills
of white-crested water,whirling in the lap of the wind to meet the ship... And then
what is left of a partially blown-out pamparo strikes them with full force.. Over
heels the ship until her lee rail is entirely submerged,the wind howls like forty

demons in her stays, and sharp peals of thunder shake her from stem to stern.. The crew grab quickly at anything which will give them a hand-hold to keep from being washed overboard, and balance themselves on the slanting decks,waiting anxiously for the ship to find herself and fight back.. Slowly like a thing alive she measures the strength of the enemy, and then finding it the weaker of the two rises to meet it. The squall is quickly over,the sky clears,and once more the stars shine down upon an even sea,the sails are set that were taken in before the storm,while high aloft in the heavens,the Creator looks down upon the shadowy outlines of a sturdy ship,speeding southward on her course.

Captain Bowden beat the ship down through Le Maire Strait, and described the rocky shores of Tierra del Fuego, as they probably were at that time of the year, dimly visable in a grey smother of storm-torn clouds. He gave them an imaginary glimpse through the spindrift just at dawn, of a beacon light perched high on the cliffs at Cape St. John. He told about the long weeks of of fighting a head wind and current on a westward passage around Cape Horn in midwinter.. Of the cold, grey-bearded seas that swept the ship fore and aft, and and of the men huddled in the sail-locker,waiting with tense expectancy for the voice of the mate.... The voice at last! ,high above the howling of the wind, and the sound of the sea striking the decks. "All hands on deck to come in stays."..
The big ship was going about on another tack ,while the sailors pulled manfully on the braces,waist-deep in the cold,green water sweeping up from the Antarctic Circle. Of Staten Land and Cape Pillar, and the master of the ship ,haggard and sleepy-eyed from many hours on the quarter-deck ,waiting for a shift of wind that seems never to come, bending over his chart and marking with steady hand his approximate position in that maelstrom of wind and sea. Of the briny drops that fall from the rim of his souwester upon its printed surface, and of other spots on other

charts ,now grown yellow with age, mute reminders of other Cape Horn passages.
The smell of wet oilskins and the salty tang of the sea, Of rounding the Horn
at last,the Evangelistas far astern . lifting their heads into a leaden sky
as the ship drives northward, the wind whistling a devil's chorus in her shrouds.
Off the Galapagos Islands... A whale spouting in the distance.... flying fish
skimming over the blue surface of the water.... an enormous turtle floating
sluggishly by.... a guano ship painted white, with black ports,becalmed off to
starboard.... a Chilean lobster schooner ,heading offshore in the direction of
Juan Fernandez (Robinson Crusoe's Island) .... a school of blackfish (wolves
of the sea) swimming close to the ship, with only their dorsal fins showing....
over the line and sailing close-hauled at night, through a tropical sea with
the Southern Cross overhead.... holystoning the decks,painting the hull above
the waterline.... taking out the hawse plugs , and bending the anchor chains
ready for bringing up... The Southern Cross now sinking below the horizon astern.,
Polaris just over the fore topgallant yard,and the ship driving northward with
a bone in her teeth. All this and a great deal more Captain Bowden told them,
and they listened with rapt attention to every word,for one had a son and the
other a sweetheart, on this ship,the movements of which he was so graphically
picturing in his imagination.

"Do you think that there will be a chance of Danny sending letters
home by some passing ship, Captain Bowden? " asked Priscilla one night, as
she and Mrs. Griswold were following the course of the Red Jacket with breathless
interest.

"They might,if they was lucky as I was once, " replied Captain Bowden
with a chuckle. "It was made to order for me to send letters home that time.

It was one night when we were down off the Diego Ramirez Islands,
beatin' our way to the west'ard around Cape Horn. The mate comes below
an' wakin' me out of a sound sleep says, 'Cap'n Bowden, there's a ship
up to wind'ard, an' if we keep on the course we're steering she's liable
to run us down!' Well, I was out of my bunk an' up on deck before you could
say scat, an' sure enough, I could hear the poundin' of her brace-blocks,
for she was running free, an' the thunderous flapping of her sails as she
rolled in the trough of a sea. 'Call all hands an' stand by to come in stays,'
I sings out. Then I grabs a belaying pin, an' hurryin' down below, lashes it
to a canvas pocket that we kept handy to send our letters home if we got a
chance, an' was up on deck again in a jiffy. She was gettin' nearer now an'
we could see her big hull looming up out of the spindrift an' darkness to
wind'ard.. I had the mate set off a flare on the poop; an' seeing it, the other
ship manuvered so that she passed about twenty feet from our stern, an' I threw
the letters onto her quarter-deck. She was the full-rigged ship "Plover", fifty-
two days out of Shanghai an' bound for Boston. There is always a chance of the
Red Jacket meeting with some homeward-bound ship, and you might be hearin' from
him any day, " the captain concluded encouragingly.

"Did you hear about the Peter's boy getting married yesterday, Captain
Bowden? " asked Mrs. Griswold, changing the subject. "He is the most bashful
young man in Eastham, and nobody ever dreamed that he would get up courage
enough to pop the question. "

"He's pretty bashful, ma'am, but I used to know a young man over on
Nantucket that was more so, " rejoined the captain in a reminiscent tone of
voice. "And if it hadn't been for his father he probably would have never got
married, not if he had lived to be as old as Methuselah. "

"If it's a story, Captain Bowden, won't you please tell it to us, " urged Priscilla with a smile. "I had no idea there could be a young man more bashful than Luther according to Annie's tell. "

"Well, I guess Ollie Higgins was, ma'am, " grinned the captain. "He's married now and master of the clipper "Comet". "But when he was younger he didn't have the courage of a bedbug when it come to poppin' the question. He was more afraid of the girls than Old Nick would be of holy water. "

"If you mean Captain Higgins that live next door to the Prebbles, I never would have suspected it, " commented Annie Griswold. "He must have outgrown it a long time ago. "

"He was different when we was boys together over on Nantucket," rejoined the captain. "He fairly worshiped the ground Addie Peabody walked on. That was the girl he finally married, but he was so bashful that he wouldn't go within a mile of her. She liked him, too, an' did everything in that modest way of hers to make him see it"

"Addie Higgins is a fine woman, " commented Annie Griswold.

"Well, Cap'n Nate Higgins, Ollie's father, was forever after Skinflint Peabody to let 'em get married, but he would always stubbornly refuse to give his consent. " 'I don't want any daughter of mine marryin' a sailor, an' what's more I'm goin' to pick out the man she marries myself, '"he would say when Nate got to pushin' him real hard about it.

" ' You won't find a better man than my Ollie if you look from Dan to Bersheba, Nate would reply stubbornly, an' that would start a long argument about the virtues of men in general.' "

"The reason they called Eben Peabody a skinflint was because he was always lendin' out money at a big interest. But he had one failin' that that had grown up with him from childhood, an' that was bettin' . He would bet on anything that come along, from the way the wind was goin' to blow the next day, to the date when the first robin would arrive. An' the best part of it was, at least to him, he was always pretty much on the right side.

Well, one evenin' when we was all down to Jabez Arey's store ,waitin' for the mail, someone speaks up an' says. ' Ain't it about time for the Mary B. Wellington to be comin' in, Nate?' Ollie was on the Mary B.'"

" ' She'll be comin' in tomorrow,'" says Nate quick as a wink. "

"' You seem pretty cock sure of that, don't you?' speaks up Eben Peabody. Anybody'd think that you had a rope hitched to her an' could pull her in anytime you wanted to.' "

"'I' ve got somethin' better than that, ' said Nate, givin' Jabez Arey a wink. 'You don't dare bet on it, Eben. ' "

"' Who said I didn't? ' spluttered "Skinflint", gettin' his dander up. "'I'll bet anything you say that she won't get in tomorrow.' "

"'All right,' says Nate with a twinkle in his eye. 'If she gets in tomorrow, you've got to let Addie marry Ollie. If she don't' ..... "Here he hesitated for a spell thinkin' of somethin' as a forfeit. 'If she don't, I'll chop wood for you all winter for nothin'. "

"Skinflint's face got redder than a beet, an' he hemmed an' hawed for quite a spell tryin' to figure a way out... "'I'll do it,' he says finally, his craze for bettin' gettin' the upper hand of him - 'An' it will be the cheapest job of wood choppin' I ever got in my life. '

"' You heard the bet' says Cap'n Nate, turning to the men in the store, with a grin on his face. 'I don't want to give him a chance to squirm out of it. Will you all be down on the wharf by noon tomorrow? '"

"'You bet we will, ' they all shouts in chorus. 'An all of us is goin' to have some money on it too¦ chimes in Ephram Prouty."

"The next day was pleasant with a strong wind from the northeast blowin', an' long before noon the wharf was crowded with people, some of 'em havin' been down there since sunrise.... Well, when it got to be two O'clock an' no signs of the Mary B. everybody started to fidgit. Skinflint was stadin¦ near Cap'n Nate; an' when someone would mention what a good chance he had of winnin¦ his face would glow like a full moon ~~~~~~ rising up from behind a whitewashed fence.

"Along about three o'clock Skinflint was as happy as a dog with two tails, for the deadline was five an' he was pretty sure of winnin'..... Then all of a sudden Ephram Prouty sings out. 'There she comes now, in by Great Point¦ '" An' sure enough, there she was comin' up the Bay with a bone in teeth. Well, you never saw such a surprised lot of people in all your born days. Skinflint just stood there as if he had been glued to his tracks, an' the rest of the people never said a word until the Mary B. was alongside the wharf with a line out.

"' Did you get the pigeon, father?' sings out Ollie through his cupped hands, as soon as they had made fast. 'I let it loose off Boon Island yesterday afternoon. '"

"' You bet your boots I did, Ollie, ''shouts back Cap'n Nate. 'Chickens always come home to roost ~son~....You get into your best bib an' tucker an' come ashore as if the house was on fire. There's goin' to be a weddin.''

"I've always wondered how a homing pigeon can find its way back after being taken so far away, " observed Priscilla. "Do you know, Captain Bowden? "

" No, I don't, Priscilla, and I never could find out from anyone either how they done it, " answered the captain. "All I know is, that the one Cap'n Nate had was pretty smart, an' when Ollie went away he gave it to him to turn loose when he was nearin' home. Ollie done it, an' the bird got back home with a message tied to its foot just before Nate left for the store that night. That was why he was so sure that the Mary B. would get in the next day. "

. . . .

In the fall Captain Bowden laid the Hornet up, and busied himself making his house and Mrs. Griswold's snug for the winter. He hauled seaweed enough to bank them both comfortably, and then turned his attention more pointedly to the possible whereabouts of the Red Jacket. Priscilla by this time had returned to Boston, in consequence of which his visits to the home of Mrs. Griswold had become more frequent. "Accordin' to all the rules of wind an' weather, Danny should be in Frisco by now; an' we should be hearin' from him no later than Christmas, " he remarked one night shortly after Priscilla had taken her departure. "I've allowed for acts of God, Ma'am, an' given 'em plenty of time. The rest of it is up to our Maker. "

"That is the best news I have heard in a month of Sunday s, Silas, " smiled the widow. "I hope that it will come true. I am almost sure that it will, if you say so. " Her faith in him by this time had become very strong and she was ready to believe anything that he said.

"The calculations may be off in spots an' places,but they ain't so far off as Lowney Dyer was once, " chuckled Captain Bowden. "Lowney started out from Vinyard Haven one day. bound over to Barnstable for a load of merchandise, an' when he got out into the sound the fog shut down so thick that he couldn't see his hand before him. Well, Lowney floated around for hours after that until he heard what he said was the fog signal at the entrance to Deep Hole Harbor. 'I guess seems the tide is runnin' that way,we'll go in there an' wait for this mess to clear up, ' " he says to the mate... " Here the captain paused to fill and light his pipe.

"Did he make the harbor safely, Silas? " inquired the widow, after the pipe was going good and strong.

" He made the harbor all right, " chuckled the captain, "But when the fog lifted he found himself right back in Vinyard Haven not ten feet from where he had been anchored before. "

After that the conversation lagged for a while, and then Captain Bowden broke the silence. "Do you believe in reincarnation,ma'am? Speakin' of fog a few minutes ago made me think of what Cap'n Lem Small told me once about a sailor by the name of Bill Bassett who was lost on the Banks. "

"I have never given it much thought,to tell you the truth," replied the widow. "I have heard,though,that the Japanese won't kill even a mosquito for fear it may harbor the spirit of an ancestor. If you have a story that would throw more light on the subject, I would appreciate hearing it. "

The captain needing no second invitation, cleared his throat and began as follows. "It was when I was on the schooner May Queen one summer,coastin' from Frenchman's Bay to Boston. We had left Northeast Harbor that mornin' an' was sailin'through Deer Island Thoroughfare,with a fair wind an' a lot of seagulls

hoverin' over our stern, croakin' like all possessed. Some of them
birds sound almost human, I says to Cap'n Lem. 'Do you suppose there's any
truth to what they say about the spirit of a drownded sailor bein' in some of
'em.?"

"'Did you ever hear of a sailor killin' one?' he asks. An' then before
I could reply he answere his own question. 'No, you never did, an' what's more
you never will' he says in a way that would lead you to believe that he knew
all about it. "

"There must be a lot of sailors drownded then," I says, "lookin' at a
thousand or so hoverin' over our wake. I'll bet there's a million of those birds
to one sailor. "

"'It's only the old ones that the spirits inhabit ' says Cap'n Lem...
'Look, there's one of 'em now! ' he exclaims, pointin' to a big one that had
poised in midair just over our heads an' was starin' down at us inquisitively.. "

"He looks old enough to be full of spirits, I says jokin'ly. Just then
the gull croaked at the top of its lungs , an' flew down so close to my head
that I was obliged to dodge to keep from bein' hit. "

"'I shouldn't wonder but what that was Bill Bassett,' says the captain
thoughtfully. 'It sounded like his voice' "

"Who was he? I asks, my curiosity aroused. "

"' An old shipmate of mine who was lost overbaard on our way home from
the Banks one trip' he says. ' I saw him turn into a seagull right before my
eyes. !"

"What had you been eatin' for supper?I asks."

"' It wasn't any nightmare, if that's what you mean. I wasn't the
only one who saw it happen, ' " he replies. "

"Seein' is believin' I says sarcastically. I guess you all had been eatin' somethin' that didn't set very well on your stomach. "

"' Well you can laugh all you want to but this is how it happened,' says Cap'n Lem, puckerin' his eyebrows into a frown. " 'We was on our way home from the Banks in the schooner"Nautilus", an' off Grand Manan we run into a nor'wester that almost blew the sticks out of her. The gale come down on us about midnight,an' by daybreak the sea was runnin' mountains high. I had been around the Horn a couple of times before that,but the weather there had been a millpond compared to it. Well along about noon that day while I was at the wheel , a sea boarded us an' hearin ' an' awful yell up forrard, I looks just in time to see it pick up Bill Bassett an' wash him over the side just like a cork. The cap'n was standin' right beside me an' quick as a flash he grabs the wheel an' says.'Get a dory over the side an' go after him,Lem'. In two shakes of a cows tail we had a dory out of its nest , an' pretty soon we was rushin' along on the crest of one of those seas like a streak of greased lightnin'".

"There ain't much use in goin' after a feller when the ~~xhsnxths~~ sea's runnin' like that I says. You don't stand much of a chance of catchin' up with him. "

"' No,you don't, ' agrees Cap'n Lem. ' But you feel better after making a try. ' "

"You sure do,I says. "

"' Well we kept on a spell longer,an' pretty soon one of the men in the bow of the dory shouts. 'There's Bill now on the crest of that big wave right ahead? We all looks an' sure enough there he was sloshing around on the crest of it like a log.' "

"Then you got him, I says. I thought you said he turned into a seagull. "

"' He did. ' says Cap'n Lem. 'I ain't finished yet. ' "

"Excuse me, I says. "

"' He disappeared before we got up to him though, an' over the spot where he went down there was a lot of gulls croaking their livers out, an' pretty soon one of 'em comes over an' lights alongside the dory an' starts carryin' on like no pitch hot.' "

"I suppose that was Bill Bassett, I says skeptically."

"' We wasn't sure of it at the time, but what happened afterwards proved that it was, ' says Cap'n Lem. "' We kept rowin' around for quite a spell after that , but no signs of Bill, an' when the Nautilus picked us up later we was sure that Bill was a goner... About three that afternoon the wind died out an' the sea went down, an' then the fog shut down so thick that we didn't know any more where we was than the man in the moon... An' then while two or three of us was standin'on the poop talkin' with the captain, a big gull flies out of the fog an' starts flappin' around over our heads croakin' like mad.

"' That bird is tryin' to tell us somethin', says one of the men after a while.' "

"' It sounds to me like the voice of Bill Bassett, an' he's tryin' to give us a course to steer by, I says after listenin' for a minute. ' "

"' What kind of foolishness is that,says the captain, You don't mean to tell me that Bill has turned into a seagull an' wants to pilot us in. '"

"'That's the how of it, I says. He was the best pilot on this schooner, an' could smell his way into almost any port. It ain't any more than natural that he should want to help us out now.'"

"' I think that you're crazy, ' says the captain. 'I ain't goin' to trust the navigatin' of my schooner to no seagull.' "

"' You listen a minute, I says, an' if he ain't sayin' steer South by West I'll eat a raw codfish. ' "

"'The gull was still squakin' an' for about five minutes all of us listened to it without sayin' a word... Well,what do you think of it now? I says to the cap'n. Ain't that the voice of Bill Bassett, an' ain't he sayin' steer South by West? '"

"' It sounds like him, says the cap'n, an' he seems to be settin' the course plain enough. But I ain't so sure that I want to depend on a seagull to pilot us in. ' "

"That ain't no seagull, I says. That's the spirit of Bill Bassett an' he's tryin' to do us a favor.'"

"'Well if you put it that way I'll take a chance, says the cap'n, turnin' to the man at the wheel. 'Steer her South by West Abija, an' if anything happens to this schooner, I have plenty of proof that Lem Small was to blame for it. '" Captain Bowden came to a full stop here and gazed up at the ceiling with a mirthful twinkle in his eye...

"Did they make port safely,Silas? " queried Annie Griswold, after waiting a reasonable length of time for the captain to continue.

"They sure did, " chuckled the captain. "The next mornin' when the fog lifted they found themselves sailin' right into the harbor of Machiasport, the town in which Bill Bassett was born an' raised. "

. . . .

Bad weather set in about a week before Christmas,and it snowed every day. From her back window,the minute it showed signs of clearing, Annie Griswold could see the sturdy figure of Captain Bowden,his kindly face almost concealed by a long woolen muffler, shoveling a path from the back door to the barn; and the pleasant feeling of security the sight gave her could only have been equaled by the actual presence of Danny.

Every morning Captain Bowden would plow his way through the drifts to Ezra Coffin's store and join the crowd asembled there, 'waitin' for the mail'. Then as the days were ticked off on the calendar and only one remained before Christmas,the doughty captain began to experience a feeling of dire uncertainty as to the outcome of his prediction. "If that letter don't come today,she won't have any more confidence in me than she would a polecat," he thought to himself, as seated on a cracker barrel in the store, he anxiously awaited the arrival of the stage-coach from Sandwich.... "This is my last day of grace,for there ain't goin' to be any more mail until after Christmas, an' if it don't come today my goose is cooked."

"What's the matter,Cap'n Silas? You act as if you had on a hair undershirt, the way you're hitchin' around on that barrel," jokingly observed Ezra Coffin as he prodded away on a sticky mass of dates with a wooden fork,while a small, freckled faced boy followed his every movement,with antipipation written on every line of his countenance.

"I'm not so easy in my mind as I should like to be, Ezra," the captain replied gloomily. "I wish that tarnation mail would get here. Waitin' for it is like settin' on the 'Anxious Seat'of a church. "

"Precious little you know about an 'Anxious Seat', " chuckled Cap'n Ezra. "If it was the freight on somethin' from Boston down here you might be talkin, but you don't know any more about an 'Anxious Seat ' than a coot. "

"Well,I've watched 'em settin' down front times enough, Ezra, an' from what I could see they wasn't what you might call settled in their minds. "

"You don't happen to be lookin' for a letter from your best girl? " grinned Cap'n Ezra. "I don't know when I have ever seen you so interested in the mail before. "

"I'm lookin' for a letter from Danny Griswold, " replied Captain
Bowden, undisturbed by the sally. "He's been in Frisco more'n six
weeks accordin' to my calculations, an' it's about time that we was
gettin' some mail from him. "

"How much time did you give her, Silas? "

"One hundred an' ten days, " was the reply.

"She ought to make it in less than that, " rejoined Cap'n Ezra.
"Arnold said he made the last voyage in ninety-six days. "

"Yes, but he was off the Horn in the summer. This time it was
winter when he made it..... Look, Ezra, there comes Sam Johnson with the
mail now, " observed Captain Bowden rising hurridly from the cracker
barrel. "An' he's got a sack of mail bigger'n a house. "

"That's the Christmas bag, Silas, and there won't be any more along
until Wednesday. I hope you get what yer lookin' for. "

. . . .

Captain Bowden, through a crack in the partition , watched Zeke
Bacon sort the mail, with breathless interest. He saw him dump the contents
of the bag out on the counter, and then reach down into it and feel carefully
around ~~for~~ for pieces that might have got stuck. Then he saw him turn all the
letters face-down and apply the cancellation stamp.... The captain thought he
would never get around to putting the letters in the pigeonholes back of him..
From where he stood he could see the one assigned to himself, and also that of
Mrs. Griswold. It seemed to Captain Bowden, that Zeke did nothing but putter
around without making any attempt to put the letters in the boxes. He would
pick up a string here, and adjust something there, take off his coat, roll up
his sleeves, and do a dozen different things but touch the letters, to the
complete exasperation of the captain. "A watched pot never boils", he muttered

finally, turning his head away. "Maybe if I put my mind on somethin'
else for a minute an' then look I'll see a letter in the box. "

"Hello there, Cap'n Silas, " greeted Moses Trott who had just come
in. "As I was sayin' to Obediah Prebble a spell back, ain't it about
time for the Red Jacket to arrive in Californee? "

"I should say it was, Moses. I should say it was, " repeated Captain
Bowden absent-mindedly. "I guess we 'll be hearin' from her soon. "

"I'm anxious to hear how Danny's makin' out, " Moses went on as
he unwound a long woolen comforter from around his neck and started to
jam it into his overcoat pocket. "It wouldn't surprise me any if he come
back mate of her. "

"It wouldn't surprise me either," agreed Captain Bowden. Moses
then moved along to the rear of the store, and the captain once more
turned his attention to the crack in the partition.. It looked now as if
the mail had all been assorted, and with the feeling of a man on his way
to the scaffold to be hung, the captain glanced in the direction of Mrs.
Griswold's box... It was empty. Then just as he was about to move away
from his point of vantage completely discouraged, an impulse suddenly urged
him to remain and watch the further movements of Zeke.. The latter, evidently
wishing to make doubly sure that he had left nothing in the bag, was preparing
to dive down into it again... Captain Bowden watched him breathlessly. "He's
goin' to find a letter from Danny in that bag", he kept repeating to himself,
and his eyes never left Zeke Bacon's arm.... Zeke was down a long time, and
when he finally straightened up something white, a letter was in his hand....
Captain Bowden's heart almost stopped beating as he watched Zeke carefully
adjust his glasses and scrutinize the inscription...Then he saw Zeke put the
letter in Mrs. Griswolds' box, and he knew without being told that it was from

Danny... In order to convince himself t'at his eyes were not deceiving him, the captain turned away and looked up and down the store several times, and then looked again in the direction of the box.. Yes, it was there, with the end sticking plainly out. He moved over to the window and with what was meant to be an air of indifference asked for his mail.. "And if there is any for Annie Griswold I might as well take that along, too, " he added.

"There ain't any for you Cap'n Silas, but there's one for the Widder Griswold from Danny, an' I bet it's goin' to perk her up considerable, seems that it's the first Christmas he's been away from home, an she' s probably feelin' pretty lonesome. "

"I guess God must have had a hand in that, Zeke, " remarked the captain reverently. "I don't know of anyone here in Eastham that's more deservin'. "

"An' to think, " Zeke Bacon returned reflectively. "There's more'n a hundred people trapsing about all over the ocean, from Eastham, right now, an nary a one of their relations have received a letter except the Widder Griswold. It don't seem possible. "

"The spirit's willin' but the flesh is weak; an' besides, there ain't many ways of sendin' mail from where they might happen to be, Zeke, " replied the captain charitably.

. . . .

"He's been made mate, Captain Silas, and says to tell you he was the only one, except a man by the name of Marshall, who stayed by the ship after she reached San Francisco. Everyone else cleared out for the gold-fields." Annie Griswold was reading portions of Danny's letter to the captain, and he was leaning forward in the chair intensely interested. "' We made the run out from Cape Cod Light to the Golden Gate in 106 days,with strong following winds most of the way. We rounded the Horn pretty well north of 60 and carried our royals all the way. In the Pacific from Cape San Lucas to the Farallone's we experienced quite a lot of fog, but as it lay close to the land we avoided most of it by making long tacks offshore. By the time you receive this,if ever? we shall be on our way to Amoy,at which port we expect to load tea and silk for Boston. Captain Bacon and Naomi send their very best to you and Captain Cowden, and Captain Bacon says tell him that we are coming home by the way of the Horn, and to be sure and have the Hornet ready to take us back to Eastham the first week in June. I know that you will give Captain Bowden all the news,Mother,but make this exceptionally strong,please. I should have been a very poor sailor but for his teachings,and the credit for my rapid promotion is his. I would have felt very much like a cat in a strange garret if he hadn't taught me what he did, and I strongly suspect of little use to Captain Bacon. We are going to have a hard time shipping a crew out here, for most everybody who can use a pick and shovel have gone up into the hills, Captain Bacon says that he is going to pick up what men he can while we are discharging, and then sail short-handed to the Sandwich Islands, where he will complete his complement with Kanakas,who are said to be very good sailors.When, and if,you receive this,please let Priscilla know right away, and I have asked her to do the same,if she hears from me first. I found two letters from you,and three from Priscilla awaiting my arrival here; and you can be sure that I was most happy to receive them. If I don't receive any more before I get home,these will all be worn out rereading over and over again. Oh yes, Sanchez arrived here about a fortnight ago in the Firefly and after selling her and everything he had,started for the gold field's. He has changed a lot since we had that row back home, and seems much more like a human-being now. I bear him no grudge and wish him the best of luck.

"You wouldn't be interested in the rest of it, Cap'n Silas, " said
Annie Griswold,folding the letter and putting it back in the envelope."He's
hauling me over the coals about Spotty, and writing a lot of nonsense about
some other subjects. "

"You can't make a sailor out of anything that comes along, " commented
Captain Bowden when she had finished, his eyes misty with tears. "Danny had
the makin's of one right from the start, an' all he needed was to get off
soundin's to bring it out. I was only,what you might call, holdin' turn for
him, Annie. He was two jumps ahead of me most of the time. "

"And to think, Silas,only a few month's ago I would have felt like
scratching a person's eyes out, who even suggested Danny's going out on a
ship. And now I just glory in what he is doing, and I am as proud of him as
can be, " confessed Annie Griswold, holding back her tears of happiness with
an effort.

. . . .

Once more the warm south winds that betoken the coming of summer, swept
gently over the Cape, and another long, cold winter was a thing of the past.
"She'll be comin' in now any day, " Captain Bowden was saying to Annie Griswold,
as seated on her front porch,they were discussing the all -absorbing subject of
Danny's arrival. "She may be off the Cape this very minute, so you had better
make up your mind to go up with me in the mornin' so's to be there when he gets
in. "

"If I was only sure that Danny would arrive within a week, I wouldn't
hesitate a minute, " replied the widow thoughtfully. Mrs. McKane has invited me
to stay as long as I would care to, but I should hate awfully to wear my welcome
out. "

"You needn't be a bit afraid of doin' that, Annie, " rejoined the captain confidently. "What Danny said about coming back around Cape Horn has given me a pretty good idea of when she'll get in. "

"A week up there would be all that I should care to stay," returned Mrs. Griswold . "I don't want to come back home here and find everything all 'sixes and sevens.' . "

"Well, let me see," remarked the captain reflectively.. "Today is Sunday... "If the Red Jacket don't get in by next Tuesday I'll fetch you back home an' give up prophesyin' for the rest of my life. "

Annie Griswold smiled. " I'm beginning to think that you know a lot about ships, Silas, and I shall be ready to go up with you in the morning, I'm so happy about Danny's coming home that I hardly know what to do with myself, " was her reply.

"I've got the Hornet all painted up slick as a whistle, and after the Red Jacket arrives I'm goin' to sell her to Luther Grant, " observed Captain Bowden after a long silence .

"Won't you feel lost without her, Silas? " queried Annie Griswold. "If you should part with the Hornet you won't have anything to pay attention to. "

"Yes, I will, if things turn out as I want 'em to, " answered the captain hurridly. "If things turn out as I want 'em to, I'm goin' to have somethin' that will give me more pleasure than the Hornet. "

"I have no idea what that could be , unless it's working in your flower garden, " replied Annie Griswold thoughtfully.

"I told you a long time ago, Annie, that I was lookin' for someone to help me stand the anchor watches, " rejoined the captain, nervously rubbing his chin. "Well, I don't have to look more'n a mile to see the one I picked out. "

"Yes, I remember that quite well, and if I am not mistaken, I recommended Sofroney Parker, " commented Annie Griswold,with a twinkle in her eye.

"So you did, " acknowledged the captain hurriedly. "But just because someone tells me to go jump into the fire ain't no sign that I'm goin' to do it, " replied the captain.

"I should say not, " rejoined Annie Griswold."I was only joking Silas. "You are no more suited for Sofroney than a rooster is for a sparrow. "

"If you want to know the truth about it,Annie, I have had my eyes on you for a good many years, " declared the captain boldly."But I always figured while Danny was home I didn't stand a chance. He'll be gettin' married himself this summer,the chances are, an' then you'll be left alone. I don't see any harm in planning our own future, Do you? You can wait until he comes home before you make up your mind. I know that he won't put anything in the way of it. " After this lengthy statement Captain Bowden settled back in his chair and gazed at Annie Griswold inquiringly...

The latter blushed and for several minutes remained silent... "I certainly feel honored,Silas, " she replied eventually. "I do not know of a soul in this world that I should feel more happy to spend the rest of my life with,except Danny," she went on. And as far as he is concerned, Silas, you need not have any fears on that score, for our happiness will always be his, " she concluded sagely.

The captain arose from his chair,his face aglow with pleasure. "Annie, I guess there ain't many men here on the Cape as happy as I am tonight, " he replied gratefully.

. . . .

The following Monday after Captain Bowden had docked the Hornet in East Boston, he bargained with the driver of a hackney- coach to take them over to the Stackpole House,where the McKanes lived. It had been previously understood that should Mrs. Griswold make up her mind to visit Boston on a moment's notice, it would not be necessary for her to stand upon ceremony, for usually there was always some member of the family at home; so on this day as the coach rattled noisily over the roughly paved streets she felt quite sure that they would be welcome.

As they wound in and out of the narrow thoroughfares leading to their destination, Annie Griswold peered curiously out at the people who thronged the sidewalks, and at the tall buildings crowded so closely together. It was her first visit to the big city, and the noise frightened her. "Why it seems just like being in another world, Silas, " she said, holding on to his hand as if afraid of being left alone in the midst of it. "I don't see for the life of me how the the people get any enjoyment living in such a place. "

"Neither do I," agreed the captain. "I wouldn't give one of my flower beds back in Eastham for the whole place. "

The coach finally came to a halt in front of a spacious building at the corner of Milk and Devonshire Street. where Captain Bowden, after paying the amount agreed upon, picked up Mrs. Griswold's carpetbag, and preceded her through the gate and across the wide front yard where they halted midway to watch the antics of a brown bear, chained to a nearby stake. The yard was well-shaded by several large chestnut trees, and a number of peacocks were strutting around on the grass, stopping occasionally to rattle their feathers and gaze inquiringly at the intruders. "The McKanes live in a pretty nice place , " remarked the captain as they entered a long hallway and paused to get their bearings. "I'll bet that it costs them as much to live here a week, as it does us a whole year in Eastham. "

"Priscilla says they have to live in a place like this on account of her father having so much company, " volunteered Mrs. Grsiwold. "They entertain them in a big sitting-room, and when they ask anyone for a meal they eat with the rest of the boarders. It is what they call a very high class boarding-house. "

"My sails are all taken aback, an' I feel like a cat in a strange garret, " commented the captain. "If I had my choice I'd much rather live back home in Eastham. Where did you say the door was,Annie? "

"Priscilla said it was the first one on the left as you entered the hall, " replied Mrs.Griswold in a low voice. "If it hadn't been for meeting Danny you would never have gotten me up here. "

"Well,that must be the one over there then, " said the captain pointing to a door on which a brightly polished name-plate glistened. They moved closer and the name Donald McKane stood revealed in black letters.

"I feel just as if someone was going to jump out and bite me, " remarked Mrs. Griswold as they stood in front of the door,gazing with awe at the imposing brass knocker...

"I feel the same way about it, " agreed the captain hoarsely. "It's like being on a lee shore with all your sails blown away. I'll give that knocker a bang an' then if there is anyone at home I'll pay my respects an' them make full sail back on board the Hornet. I'm plumb off my soundin's in a place like this! With that the captain gave the knocker several sharp raps,and then after waiting a reasonable length of time and receiving no reply,he repeated the performance.... This time he had better luck, for they heard steps approaching. "That woke 'em up! " exclaimed the captain. "You get in front,Annie,so that whoever it is will see you first. "

Annie Griswold complied, and as the door swung slowly open the smiling face of Mrs. McKane confronted them. "Well of all things! " she exclaimed. "Annie Griswold and Captain Silas. Come right in. This is indeed a pleasant surprise. "

"Captain Silas has it all figured out that the Red Jacket is due no later than Thursday, so I thought it would be a good time to pay you a visit, " said Annie Griswold as they were ushered in.

"Priscilla is going to be very pleased when she hears that, " smiled Mrs. McKane. "But I'm sure no more pleased than Donald and I, " she added quickly. "Annie tells me that you are a regular oracle when it comes to predicting the arrival of a ship, Captain Silas, " she went on turning in his direction. "I hope that there will be no error in your calculations this time, for if there is you will have several very disappointed people to deal with, and I shall not answer for the consequences. "

The captain grinned sheepishly. "I guess I've got myself into a pretty kittle of fish, " he remarked. "But I'm goin' to stand by my guns, ma'am, an' even go so far as to predict that you may see the Red Jacket comin' in through the Narrows tomorrow afternoon. "

"Did you hear that, Annie, " said Mrs. McKane. "Do you suppose the captain really knows how terrible the wrath of three disappointed women can be?. "

"He has raised my hopes clear up to the masthead, as John used to say, and if he proves wrong I shall feel very sorry for him, " rejoined Annie Griswold, feigning deep concern.

"Where's Miss. Priscilla, ma'am? " asked the captain. "I'll bet if she was here I'd have someone on my side. "

"I am quite sure of that, " smiled Mrs. McKane. "Priscilla is out shopping but is expected home any minute, and will be overjoyed at seeing you both. "

"I hope that you will not think me bold, paying you such an unexpected visit, and lack consideration, " voiced Annie Griswold apologetically. "I only made up my mind to come at the last moment. "

"Why of course not, Annie. How could you ever think of such a thing? Priscilla and I urged you to come whenever the spirit moved, and we meant it. "

"I was quite sure of that,otherwise I would have stayed at home,
and waited for Danny there, " Annie Griswold replied,her eyes filling
with tears.

"Here comes Priscilla now! " exclaimed Mrs. McKane, as the sound
of a closing door reached their ears. "I'm in here with some very good
friends of yours, Priscilla. Hurry up and join us, " she called out.

"I shall only be a minute, Mother, " they heard her reply, and then
she came bursting into the room,radient with youth and vitality. "Oh,I'm
so glad to see you,Mother Griswold! " she exclaimed, throwing her arms
around the latter and kissing her tenderly on the cheek. "It seems an age
since I left Eastham. "

"You have no idea how much I have missed you,Priscilla, " returned
Annie Griswold. "If it had not been for Silas and his stories I should have
been desolate. "

"I've missed you and the stories as well, Cap'n Silas, " said Priscilla,
as she turned her smiling face in the captain's direction. "You must tell us more
of them tonight after father comes home. "

"When a girl like you says she misses an' old coot like me, it's somethin'
to be proud of, an' I ain't goin' to forget it right away, Priscilla, "replied
the captain, his admiration for her reflected on his honest face.

"Just for that I am going to give you a good big kiss, Cap'n Silas, and
I hope that it will not be the cause of making anyone jealous, " remarked
Priscilla, glancing slyly in Annie Griswold's direction.

"How did you know that she would be interested?" queried the captain,
blushing a deep-red. "It beats all creation how quick wimen catch on to things! "

"Are you up here on your honeymoon? " asked Priscilla in a low voice, after she had kissed him. "If you are,it wasn't very nice of you not to let us know in advance about it. "

"No,we ain't done it yet,but we figure on doin' it any day now, " was the whispered reply. "I sort of figured that we would be able to make it a double one ,after Danny comes home. "

"When do you think the Red Jacket will get in,Cap'n Silas? " asked Priscilla.

"If I ain't wrong in my calculations,she'll be coming in tomorrow afternoon, " was the captain's confident reply. "You tell your father to keep his eye on the signals that go up on Telegraph Hill about noon. After we get them signals,we can all go down to India Wharf an' watch Captain Bacon an' Danny dock the Red Jacket. "

"Don't take too much of what he says for granted,Priscilla, " called out her mother teasingly. "We have just been telling him that he should be careful about raising our hopes too high regarding the Red Jacket's arrival, for if we are disappointed it will be just like stirring up a hornets nest. "

"Come now,Cap'n Silas, confess that you have received news regarding the Red Jacket from some ship which has but lately arrived, " observed Priscilla smilingly.

"She ain't been reported by any ship or you would have read about it in the newspapers, " was the reply. "But there's other ways of killin' a cat besides chokin' it to death with butter, " the captain added mysteriously.

"What do you suppose he means by that, " observed Priscilla thoughtfully, as she gazed inquiringly at her mother and Annie Griswold. "Do you think that he is keeping something back from us? "

"I haven't the slightest idea, Priscilla, " smiled Mrs. McKane. "All I can say is that he is a very resourceful individual, and will bear watching. "

"I guess I had better be movin' along before I get into trouble, " remarked the captain, giving Priscilla a friendly wink. "If your father was here, I might stand some chance of holdin' my own; but a modest seafarin' man like myself ain't good for nothin' but holdin' turn , when he's alone with a parcel of wimen. "

"But you are going to stay for supper, Captain Bowden, " observed Mrs. McKane warmly. "Donald would never forgive me if I let you go away like this, and I am not going to take no for an answer. "

"I've got a lot of chores to do on the Hornet, but maybe I can make it, " was the reply. "My mate is like a dog without a tail when I am not on board ma'am. "

"Don't you believe a word he says, Mother. He's an old fibber, " exclaimed Priscilla teasingly. "I have known him to leave the Hornet in charge of his mate for days at a time, and forget all about her. "

"Then we shall expect you, Captain Bowden, " said Mrs. McKane decidedly. "We shall have supper at six, so please come the minute you have finished those chores, " she added with a smile.

" You had better do it, Silas, " remarked Annie Griswold in an undertone. "It will make things a great deal more cheerful if you are here to keep us company. "

. . . .

"The ladies tell me that you are expecting the Red Jacket in tomorrow, Captain Silas " observed Donald McKane, after they had all seated themselves in one of the private dining-rooms of the Stackpole House, that evening, and were awaiting supper to be served.

"According to my calculations she should be passin' in through the Narrows about noon, " replied the captain without a moments hesitation

Donald McKane gazed at the speaker for quite sometime after that, with a look of incredulity stamped on every line of his features. "I know that you are a good sailorman, Captain Silas, and can probably guess as accurately as anyone the approximate time it would take the Red Jacket to make it, but when you mention the day and hour I challenge your methods of calculation. Why man! The Red Jacket hasn't been spoken once since she left Amoy. "

"She ain't been spoken in one sense of the word, but just the same, barring accidents, she'll be comin' in tomorrow, " replied the captain stoutly.

"Would you stand by that assertion regardless of all arguments to the contrary, Captain Silas? " queried the shipbuilder with a smile.

"I'm so sure of it, that I would be willing to bet the Hornet that she will, " was the confident reply of Captain Bowden.

"Donald, please do not indulge in your proclivity for betting, even if Captain Bowden has given you the opportunity, " admonished Mrs. McKane with a complaisant smile.

"Oh, let them wager something, Mother. It will make it all the more interesting, " urged Priscilla eagerly. "Can't you see that father is baiting Captain Silas? "

"You are right in a way, Priscilla, " observed the shipbuilder with a smile. "Anyone so cock-sure of a thing as Captain Silas should be taken down a peg. "

"Do be careful, Silas, " cautioned Annie Griswold in an undertone. "We cannot be too sure of anything, these days. "

"Don't worry, Annie, " the captain replied. "I've still got all of my wisdom teeth, and regardless of how foolish it sounds, I know what I'm talkin' about. "

Donald McKane contracted his heavy eyebrows in a puzzled frown. "I cannot see, for the life of me, what reasons you have for being so sure of it, " he said finally. "If the Red Jacket had been spoken by some faster homeward-bound ship it would have been common knowledge by now. I didn't build her, but she can show her heels to almost any of the ships that are afloat today. Yes, I would be willing to wager anything in reason , Captain Silas, that she won't be in tomorrow. "

On Captain Bowden's weather-beaten face there appeared a look of intense satisfaction, which he was trying very hard to conceal, and it seemed quite obvious that the baiting referred to by Priscilla was not confined entirely to the shipbuilder. "Ain't there some talk of givin Cap'n Bacon command of the "Flying Cloud", when he gets in? " casually enquired the captain.

"Yes, it has been practically decided that he will be given command of her as soon as he arrives in port, " was the reply.

"In that case the Red Jacket will be without a captain for a spell, " observed Captain Bowden thoughtfully.

"She will until we have decided who will go out master of her, " was the the reply. "Several men have been suggested, but none as yet agreed upon. I presume the mate will take charge of her temporarily. "

"Well in that case I guess we can get together an' make a bet that will be satisfactory to all hands an' the cook, " rejoined Captain Bowden.

"Are you intimating that you would be interested in taking the Red Jacket out, Captain Silas? " asked the shipbuilder in surprise. "If that should be the case, perhaps it could be arranged. I am positive that all my associates would have complete confidence in your ability. "

Captain Bowden chuckled... Maybe ten years ago I might , but I ain't
conceited enough to think that I am the man you would want now, " he
replied. " I had her mate in mind, Danny Griswold. "

"Don't you think that he is going to have trouble enough looking after
my daughter, " smiled the shipbuilder... "And wouldn't it seem a bit partial
if I should reccommend a prospective son-in-law for the berth, Captain Silas? "

"They ain't goin' to care one way or 't'other' if he's capable. And he is. "
replied the captain emphatically."If the Red Jacket gets in tomorrow, all
you've got to do is use your influence to make him captain of her. "

"And if she don't get in? " smiled the shipbuilder.

"I'll sell the Hornet an' give what I get for her to Priscilla an'
Danny as a weddin' present. " rejoined the captain quickly. "I was goin'
to do it anyway, so it don't make any difference. "

"How old is he, Annie? " questioned the shipbuilder, turning to Danny's
mother.

"He will be nineteen in August," she answered, glancing proudly in
Captain Bowden's direction.

"Shouldn't you think that he was a bit too young for such a responsible
position, Silas? " observed the shipbuilder mildly.

"No, " answered Captain Bowden quickly. "He's a man, an' can handle
a ship with the best of 'em. You ask Cap'n Bacon when he gets in, If he says
Danny is capable what more do you want? "

"I haven't the slightest idea, " returned the shipbuilder thoughtfully.
"But it strikes me that the owners will look for a man with a great deal more
experience than Danny can lay claim to. How shall we ever get around that,
Silas ? "

"Tell 'em that Danny's ancestors was all seafaring men,who wouldn't take a back seat from anybody where the sailin' of a ship was concerned; an' ever since he was knee high to a grasshopper he's had Sailor Eyes like all the rest of us on the Cape, " rejoined the captain.

"I guess you are right,Silas, " answered the shipbuilder reflectively. "There will be a directors'meeting next week, and if the Red Jacket is in by that time, which you have almost made me believe she will, I shall have Captain Bacon there to recommend him. "

"One could almost imagine that Captain Silas was gifted with second sight,he seems so positive regarding the Red Jacket's arrival, " commented Mrs. McKane . " I wonder if hea could go so far as to predict the state of their health, " she concluded with a smile.

"I can do that as easy as fallin' off a log,Ma'am , " said the captain without a moment's hesitation. "They are all well an' happy as larks. "

"Silas,don't you think that you have carried this joke far enough, " admonished Annie Griswold. "You couldn't be sure of that unless you are gifted with supernatural powers, and I am quite sure that you are not. "

"I ain't said nothin' about this before,but once when I was out in India I took some lessons from a Yogi, an' I can figure out almost anything I have a mind to, " said the captain,with a sly wink at Priscilla.

"Well, I see where I am going to lose a daughter much sooner than I expected , " observed the shipbuilder,feigning a look of disappointment."In a weak moment I promised Priscilla that she could marry Danny just as soon as he was given command of a ship, and it looks very much as if that time was near at hand. "

"Only three or four days, Donald, " chuckled Captain Bowden.

"Why it is positively uncanny the faith that man has in his predictions, " observed Mrs. McKane with a puzzled frown. "I am almost tempted to believe that he is in league with the spirits. "

"Speakin' of spirits, Ma'am, reminds me of a time when I had what you might call some dealin's with 'em, " observed the captain in a reminiscent tone of voice. "I was standin' one night with a shipmate, in front of the Town Hall in Eastham, lookin' at a sign that read 'Tonight at eight o'clock Professor Horatio Wintergreen, will, through his spirit, guide Big Chief Weeping Willow, bring back for a few minutes of social discourse, various an' sundry relatives who have departed this sphere, for the small sum of fifty cents.'"

"Well, what do you think of that, I says to Lowney. Do you want to go in an' lissen for a spell? It ain't goin' to cost anything unless you talk to somebody. "

"' I don't mind' Lowney says. 'It would be worth fifty cents to hear the voice of Uncle Thad, an' find out how he an' his hoss Ben's gettin' along.' "

"You don't mean to say that you're goin' to try it? I says. "

"'Why sure, ' he says. ' I ain't afraid of spooks. Less go in an' find out what Uncle Thad is doin' in the spirit world. "

"An' so we entered the hall , an' marchin' down the middle aisle, seated ouselves in the front row as bold as you please, right where we could almost reach out an' touch the stage. "

"What did you come way down here for? I says, lookin' back over my shoulder at the rest of the audience that was seated further back. Why couldn't we have set back there with the other people? "

"' I was thinkin' of making it easier for Uncle Thad' says Lowney. 'If he brings his hoss with him, he won't have so far to go with it'. "

"It didn't say anything on the handbill about bringing back animals," I says. "It just said relations. "

"'Well ain't animals relations?, ' he says. 'Didn't we all spring from monkeys?' "

"You might, but I didn't" I says. Then the argument was stopped by the appearance of the professor, who walked close to the edge of the stage an' gazed down at us with a far away look in his eyes. ' I take it that one of you gentlemen wish to commune with a dear, departed spirit, ' he says in an oily voice...'Was it you?' he asks, pointin' in Lowney's direction.. 'Yes it was' he says, answering his own question.'I can distinctly feel your vibrations. ' "

"' I did have some idea of speakin' to my Uncle Thad, ' says Lowney bold as brass. ' But there ain't no hurry. Maybe someone else would would like a try at it first! I'd just as soon wait. ' "

"'I can feel the spirit of your Uncle Thadeus hoverin' over me now,' says the professor, rolling his eyes toward the ceiling. ' I shall summon Chief Weeping Willow at once so that you can commune with your dear, departed uncle. ' "

"' I ain't in any hurry, ' says Lowney. ' There may be a lot of people ahead of me. ' "

"'It's too late now, ' says the professor. 'The vibrations of your Uncle Thadeus are so strong that they have scared all the other spirits away. ' "

"' All right',says Lowney. 'If it's my Uncle Thad,there wouldn't be any use tryin' to stop him. ' "

"Do you think it's him? I says in a stage whisper. "

"' I don't know' says Lowney with a puzzled frown. 'I can tell better after I hear him talk. Maybe there's somethin' to this business after all. ' "

"After that the professor lost no time goin' into action. The lights was lowered,an' he got behind a big sheet that was hung up on the stage ,while everybody held their breath... Pretty soon a regular bedlum broke loose behind the curtain,tambourines banged, banjo's twanged, and between the two of 'em,they made noise enough to wake up the spirits,even if they was as deaf as a post. "

"' That must be Uncle Thad comin' now' says Lowney. 'He had the reputation for bein' the noisest man in Barnstable County. ' "

"Lowney had no sooner said it,when up from behind the screen popped a figure draped in a sheet. ' I am the spirit of Thadeus Phipps an' I would commune with my dear nephew, , ' says the figure in a sepulchral voice. ' Is his aurora attuned to my vibrations?' "

"' I don't know anything about what you just mentioned,but I'm settin' right out here in front of you, ' says Lowney. 'How's things over on the other side Uncle Thad?' "

"' Wonderful! ' exclaimed the shade. ' It's a land overflowin' with milk an' honey. A veritable paradise of sunshine an' flowers, my dear nephew. '"

"' Did you bring Ben with you, Uncle Thad? ' inquires Lowney after a long silence. "

"' Ben? ' replied the shade,in an inquiring tone of voice, as if
it had forgotton for the moment the person referred to.'. "

"' Your hoss, ' prompts Lowney. 'The one that died about the same
time you did. ' "

"' My hoss' repeats the shade, as if he still didn't understand what
Lowney meant.. 'Oh,you mean my hoss. Ben? ' he says after a moment's silence.
"'Why the dear,gentle creature. is right here beside me, after a period of
grazin' in the Elysian Fields. '"An! then as if to prove it someone back of the
sheet tried to imitate the whinny of a horse,which sounded like the squeals
of a pig havin' its throat cut... "' There, did you hear that'? says the shade
of Uncle Thadeus. ' The noble creature is actually overjoyed at seein' you.' "

"' I guess he's havin' another one of his tantrums, ' says Lowney. 'If
I was you' I would put him back in the barn before he kicks another one of
your ribs out, Uncle Thad. ' "

"The shade of Uncle Thadeus wabbled around for a minute an' then
disappeared like a Jack-in-the box ..."' Well I guess that's the last of him'
says Lowney. 'He's probably ridin' that hoss of his back to them fields he was
talkin' about.' ".

"Do you suppose there's anything to this spirit business? I says to
Lowney after the seance was over. "

"'Well,you can judge for yourself, Silas, ' says Lowney, after he had
relieved himself with a good hearty claugh. ' There wasn't a man in the whole
township who could cuss like my Uncle Thad. An' as for his hoss,it was the
most vicious critter you ever set eyes on. It was due to a kick that animal
gave him,that he is where he is now.' "

After the story was finished, Captain Bowden glanced quizzically around the table,his blue eyes twinkling with amusement. "When I get started on a story no one else can get a word in edge-ways, " he grinned. "You folks gave me credit for having second sight,but still I ain't got sense enough to hold my tongue. "

"Why,Captain Silas,how can you say such a thing? " observed Mrs. McKane. "I could listen to your stories for hours. Please tell us another one. "

"Yes, do, " urged Priscilla.

"He never runs dry of stories,like Phoebe Frost's well never runs dry of water, " added Annie Griswold with a smile. I don't know what I should have done last winter but for them. He could have a new one for every hour in the day. "

"I could stand another very nicely,smiled the shipbuilder. I have talked so much myself today that I'm perfectly willing to sit back and give someone else a chance. "

"All right, " said the captain good-naturedly. "I'll tell you about a joke the mate of the Hornet played on Lowney Phipps, the man that I went to that spiritual seance with, once while we was in Boston.Lowney was the cook at the time, and the Hornet was layin' sandwiched in between to big foreign freight steamers."

"The dock was fairly alive with customs men on account of there being so many foreign ships moored to it, and Lowney was standin' by the rail lookin' down at one of 'em suspiciously.... The man in question stood with one foot on the capsill of the wharf in conversation with a stevedore, an' every now and then he would cast what appeared to be an inquiring glance in Lowney's direction. 'Dodgast that feller's hide;he's spying on me, ' Lowney was muttering.

" ' Now what are you grumbling about?'says the mate, comin' to a halt
beside him . One would think that you had money in the bank by the way you're
carryin' on. ' "

" ' I've got more'n you have, ' answered the cook. 'I don't go an' throw
it away on fiddle diddles the way you do. ' "

" ' You don't say, ' replied the mate with a sneer. ' How about them
two canaries you brought on board from off that freighter? ' ".

" 'That's different, ' says the cook. 'I got 'em cheap,an' after supper
I'm goin' to take 'em over to a friend of mine in Medford. ' "

" 'What do you call cheap? ' says the mate. 'You don't know anything
about canary birds, Lowney. ' "

" ' I know that a dollar for a pair of Hartz Mountain Rollers is cheap,'
replied the cook.'I can get five for 'em just as easy as sittin' down in a chair. '"

"The mate was silent for quite a spell,thinkin' of some way to get the
best of the cook... ' You'll have to pay duty on 'em, '"he says finally".

" ' Who said I would? ' sneered the cook . '

" ' I did, ' said the mate, 'If you don't,they'll fine you fifty dollars
an' put you in jail besides, ' "

" ' They'll have to catch me first, ' says the cook.'I ain't goin' to
pay any duty on a couple of skinny canary birds.' "

" ' You don't mean to say that you're goin' to smuggle 'em ashore,' says
the mate assuming an air of righteous indignation.'That would be cheatin' Uncle
Sam. '"

" ' Uncle Sam's got plenty of money an' I ain't goin' to worry about him
any,' says the cook."

" 'But you couldn't smuggle that cage ashore even if 'tis small,' says the mate. 'It would stick out from under your coat like a sore thumb.' "

"' I ain't goin' to take 'em ashore in any cage, an' if you had the sense of a bedbug you'd know I wasn't, ' replied the cook. "

"' Well how under the sun are you goin' to do it then? ' asks the mate. 'A feller can't even smuggle a toothpick ashore these days wit' out bein' caught, ' "

"' They don't hold up everybody,' says the cook. 'I've seen dozens walk right out the gate an' the man never looked at 'em.' "

"' That was because they wasn't smugglin' anything, They can tell by a feller's face, if he's doin' somethin' crooked, ' says the mate. "

"'Well it wouldn't show in mine, ' says the cook boastfully. "

"' I wouldn't be so sure of it if I was you, ' says the mate. 'You know what they say about a guilty conscience. ' "

"The mate just as soon as he had finished supper that night, went up on the poop. an' began to walk back an' forth with his eye peeled on the cook's galley. 'I'll fix that walrus-faced pot-boiler, ' he chuckled. "

"Finally he saw the cook come out of the galley dressed in his shore-goin' clothes, an' after unhooking the bird-cage that hung just outside the door, carried it inside. 'Now I'll find out how that old coot is goin' to take 'em ashore, ' he says to himself, an' suitin' action to the word, he tiptoes forrard, an' peers cautiously in the galley winder.... He stood there for quite a spell watchin' the cook's movements, an' then he goes over to the rail an' motions to a customs man on the dock.

"' The cook's tryin'to smuggle somethin' ashore,' he says to the man as soon as he arrived within ear-shot. 'Don't you want to come up here with me an' watch the fun?' "

"The customs man come up on deck, an' takin' his place beside the mate gazed sternly in the direction of the galley. "

"'There he comes now, ' says the mate. 'He'll be scared out of his wits when he sees you standin' here with me. ' "

"When the cook rounded the corner of the galley,he was whistlin' as big AS you please, but when he saw the customs man the whistlin' stopped as if he had choked on a hot pertater. He kept right on goin' though,but his movements wasn't much faster then a turtles,an' the look on his face was anything but inocent."

"'Hello , cookie', says the mate,havin' all he could do to keep his face straight. 'Goin' for a walk?' "

"'Where did you think I was goin', ' says the cook. 'Up in the crosstrees. 'Can't a feller go on about his business without you buttin' in?' "

"' Ain't you afraid the wind'll blow your hat off? ' says the mate. There wasn't hardly a breath of air stirrin', but still the cook kept reachin' for his hat nervously. "

"' No,I ain't, ' says the cook, his walrus- mustache bristlin' with indignation. But at the same time he reached up an' pulled his hat down more firmly over his ears. "

"' I wonder how I would look in a hat like the cook wears, ' says the mate,givin' the customs man a sly wink.'I've a good mind to try it on. ' "

"'That would be a fine idea, ' says the customs man. 'Go ahead an' do it, an' I'll tell you how it looks. ' "

" 'I will,' says the mate. With that he reaches up quick an' pulls off
the cooks hat. Then in their ears sounded a series of startled peeps,an'
the fluttering of wings, as the two canaries the cook had hidden away in it
kixxkxt, rose high in the air, an' after circling the dock-shed a couple of
times,headed in the direction of Massachusetts Bay."

" 'Well,I'll be darned! ' exclaimed the mate,assuming an attitude of great
surprise . 'Didn't you know that a couple of canary birds had gone an' built
a nest in your hat, Lowney?' "

There were several smiling comments made on the cooks method of smuggling,
after the captain had finished his story,and then,supper being over they all
adjourned to the McKane's sitting-room, where they continued their conversation.

"I shall never rest until I find out how you come to know so much about
the arrival of the Red Jacket,Captain Silas," smilingly remarked Mrs. McKane
after they were seated. "You know how inquisitive all of us women are, so you
had better tell before you get into trouble. "

"Well ma'am,it's a case of 'castin' your bread upon the waters'" replied
the captain. "I did a favor for somethin' once an' that is how it paid me back. "

"Can you make anything out of that,Donald? " observed Mrs. McKane,glancing
at her husband quizzically. "Captain Silas certainly likes to keep us on tenter-
hooks. "

"It's the Yankee in him, " smiled the shipbuilder. "He'll come out with
it in due season. Just give him time. "

"You can't rush him, " added Priscilla. "He's as stubborn as a mule
when it comes to that. "

"I, should say he was, " voiced Annie Griswold. "Silas, if you don't tell us how you know so much about it, I shan't speak to you again for a month. "

"Well I guess in that case I had better tell, " said the captain, drawing a small piece of paper from his coat pocket, and fingering it gingerly. "It's all down here in the handwritin' of someone you've all heard of. "

"Silas,if you don't get started pretty quick I shall fly right up through the roof! " exclaimed Annie Griswold impatiently. I don't blame the folks for being on pins and needles. "

"Well, it all started one mornin' when I picked"Gloccus"up on the beach with his wing broken, " said the captain,gazing from one to the other of his audience appraisingly.

"For heaven's sake,Silas,what has a bird got to do with the Red Jacket's getting in? " questioned Annie Griswold.

"If you will hold your hosses for a minute, I'll tell you just how it was, Annie, " replied the captain,not in the least bothered by her question. "I was just workin' up to it. "

"I should advise all of you to leave him alone,otherwise he will keep us all in suspense for the remainder of the evening, " smilingly warned the the shipbuilder.

Captain Bowden cleared his throat once more and then with a smile of satisfaction, continued. "Gloccus was a young seagull, an' as pert a bird as you ever laid eyes on. An' when I took him back home with me that mornin' an' fixed up his wing,from that day on he followed me around like a dog. Then one day I says to myself, I'll take him on board the Hornet an' see what he'll do there. I kept him in a crate for a spell until he got used to the schooner, an' then one day on our way up to Boston I turned him loose. It will be the last of him I says to myself ,but it wasn't,for after flyin' around with the rest of the gulls for a time, he came back to the Hornet an' went into his crate. Well , I says to myself,he knows which side his bread is buttered on, so after that he had the run of the ship. He knew the minute that I would leave the Hornet, after we had docked in Eastham , an' when I got home I would find him on the back-door step waitin' for me. He must be the reincarnation of some old sailor, I says to myself, and would enjoy a good long voyage to sea, so I gave him to Danny the day he sailed on the Red Jacket . I says you take the old son-of-a - gun an' try to keep him on board until you get back off the Cape. Then you turn him loose an' see what will happen.... Well last Sunday morning when I opened my back door,there he was as large as life, an' when he saw me he began to flap his wings an' carry on like all possessed."Hello Gloccus"; I said as I reached down to pick him up. How did you find the weather off Cape Horn? Then I noticed that he had a message tied to his leg , an' here 'tis, Annie,"the captain concluded handing her the piece of paper.

With an exclamation of surprise Annie Griswold reached for the paper, and with trembling hands held it to the light so that she could more easily decipher the message that it bore, and here is what she read. "Dear Cap'n Silas. We are all well, and if this breeze holds out should be coming in through the Narrows about noon Tuesday. Try to persuade Mother to go up with you to Boston so that she will be there when we arrive. Love to all. Danny. " Then with her eyes dim with tears Annie Griswold silently passed the note to Priscilla, who eagerly read it over several times to herself, and then out loud to the others. "Do you think that was nice,Captain Silas, keeping us in suspense so long after you had received it? " admonished Priscilla after she had finished.

"It wasn't very nice that's a fact, " acknowledged the captin sheepishly. "But I wanted to wait an' get you all together so's it would be more sociable. I almost had to tie a knot in my tongue to keep from tellin' Annie though, " he concluded.

"I should like very much to see that gull you call Gloccus, " voiced the shipbuilder. "It don't seem possible that a bird of his description could be carried all the way out to China and back without being lost. "

"I was pretty sure you would, so I brought him along, " replied the captain. That was why I went back on board the Hornet this afternoon. He's down cellar now with the porter. If you'll wait a minute I'll go fetch him. "

"Did you ever in all your life, hear of such going's on? "observed Annie Griswold, after the captain had left the room. "Silas is one of the most lovable and resourceful men that I ever heard tell of. "

"If he was twenty years younger I wouldn't give much for Danny's chances of going out master of the Red Jacket, but I don't suppose a team of oxen could drag him off soundings now, " commented the shipbuilder, "He was a very capable sailor in the old days, and still is. "

"He says that he has swallowed the anchor, and is going to devote all his time to making a certain person who is not far away, 'as happy as a clam at high water', " remarked Priscilla, as she glanced with a smile in Annie Griswold's direction.

"And that is as it should be, " added Mrs. McKane with an air of complete satisfaction. "I couldn't think for the life of me, of two people who are more suited for each other. "

They were interrupted at this point by the entrance of Captain Silas.
"Here's the old son-of-a-gun! " the latter exclaimed, gently removing the
gull from his shoulder and placing him on a rug in the center of the McKane's
sitting-room. "I'll leave him here an' then set down an' see what he does. "

Gloccus stretched his wings, ruffled his feathers, and then standing
with one foot hauled up under him eyed the audience curiously. "He don't know
quite what to make of it yet, " volunteered the captain. "We've got to give
him time to get his bearin's. "

At the sound of the captain's voice, Gloccus cocked his head knowingly
in his direction and started toward him with a roll that would have done
credit to a Western Ocean sailor, and on reaching the captain's side, grabbed
his coat in his beak and pulled himself up onto his lap, where he paused for
a moment and then fluttered to his shoulder. "He's a smart bird, an' knows a
heap sight more'n some humans I've met in my day, " observed the captain.

"Look, Mother, Gloccus has fallen asleep on the captain's shoulder, "
exclaimed Priscilla. And sure enough the gull at peace with all the world,
after its long voyage in the Red Jacket, had settled down on its benefactor's
shoulder, satisfied beyond the question of a doubt that its days of wandering
were over.

"He'll stay there until I get ready to leave, " said the captain
proudly. "In the meantime I'll tell you a story about a parrot an' then head
for the Hornet. We're goin' to have a big day tomorrow. "

"I shall be all ears, " remarked the shipbuilder.

"And so will I" echoed each of the ladies in turn.

"It was when I was master of the bark 'Auburndale' an' we were dischargin' cargo at the mates home-port, where I had left him in charge for a spell an' come back home. Well, no sooner had I left the ship then his relatives begin to come on board, an' make themselves right at home, much to the annoyance of the cook, Lowney Phipps. "

"With the first streaks of dawn, an' they come pretty early, for it was in the month of June, some of them would climb on board an' sniff hungrily at the smell of food comin' from the galley, which usually ended up in the mate's inviting 'em to breakfast. "

"Well the cook stood it for a day or two without a murmer, but when they got to comin' on board for all their meals, he got madder'n a hornet.

"'That was a pretty good breakfast cookie,' says the mate one mornin' after two of his cousins, an' his Uncle Charley had finished an' pushed their chairs back from the table. 'We'll be seein' you again at noon.' "

"' Not if I've got anything to say about it, " replies the cook. 'Cap'n Silas didn't have them stores put on board to feed your relatives with.' "

"'It ain't no skin off your nose,' says the mate. 'You don't have to pay for 'em. ' "

"' It makes extra work cookin' 'em, ' retorts the cook, an' I don't get paid for runnin' a boardin' house.'"

"' It makes up for all the loafin' you do while we're at sea, ' says the mate. 'While us sailors are reefin' an' steerin' you're down below gettin' forty winks. ' "

"Well, it come Sunday an' the mate was standin' on the poop talkin' to a Mr. Scoggins who had stepped on board for a friendly visit on his way home from church. In a cage on top of the wheel-house a large green an' yellow parrot sidled back an' forth on its perch, pausin' at intervals to ruffle its feathers an' gaze at them owlishly out of half-closed eyes. "

"' It would take a lot of money to buy that bird,' says the mate casually,as he noted Mr. Scoggins glancin' in its direction. At the same time he would have snapped at an offer of five dollars like a hungry fish."

"' You don't say, ' remarked Mr. Scoggins, glancin' at the bird with added interest. 'Do you consider it a valuable one,Mr. Pomroy?'"

"' There ain't any more valuable around these parts,' boasted the mate. 'It would take a lot of cold cash to tempt me to sell it. ' The truth of the matter was, he had bought the parrot for two dollars,the voyage before from a drunken sailor on Commercial Street in Boston."

"Then,all of a sudden the parrot stretched out its neck an' burst into a song, at least that was how the mate interpreted the sound to Mr. Scoggins. ' That's a Portugee love song,' says the mate, 'an' the feller that I bought it from,says it sings 'em like a concert-hall artist. ' "

"'Wonderful! ' exclaims Mr. Scoggins.

"Then the parrot satisfied with its exibition settled down on its perch for a nap."

"' My wife always wanted a parrot,' says Mr. Scoggins, givin' the bird another admirin' glance. 'An' tomorrow is her birthday. ' "

"The mate anticipatin' a sale,poked the parrot gently with a stick he was whittlin',makin' a cluckin' noise with his tongue,after which the bird suddenly come to life an' cockin' its head knowingly to one side,croaks 'Hello,Cousin Wet'. "

"To say that the mate was surprised wouldn't have half expressed it, for previous to that time the bird had never spoken a word that anybody could have understood, an' he stood there completely flabergasted for almost five minutes."

"' Remarkable! ' exclaims Mr. Scoggins. "

"' It is one of the best birds ever brought out of the wild jungles of Brazil,' says the mate,after he had partly recovered from his astonishment. 'The man I bought it from says it speaks three or four different languages.' "

"' Would you take ten dollars for it? ' questioned Mr. Scoggins eagerly."

"' The mate gazed at Mr. Scoggins for a minute in goggle-eyed surprise, an' was afraid to answer for fear he might show his eagerness to part with the bird for that price. "

"On the other hand, Mr. Scoggins,thinkin' that it wasn't enough,quickly raised his offer to fifteen dollars. 'I'll pay you that an' not a cent more,' he adds firmly. "

"By this time the mate's eyes fairly bulged from his head,for he could hardly believe his ears. 'I'll take it,'he says finally. "

"' Very well,' says Mr. Scoggins. 'I'll be down tonight an' take it home,for I don't want Mrs. Scoggins to see me with it.' "

"The mate now in a happy frame of mind called loudly for the cook, an' while waitin' for him to appear invited Mr. Scoggins to supper.' Lowney ' he says,when the cook made his appearance ,'I want you to fix up somethin' good for supper - somethin' that will tickle the appetites of me an' Mr. Scoggins.' "

"With his face wreathed in smiles,the mate faced Mr. Scoggins that night at the supper table,an' the ways an' means of spendin' that fifteen dollars he was goin' to get after the meal was over was almost numberless. In front of them rested plates containin' what appeared to be stew,from which arose a very appetizing aroma. 'What is this here concoction,Lowney? ' asked the mate, as the cook passed his chair on the way to the pantry.'I hope that it tastes as good as it smells.' "

"' It's Brazilian partridge,'" answers the cook. ' I got it from a friend of mine who has just got in from South America. ' "

"' I've never heard of any bird by that name before,' observed the mate, smellin' the contents of his plate suspiciously.'Did you Mr. Scoggins? ' "

"' No ,I shall have to admit that I haven't,' answered Mr. Scoggins as he speared a piece on the end of his fork an' tasted it gingerly. "

"' It don't taste so bad at that, ' remarks the mate,after he had carved a piece from one of the legs,an' with a great effort, succeeded in swallowin' it. 'But I ain't ever been much for newfangled dishes.' "

"' It is not what you might call tender, ' contributed Mr. Scoggins."

"' I never did like game birds very well, ' added the mate. 'Besides I guess they didn't fat this one up very well. ' "

"An' so it went on until they had finished supper,an' had sat around in their chairs for a spell discussing various subjects... 'Well I guess it's time that I was goin, ' says Mr. Scoggins after a while,lookin' up at the clock, an' reachin' for his pocketbook. If you have that parrot handy,I'll relieve you of it, Mr. Pomroy' "

"'It's still up on top of the wheel-box,' says the mate,smilin' with satisfaction at the thought of the money he was goin' to get. 'We'll get the bird on our way up.'"

"'No,you won't,' says the cook, who had been standin' close by listening to the conversation. 'The cage is there but it ain't got any parrot in it.'"

"'There ain't no parrot in it,' echoes the mate,his face the color of a boiled lobster. 'Where in thunderation did it go to then?'"

"'Down your gullet in that stew,' answers the cook,jumpin' back into the pantry an' closin' the door behind him with a bang. "

As the captain finished his yarn Gloccus opened his eyes and stared sleepily around the room,after which he ruffled his feathers,uttering a hoarse croak. "He says it's time to go on board, " the captain remarked with a smile. "He ain't used to keepin' late hours. "

"You don't have to go on board tonight unless you feel like it,Silas, " remarked the shipbuilder . "I am quite sure that we can find a place to put you up. "

"Why of course we can," added Mrs. McKane. "I had planned on his staying and everything is all ready. "

"It's awfully nice of you ma'am, an' Donald here, to suggest it,but if you don't mind I'll take Gloccus in tow an' we'll be makin' tracks for the Hornet, " said the captain. "I'll be seein' you all at'Topliff's' about ten o'clock tomorrow. "

"You are a lucky woman,Annie, " the shipbuilder remarked after Captain Bowden had taken his departure. "You may have lost a son in one sense of the word,but you are going to have in his place one of the finest men it has been my good fortune to meet. "

Annie Griswold blushed like a schoolgirl at the reminder that she was about to become Mrs. Bowden, and for a moment maintained an embarrassed silence... "You are right as far as you have gone, Donald," she remarked finally. "But you have neglected to add that I am going to have a fine daughter-in-law, and two of the most faithful friends that a women could wish for besides."

....

The day scheduled for the arrival of the Red Jacket dawned bright and fair with a sea-turn in the wind. At ten o'clock Captain Bowden paused near the entrance to Topliff's News Room, and all smiles awaited the coming of the others. He had already observed the signals on Telegraph Hill, and knew that the Red Jacket would soon be coming up the Bay.

"Have they sighted her Silas," queried Annie Griswold, almost out of breath as she came hurrying up with the others. "Is it the Red Jacket?"

"Yes, Annie. It's Danny's ship comin' into port, an' pretty soon you are goin' to see what makes all of us on the Cape have 'Sailor Eyes'," answered the captain proudly.

At the mention of Danny and his ship, Annie Griswold's heart almost stood still, for now that his coming was assured her mind was in a daze, and her thoughts too full for utterance. A vibrant summer breeze droned in her ears, and a warm, restful feeling wrapped itself around her.. Silently she listened to the remarks of the others, and tried to picture how Danny would look after being gone almost a year.

Mrs. McKane on the other hand was thinking of her daughter, and how it would be possible to get along without her, now that she was about to become a part of the sea. But her thoughts were far from being selfish however, for she was perfectly well-aware that she was about to gain a son-in-law of whom she could be very proud.

"She'll come streakin' up the Bay with this wind! " exclaimed
Captain Bowden excitedly. "We had all better go down to India Wharf
where she's goin' to berth an' watch her come in. "

With the effortless speed of a seagull the Red Jacket came driving
up the Bay with a bone in her teeth, and just before reaching the Narrows
between Georges and Gallops, luffed a few points and boom-ended her studdin'
sails in order to negotiate the narrow passage between the islands. As she
drew nearer one would have thought that she had just left some port after a
thorough overhauling, so trim and shipshape did she appear, as she raced up
the Bay, with her brightwork and freshly holeystoned decks gleaming in the
noonday sun, in keeping with the snowy whiteness of her billowing canvas.

"By Tophet! It looks as if Cap'n Bacon was goin' to carry his royals
right up to the wharf, " remarked Captain Bowden. "I'll bet that he's had
'em on her ever since he left China. "

But no sooner were the words out of his mouth, when men were seen
hurrying aloft on the Red Jacket, and the sails referred to were clewed-up like magic.

"I have never seen a sight like that in all my born days, " observed
Annie Griswold in an awed tone of voice. "And to think that my son Danny is
on that beautiful ship. I have never quite appreciated before how wonderful
they look under full sail. I shouldn't be at all surprised but what they had
souls like us human beings. "

"I have felt that way for years Annie", agreed Donald McKane reverently.
"God gave them a soul like the rest of us, even if they are made out of wood
and iron. "

"You can count me in on that too, " added Captain Bowden solemnly.

In the meantime the Red Jacket was coming nearer to the wharf,
and comments were flying thick and fast regarding her appearance,as
necks were craned to catch a glimpse of some member of the crew...
Boarding house runners, Ann Street hussues, and ship chandlers,rubbed
shoulders with each other, all prepared to greet Jack and offer him
hospitality of sorts.

Nearing the wharf the Red Jacket rounded up into the wind with a
graceful curve,and backing her topsails to check her headway,let go
her port anchor with a splash.. Then followed the harsh rattle of chain
as it cleared the hawsepipe,and like a spirited horse which has suddenly
been reigned-in,the lofty ship shuddered as she felt the weight dragging
at her bows, and then as her ground-tackle became firmly embedded in the
mud, she stopped less than fifty feet from where they were standing.

Annie Griswold could hear Danny's voice ordering the men aloft to
furl the sails,and soon she saw him on the forecastle-head.. Instinctively
so it seemed,he looked in her direction,and she waived her hand. He
recognized her at once and waived in return.. "How big and strong he looked,
standing there", she thought. "He was a boy no longer in her eyes, but a full-
grown man. To think that less than a year could make such a change in him." It
was then that she turned and smiled at the others through tears of joy.

A warp leading from the capstan was sculled ashore by a boatman and
made fast to a bollard on the wharf,and then the sailors on the Red Jacket
began to walk around the capstan to the tune of

> "Oh times are hard and wages low.
> Leave her,Johnny, Leave her.
> I'll pack my bag and go below.
> It's time for us to leave her. "

....

And now dear reader it is also time for us to leave the characters in this story. They are all fictitious, and only the product of a modest attempt to portray the thoughts and action of people whose counterparts lived in the villages of Cape Cod and elsewhere on the New England coast, during that era and went down to the sea in ships.

The similarity of the shipbuilders name to that of Donald McKay was intentional, for he lived in a day that the residents of Massachusetts can well look back upon with pride, for he and other sturdy men who built and manned clippers of that period had "Sailor Eyes", and helped to make North America what it is today. So in bringing this story to a close I shall quote as an eulogy to a great man, a paragraph from Samuel Eliot Morrison's, Maratime History of Massachusetts.

"The master builders, reluctant to raise barnyard fowls where they had once raised eagles, dropped off one by one. Donald McKay died almost in poverty after a career that should have brought him wealth and honor, sleeps at Newburyport, Massachusetts, among the comrades of his young manhood. The Commonwealth , so generous in laurel to second-rate politicians , and third rate soldiers, contains no memorial line to this man who helped to make his name imortal. But in the elm branches over his grave the brave west winds that he loved so well, murmer soft versions of the tunes they once played on the shrouds of his glorious ships. "

There has been a great deal written and screened about the
covered wagon,and the hardships of those sturdy pioneers who treaked
westward overland, but little about the people of New England who, having
"Sailor Eyes" , used them to build ships and blaze a trail to every
port of the seven seas. I had them too, and know how it feels to beat a
ship around Cape Horn in midwinter. Only the ghosts of the old clippers
sail in and out of the Golden Gate today, and few people remember them
either in song or story,but they played a very important part in our
history, and may all the men who went down to the sea in them, and all the
women who patiently awaited their return,rest in peace, for they have earned
it.

The End

ALEXANDER HACKETT
1732 WASHINGTON STREET
TOLEDO 2 OHIO

Alex. Hackett

Present address
1025-3rd Street North
St. Petersburg 1, Florida

www.ingramcontent.com/pod-product-compliance
Lightning Source LLC
Chambersburg PA
CBHW080819250626
47159CB00011B/3442